The SILVER SUITCASE

The SILVER SUITCASE

TERRIE TODD

Waterfall
PRESS

This is a work of fiction. Names, characters, organizations, places, events, and incidents are either products of the author's imagination or are used fictitiously.

Scripture references are from the King James Version, public domain, except for those that occur during parts of the story that take place in the 21st century, where the New International Version is used.

Grateful acknowledgment is made to reprint the following hymns:

Berg, Lina Sanell, 1832–1903, "More Secure Is No One Ever"

Crosby, Fanny J., 1820–1915, and Lowry, Robert, 1826–1899, "All the Way My Savior Leads Me"

Tullar, Grant C., and Breck, Mrs. Frank A., "Face to Face," 1927

von Schlegel, Katharina, "Be Still My Soul," 1697, translation by Jane L. Borthwick, 1813–1897, and Jean Sibelius, 1865–1957

Published by Waterfall Press, Grand Haven, MI

www.brilliancepublishing.com

ISBN-13: 9781503950498
ISBN-10: 1503950492

Cover design by Laura Klynstra

Printed in the United States of America

Dedicated with love to my mother, Norma (Oswald) Klassen.
In the classroom of life, she teaches me still.

The SILVER SUITCASE

And the Lord answered me, and said, "Write the vision, and make it plain upon tables, that he may run that readeth it. For the vision is yet for an appointed time, but at the end it shall speak, and not lie: though it tarry, wait for it; because it will surely come, it will not tarry."

Habakkuk 2:2–3

PROLOGUE

Manitoba, Canada
1981

Benita Gladstone's best friend would soon turn sixty years old. Which might not be remarkable if Benita weren't ten.

She crossed the elementary school playground and looked at the bright blue of the Winnipeg sky. In three more weeks, grade five would be history. Once the school year was over, she could again spend long days at Gram's house, which she still thought of as home all these years after her mother had insisted it was time to move out. With her ponytail swinging, Benita kicked a stone and kept kicking it down the sidewalk all the way to her grandmother's.

"Because you're in school now, honey," Grace Gladstone had explained at the time. "You don't need Grandma Cornelia to babysit you while I'm at work anymore."

"But if I had a daddy, you wouldn't have to work. Becky's mom stays home with her."

"Your daddy left us, sweetheart. Men cannot be counted on. Besides, you can still go to Gram's every day after school, until I'm off work."

"Then why can't we stay at Gram's all the time?" Benita wanted to know.

"It's better for grown-ups like me to not live with their parents, that's all. You and I need to be our own little family, and we can do that best if we live in our own home. You'll understand one day."

But Benita still did not understand, though four years had passed. When she reached Gram's front gate, instead of pushing it open and walking through, she tossed her backpack into the yard and climbed over. She then scooped up the backpack again and ran around to the backyard, where she knew she'd find her best friend in the garden.

"Hi, Gram!" Benita swung the garden gate open. Benita had watched Uncle Jim and Gram build the chicken-wire fence, designed to keep rabbits and squirrels out of the carrots, lettuce, and nasturtiums. Even deer could sometimes be seen in the city, nibbling on beet leaves or spinach.

Gram stood from where she'd been kneeling in her row of radishes and stretched. Her gray-blue eyes still sparkled as she looked at her granddaughter. "You'll never guess what," Gram said as Benita launched herself into her arms with abandon.

"Yes, I will. I'm the smartest granddaughter you ever had."

"Well, yes, you are. But that's not what I intended to say." Gram laughed.

"The prettiest?"

"You're that, too. But that's not it, either."

"What then?" Benita danced around the yard, stopping to pick a daisy and stick it behind her ear. She picked another and ran back to Gram.

"I have a surprise for you." Gram submitted to the flower being tucked behind her ear. "My brother came by today with some fresh cream straight from the farm. You know what that means."

"Ice cream!" Benita yelled. "I scream, you scream, we all scream for ice cream. What kind?"

"After Uncle Jim left, I went to the store and bought some fresh strawberries. Guess where they were grown." Gram gathered the tools and headed for the house while Benita started guessing.

"BC? Nova Scotia? Oh, I know, I know! Ontario! It's not too early for strawberries in Ontario, right?"

Gram washed her hands in the kitchen sink and pulled the container of strawberries out of the fridge. She held it out so Benita could read the label for herself.

"California?"

"I'll get the ice-cream maker while you find California on the map."

Benita pulled a large road atlas from a shelf above Gram's desk and opened it on the old wooden kitchen table. Using the index in the back like Gram had showed her, she quickly located California on the list and turned to the right page.

"Got it?" Gram asked, cutting strawberries into a bowl.

"Yup."

"Yes."

"Yes. It's right here." Benita tapped a finger on the map. "Can I start turning the crank now?"

"Not so fast. First we pour the cream and sugar into this part, and where does the ice go?"

"In the bucket part." Benita watched as Gram dumped the ice cubes in.

As the two poured ingredients into the machine, Benita responded to Gram's off-the-cuff geography quiz.

"Is California in Canada?"

"No, silly," Benita said. "The United States."

"West or East Coast?"

Benita thought for a second. "West."

"And what else grows there?"

"Mmm. Grapes?"

"Yes. And oranges, and tomatoes, and broccoli, and lots of other good things." Gram smiled at her granddaughter as they began cranking the handle on the old ice-cream maker.

"Broccoli is not a good thing." Benita waggled her head. This was not even up for discussion.

"What did you do in school today?"

"Oh, the usual stuff. Can we play crazy eights while we eat our ice cream?"

"Probably. One round. But then it's homework time."

"Aww." Benita knew there was no point in complaining too loudly. Besides, she'd much rather finish her homework while Gram was around to help. If she left it until after her mother picked her up, she would have to do it on her own while her mother took care of household chores or worked on her own studies. Mom called them "correspondence courses," but Benita wasn't sure what that meant, only that it kept her mother preoccupied.

"What did you do in math class?" Gram asked.

"Finding . . . the lowest . . . common . . . denominator." Benita talked in rhythm with the cranking of the handle.

"Really? You mean to tell me it's 1981 and they still haven't found that thing?" Gram smiled. "I remember looking for it when I was a kid."

Benita started giggling until her cranking weakened into pathetic slow motion.

"I think you're trying to weasel out of work." Gram grinned. "Here, let me have a go at that handle." With Gram's strong arms at work, the ice cream thickened in no time, and the two sat down to enjoy two bowls filled with the icy pink treat.

"Mum ish gonna shay you ruined my abbethithe again." Benita talked around a big mouthful.

"I put a bowl in the freezer for her, too. I think she'll be okay with it. Now, tell me what you learned in English class."

"I don't remember." Benita shrugged. "Something about adverbs and adjectives."

"What about history?"

"Oh, Gram, I almost forgot!" Benita ran to the back door, where her schoolbag still lay. She dragged it to the table and pulled a notebook from it. "School's out in three more weeks and Miss Stokes gave us a project. We can either do it on the Great Depression or World War II."

"Oh?" Gram raised her eyebrows. "What precisely do you mean by 'we'?"

"You can help me, Gram. You were there!"

"I was, was I?" Gram smiled.

"Of course you were."

"I wasn't exactly *there*, at World War II. I was safely back here, in Canada."

"Well, okay, but you lived through it, right? You can talk and I'll write it all down." Benita opened her notebook to the first clean page and sat with her pen poised, waiting.

"Hmm, I don't think it's going to be quite that easy." Gram cleared the ice-cream dishes from the table and began to rinse them in the sink. "Why don't you go find a couple of encyclopedias and bring them to the table?"

Benita moved to the living room, where Gram's books covered one entire wall. The encyclopedias were on the bottom shelf.

"Which ones should I bring?" she called out.

"Well, think about it. What are you looking up?" Gram stood in the doorway, drying her hands on a dish towel.

"World War II. So . . . *W*?"

"Sure, we can start with that."

Benita hefted the book to her chest and lugged it over to the kitchen table, dropping it with a thud and a grunt.

"My, so dramatic!" Gram grinned. "Can you find it?"

Benita flipped pages, getting distracted every few moments by photos of walruses and watermelons and wigs. When Benita finally reached the section about World War II, Gram laid the dish towel aside and joined her at the table. The girl began to read aloud, pausing occasionally when she stumbled over an unfamiliar word.

"'Though conflict had been brewing in Europe for many months prior, World War II officially began at 5:20 a.m. (Polish time) on Friday, September 1, 1939, when the Germans bombed Puck (pronounced "Pootsk"), Poland . . .'"

With a giggle, Benita practiced the funny-sounding name. "Pootsk. Pootsk! '. . . a fishing village and air base. In the war's first five days, over fifteen hundred noncombatants died. On September 3, the United Kingdom and France declared war on Germany.

"'Canada, a country of large land mass but only eleven million people, began the war with an underequipped militia of only five thousand men. Nevertheless, men from across the country began volunteering to serve king and country.'"

Benita paused in her reading and looked up. Gram was gazing out the window, a faraway look in her eye.

"Gram?"

Gram's gaze slowly turned toward her granddaughter's face, but she remained silent.

"How old were you in 1939?" Benita knew full well her grandmother would make her figure it out for herself.

"You do the math. I was born in 1922."

Benita pulled a small calculator out of her bag and started punching in numbers.

"Now where on earth did you get that? Surely they don't let you use calculators in school at your age."

"Of course they do." Benita didn't even look up. "You were seventeen years old."

"Yes, I was, but I'd certainly feel better knowing you could figure that out on your own."

"I can." Benita shrugged. "Just not as fast." She turned back to her encyclopedia.

"Oh, here's what I need. 'A few brief facts. Canada was the first Commonwealth country to send troops to Britain in 1939.'"

"That's true," Gram said. "I remember."

"'From 1939 to 1945, hundreds of thousands of Canadians enlisted: more than 40 percent of the male population between the ages of eighteen and forty-five. Virtually all of them were volunteers.'"

"Yes, that's true, too," Gram agreed.

"Did you know some guys who signed up?"

"Oh, plenty. There were hardly any boys left at home. I thought it awful, but some of my girlfriends grabbed the chance to take jobs and learn new skills they wouldn't have had the opportunity to learn otherwise."

Benita turned back to her list of facts: "'The first Canadian infantryman to die in World War II was Private John Gray. He was captured and executed by the Japanese on December 13, 1941, in Hong Kong.'"

She looked at Gram expectantly, but Gram was staring out the window again. She drew in a deep breath and mumbled something Benita couldn't make out.

"What's that, Gram?"

"It isn't true," Gram said softly. "John Gray was not the first to die."

"What do you mean? It says so right here."

"The first Canadian soldier to be killed in World War II never saw a battle. He died in a train accident on December 10, 1939, on his way to Halifax to ship out to England." Gram spoke as if reciting a fact she'd memorized long ago.

"How do you know, Gram?" Benita couldn't believe that her dear grandmother dared to contradict one of her sacred encyclopedias.

"I just know."

PART 1

Cornelia

For I know the thoughts that I think toward you, saith the Lord, thoughts of peace, and not of evil, to give you an expected end.

Jeremiah 29:11

CHAPTER 1

Roseburg, Manitoba
January 1939

Seventeen-year-old Cornelia Simpson lifted a mirror off the attic wall and brushed away chips of paint that stuck to her fingers from the wooden frame. Concealed behind the mirror hung a pocket-size picture of Jesus—a prize she'd won for perfect Sunday school attendance years before. Cornelia scrutinized it. With her tongue poking out between her lips, she pushed a thumbtack straight into Jesus's left eye.

"Liar, liar, pants on fire," she whispered. "One day, I'll tell the world the truth about you."

Cornelia replaced the mirror with care, making sure it hid the picture. At her feet lay an untidy bundle of papers tied together with string. She penned *Diary, 1938* on the top sheet and waited for the ink to dry. Then she carried it to the far corner of the attic and placed the treasure into the bottom of an old silver suitcase, deep under a quilt, where prying eyes would not discover the darkest secrets she had recorded. As she began to close the lid, she suddenly reconsidered.

Carefully lifting out the colorful quilt and spreading it on the attic floor, Cornelia looked from piece to piece. The squares represented an array of color, each one holding a memory of her mother. She recognized bits of the flannel nightgown she'd worn as a preschooler, the dress she'd worn her first day of school, her mother's favorite apron, her brother's shirt. Or was it Daddy's?

This pink square, she knew, came from a dress she'd worn the summer she turned twelve, the summer her mother passed away. The dress had been a favorite of Cornelia's, though her mother had fashioned it from one of her own.

In one corner, there survived a patch from a little gray coat her parents had presented to her the Christmas she was ten: yet another item of clothing that had been lovingly made by her mother. Although Cornelia had hated the color, she'd never let on to her parents that she longed for a red coat like her friend Agnes's.

Cornelia ran her hand over the quilt's softness and closed her eyes, as though touching it might bring her mother closer. Five years. Cornelia had lived a lifetime since her mother's death—growing from girlhood to womanhood.

The thud of a door slamming below shook Cornelia. "Corrie?" her father called from downstairs.

Her father was in from doing chores and ready for a hot lunch. With her little brother back in school after the Christmas break, barn chores now took Daddy longer. So far, he had not recruited her to take Jim's place, and she wasn't about to volunteer. She stuffed the quilt back into the suitcase, closed the lid, and hurried back toward the ladder. A quick glance in the mirror as she passed told her she had tangled with more than one cobweb. She paused long enough to brush a hand over her light brown hair. Others often commented on her resemblance to her father's side of the family, but she saw her mother's gray-blue eyes looking back at her.

"Coming, Daddy." Cornelia scrambled down the ladder to the second floor, where the family's bedrooms were located. Then she hurried down the stairs to the first floor. In one smooth motion, she grabbed an apron from behind the kitchen door at the bottom of the stairs and began stoking the fire in the old cookstove.

"Soup's hot. Bread's cool enough to eat," she called over her shoulder.

"Good girl." Her father scrubbed his hands at the tin basin by the back door, hung the towel neatly back into place, and took his seat across from Cornelia at their kitchen table. Charles Simpson's receding hairline, graying temples, and weathered skin made him appear older than his forty-two years.

"Well, now. Why don't you say grace for us today?" He smiled at his daughter.

Cornelia had this down to a routine. Crossing the fingers of both hands under the table, she bowed her head. "Come, Lord Jesus, be our guest; let this food to us be blessed. By his hand we all are fed; thank you, God, for daily bread. Please watch over Jimmy at school, and thank you for the shelter for us and for our animals in this winter weather. Amen."

With her father's heartfelt "Amen!" they began slurping the simple soup and devouring the homemade bread.

"Won't be long till we have butter and cheese to go with this," Charles said.

Cornelia looked up from her soup. She'd gladly forgo butter and cheese if it meant prolonging the reprieve from milking, separating, churning, and cheese making. But she kept her opinion to herself.

"Why? Is Hazel having her calf?"

"Anytime now. And she always provides more than enough milk." Charles's chest grew noticeably broader at this declaration.

Cornelia hoped the calf would wait for a break in the weather, both for its sake and for hers. With the meal complete, she dipped hot water from the reservoir on the side of the stove into a basin and began washing both the breakfast and lunch dishes while deep in thought. *Is this to be my life, then?* She sighed. *The days running into each other, each one repeating the same cycle, like the hands of the clock on the mantel? The activities never changing except perhaps as dictated by the seasons? Different chores, slight variations in diet, but otherwise the same endless cycle?*

As she dried a chipped plate, she wandered over to the window and breathed on the glass to clear a peephole through the frost. The blinding sunlight reflecting off the snow made it hard for Cornelia's eyes to adjust. She was thankful to be safe and warm inside. Still, something restless stirred inside her, and she envied her little brother's opportunity to continue his education and see his friends each day. They'd argued about it last night as Jimmy anticipated returning to school.

"You're lucky, Corny. You get to stay home."

"Stop calling me Corny. And you're the one who's lucky."

"No, I'm not. Stick me on the tractor any day of the week. You can even stick me on a milking stool. It's still better than those teeny little desks at school. And you get to sit here inside and stay nice and warm, Corny."

"I said stop calling me Corny!"

"Corny, Corny, Corny."

It escalated into a tea-towel-snapping chase around the kitchen, during which Cornelia realized her baby brother was quickly gaining on her in both strength and stamina. Maybe she shouldn't let Jimmy's teasing get under her skin, but where was the fun in disappointing him by not reacting?

Now, from the living room, the radio crackled with a weather report, bringing Cornelia back to the moment. She knew her father would soon doze off in his favorite chair, as he did every afternoon in the winter months. She dried the last dish and bundled herself into warm boots, coat, and hat. Outside, a clothesline full of frozen long johns and towels waited to be relieved of its icy burden, and Cornelia needed some fresh air. She stepped out into the brightness and stood still long enough to blink and suck in her breath before hustling over to the clothesline. Even old Shep, their border collie, hid in some straw under the back steps instead of tripping her up today.

Fumbling with mittened hands, Cornelia freed the clothing from the grip of the pins and laid each piece in a pile on the snow. They looked like a stack of mummies. By the time she added the last one, her freezing fingers could barely manage the clothespins. In a rush to thaw her fingers, she abandoned the bucket of pins, picked up the clothes, and panted back to the house. This was ridiculous. It had not been nearly this cold when she'd hung the clothes out the day before. At least the bright sunlight had whitened them, as she'd hoped.

"Are you proud of me, Ma?" Cornelia whispered.

Back inside, she dumped her load unceremoniously on the kitchen table to thaw, and removed her winter wear. She threw more wood into the kitchen stove and filled the teakettle, rubbing her hands together over the stove while she waited for the water to heat up.

Once the tea was ready, Cornelia filled one of her mother's pink china cups and carried it upstairs to her bedroom. Humming "Side by Side" to no one in particular, she wrapped a shawl around her shoulders and then sat at a small desk by the window. She reached into a drawer and pulled out the brand-new diary she had unwrapped on Christmas morning. Like every other diary she'd received on Christmas mornings since the age of twelve, this simple school notebook held a thousand possibilities. And like her previous diaries, this one would no doubt fall apart and need string to hold it together before the year ended. But for now, it represented a world of pristine potential. *Surely, somehow, this year my story will finally begin,* she thought.

While her tea cooled to a drinkable temperature, Cornelia dipped her pen in its inkwell, opened the diary to its first page, and wrote *January 5, 1939*.

CHAPTER 2

May 1939

Cornelia buried the last of the seed potatoes in dirt, making a little hill with her hoe the way Daddy had taught her years before. It was mid-May and only the delicate tomatoes remained to plant. Now if it would only rain. *If I hurry, I can take a bath before starting supper,* she thought, gathering her hoe and empty gunnysack. But as she rounded the corner of the toolshed, she was surprised to see a bright red car in the farmyard. A tall young man climbed out of the driver's seat while an older woman emerged from the passenger side.

"Is this the Simpson place?" The woman looked vaguely familiar.

"Yes. I'm Cornelia Simpson." Cornelia glanced over at the driver and back to the woman, then brushed dirt from her clothing before hiding her blackened hands in her pockets.

"Pleased to meet you, Cornelia. My name is Eva Roberts and this is my son, Henry." Henry nodded in her direction, and Cornelia merely nodded back. His neatly combed hair, clean clothes, and shiny shoes emphasized her dishevelment.

"Actually," the woman continued, "we've met before, when you were small."

Cornelia waited for her to continue, trying to puzzle out where she'd seen her.

"Your mother and I were friends as girls. I was so sorry to hear of her passing."

"It's been five years, ma'am." Cornelia tried not to sound rude, but it seemed a strange time to pay one's respects.

"Yes. I so badly wanted to come sooner." Mrs. Roberts looked at her shoes. "The economy being what it's been . . . well, I haven't been back to the area in nearly fifteen years."

Cornelia wasn't sure what to say next.

"Is your father home?" The woman glanced around the farmyard.

"He—um, had to go to town for seed and will probably pick up my brother from school on the way back. They should be here any minute. Would you like to come in?" After fifteen years couldn't they have waited an extra fifteen minutes and given her time to clean up?

"Thank you, that would be lovely." The woman turned to her son. "Henry, please bring the package."

Cornelia stepped onto the front porch, with Mrs. Roberts following.

"Please excuse me, I've been planting the garden. I must be quite a sight."

"Perfectly understandable, dear. Good for you. And you look lovely. I saw your father in you right away. If you like, we can wait out here and give you a chance to clean up."

Feeling relieved, Cornelia remembered the manners her hospitable mother had ingrained in her. "Let me at least bring you a drink first. Coffee or a cold glass of water?"

Once the two strangers were settled on the front porch with their water, Cornelia washed as quickly as she knew how. It was not the hot bath she longed for, but it would have to do. She changed out of her denim overalls into a brown straight skirt and a soft, short-sleeved pink sweater. She swept a teensy bit of rouge on each cheek and ran a brush through her hair, which Aunt Nonie had cut into a stylish bob just last month.

As she returned to the porch, Daddy and Jim were just pulling up, with puzzled looks on their faces. They climbed out of her father's old truck, and Jim hung back to admire the Robertses' car while Daddy ventured forward.

"Good afternoon, ma'am."

"Charles! It's so good to see you." Mrs. Roberts stood but offered nothing by way of explaining her identity.

Cornelia watched, wondering whether she should introduce the two visitors. Her father stared at the woman. Did he know her or not?

"Eva Holston!"

She smiled. "Eva Roberts now. I'd like you to meet my son, Henry. We're in the area visiting family, and I just had to come by and see you. We were so sorry when we heard about Mary."

"Thank you. Uh—this is my daughter, Cornelia, and my son, Jim."

"Yes, Cornelia has already been very gracious. Hello, Jim."

Jim shook Henry's hand and turned back to the woman. "I think I've seen you in pictures."

"Mrs. . . . uh . . . Roberts, was it?" Daddy asked, and she nodded. "Mrs. Roberts was your mother's maid of honor at our wedding, Jim. You've seen her in our wedding picture."

Now a light switched on for Cornelia. She had seen her parents' wedding picture, too, of course. But she had also seen a picture from this woman's wedding, in which Cornelia's mother had been the matron of honor. She remembered her mother faithfully writing letters to her friend Eva, and speaking of her on many occasions.

"Can you stay for supper?" her father asked.

After offering the obligatory protests about not wanting to impose, and after Cornelia had provided equally obligatory assurances that their staying would be no bother, the Robertses agreed to stay. Cornelia excused herself to the kitchen where the three small chops she had planned to fry waited. She put on her apron and began cutting the meat into cubes for stew instead.

Jim followed her inside a few minutes later. "Dad says I should help you."

"Fetch some potatoes, onions, and carrots from the root cellar." She handed him a bucket. "Oh, and here's a second bucket for apples. After that, you can start peeling. I'll make apple crisp for dessert."

Cornelia set the table while the meat began to simmer. She jumped when she realized Henry was standing in the doorway.

"Sorry. Didn't mean to startle you."

"You didn't," Cornelia lied. "How long have you been there?"

"Not long." His brown eyes studied her. "I remember you, you know. Do you remember me?"

"No. I mean, yes. Well, not really." Cornelia remembered seeing a photo of her mother posing with Eva, a two-year-old Cornelia, and a dark-haired little boy who could only have been Henry. "We have a photo of our mothers together, with you and I," Cornelia stammered. "Me, I mean. You and me. But I only figured that out now. That it was you and your mother, I mean. I was just a toddler." Cornelia bit her lip in an attempt to stop stumbling over her words.

"I remember the visit." Henry grinned. "You came to our home with your mother, and you wore a bright red dress. We chased the cat. You tripped on the stairs and skinned your knee, but you didn't cry."

Cornelia's eyes widened. "You have an awfully good memory."

"Well, I was probably just older. About four, I think. I'm nineteen now."

"And I'm seventeen."

"That explains it." Henry leaned against the kitchen counter, his arms crossed, one ankle casually resting atop the other, as though he talked to girls all the time.

"Yes, that explains it," she muttered, wondering why it was so easy to talk to her brother but talking to this stranger made her heart pound. She sighed with relief when Jim came up the cellar ladder and handed her the pail of vegetables.

"Let me give you a hand with those." Henry reached for a bucket.

Jim gave Henry the apples, and the pair went to work peeling and cutting while Cornelia prepared the crisp part of the dessert. She was thankful that the boys talked easily about boy things, like baseball and cars. She wasn't good at one-on-one conversations with people she didn't know. Especially male people.

Once the stew was simmering and the apple crisp baking, they returned to the porch, where her father and Mrs. Roberts were deep in conversation.

"So you can see why it was worth the extra time to drive out here, Charles," she was saying. "I'm sorry I waited so long. I should have sent this as soon as I heard about Mary's passing—as soon as I learned of her illness, really—but I didn't feel right putting it in the mail. It seemed to me it deserved a personal delivery."

Eva Roberts gave Daddy the package Henry had carried from the car. Daddy sat holding it and Cornelia thought he looked almost afraid to open it.

"I don't know what to say, Eva. I didn't know this still existed. Are you sure?"

"It's yours now, Charles. To pass on to your children."

"What is it, Dad?" Jim couldn't contain his curiosity.

"Is supper ready, Corrie?" their father asked.

"Almost."

"Sorry, son," Daddy said with a grin. "But I'm afraid you're going to have to wait and see."

CHAPTER 3

While the others enjoyed her hot apple crisp topped with fresh cream, Cornelia slipped away from the table and returned with a box of photographs. As her father poured coffee for everyone, she opened the box.

"I thought you might enjoy looking at these." She pulled out an assortment of framed and unframed photographs of various relatives, dressed in their finest and staring at the camera in a most serious manner. Cornelia picked up her parents' wedding picture and handed it to Eva Roberts. *August 1917* appeared in faded ink on the back.

"Ah, yes." Eva sighed and gave a little smile. "Look how young we all were! Of course, this wasn't the actual wedding day, you know."

"It wasn't?" Cornelia raised her eyebrows.

"Oh, no," her father said. "Back then you did your picture taking whenever the photographer came around with all his equipment and set up a studio."

"And you did your marrying whenever the preacher came around." Eva laughed. "The two events *never* happened at the same time."

"Weddings were held after church on Sunday," Charles said. "And in Roseburg, we only had a preacher every other Sunday, when it was our turn. The wedding would be announced a month or so in advance.

Then on the big day, everybody brought something for a grand potluck and stayed after church to witness the ceremony and eat together."

"No such thing as honeymoons, either," Eva added.

Charles nodded. "Well, maybe for the rich. Most grooms simply took their new brides home—if they were fortunate enough to have a place of their own."

"Did you?" Jim asked.

"Not right away. Your mother and I stayed at the old Thompson cabin five miles north of town. We didn't move to this place until five years later. By that time you had arrived, Corrie."

"So then when was this picture taken?" Jim studied the photo.

"About a month after the wedding, I think," Eva said. "Your mother and I had sewn new dresses for the wedding, and it killed us that we hadn't yet had a chance to wear them a second time. We couldn't wait to dress up again and pose for the picture. The men took a little more coaxing."

Henry took the photo from Jim. "Who's the best man?"

"That's my brother, Bill." Cornelia's father gazed at the picture with a distant look in his eye. "We lost him in the war a few months later."

Cornelia reached into the box and pulled out another unframed photo: the one in which she and Henry appeared as small children, seated on their mothers' laps. When she turned it over, she could barely make out her mother's handwriting. "'Cornelia and I with Eva and Henry in Winnipeg, June 1924,'" she read out loud. "'A very pleasant visit.'"

They passed the photo around the table. "Was that the last time you saw Mary, then?" Charles's voice held a slight quiver.

"Yes," Eva said, sighing. "If only I'd known. She met my Samuel just that once. He would have loved to come with us on this trip, but his printing business keeps him much too busy."

"I understand," Charles said, but Cornelia wondered whether he really did. His own planting was no less important, yet he had sacrificed several hours of precious daylight to sit here and visit with this old friend.

"Here, Mrs. Roberts. You may as well keep these." Cornelia pulled a stack of letters from the bottom of the box, wrapped in a ribbon. "Your letters to my mother. I'm sure they are even more precious to you than they are to us."

"Oh my—look at that! She saved them." Eva took the bundle and held them to her heart, her eyes glistening.

"You were always special to her." Charles smiled, then turned to Jim. "And son, I know you've been dying to know what's in the package these good folks brought. I think it's time."

Jim needed no further encouragement. He picked up the box from where it had sat at his feet since before supper, when his father first instructed him to be patient. In a flash, Jim opened the box and pulled out a bucketlike contraption with the words *North Pole Freezer* printed on the side and a crank handle with *1910* stamped on it.

Jim's eyebrows came together like a puzzle. "What is it?"

Charles and Eva laughed. "It's an ice-cream maker!" she said, as though it were the sort of thing everyone should know.

"Ice cream?" Jim looked stumped. "Well, I love ice cream. I mean, I've only tried it a few times, when the fair comes to town. But what they make it in doesn't look anything like this."

Charles explained how the machine worked: A person placed the cream and sugar in a cylinder inside the bucket, then added ice or snow around the cylinder, plus salt to make the ice melt faster. Then they turned the crank continuously while melted ice leaked out the little hole in the side of the bucket.

"Well, we've got plenty of cream . . . but where can we find ice this time of year?" Jim examined the gears.

"I think we can manage to round some up," Charles said. "But first, you all need to hear the story behind this gadget."

"I thought you'd never get to that part." Cornelia turned to Eva. "Why did you say this belonged to us?"

"I'll let your dad tell it," Eva replied, and smiled in Charles's direction.

"Let's see if I can remember all the details right." Charles paused and looked at his children with a grin.

"Mrs. Roberts, your mother, and I were all in the same Sunday school class at Roseburg Christian Church. We were, what, about twelve or thirteen?"

Mrs. Roberts nodded.

"The Sunday school superintendent was Old Man Jacob, Elsie Jacob's father. Somehow he'd acquired this fantastic ice-cream maker and offered it as a prize to the student who could memorize the most Scripture over the course of the year."

Cornelia tried to picture her father at Jim's age, knowing Jim's dislike for memorization of any kind.

"Old Man Jacob made the offer in September and the ice-cream maker would be presented at the Sunday school picnic in June," Charles continued. "Naturally we all wanted it, although some of us were a lot more disciplined about memorizing than others."

"Most of all, we didn't want Elsie Jacob to win it." Eva laughed.

"Well, now, that's true, too. Old Man Jacob was convinced his daughter was the smartest, finest young lady in the whole Sunday school and would win the machine hands down. He figured he'd be able to enjoy the ice cream while still looking like a hero for having come up with such a great prize." Charles chuckled. "Poor girl probably never felt so much pressure in her life."

"Poor girl?" Eva interrupted. "Her opinion of herself was even higher than her father's. Nobody wanted to see her win. Your mother and I went to work memorizing verses immediately, quizzing each other at every opportunity . . . recess time, mostly. But I'm sorry, Charles, you're telling this."

The three youthful faces around the table all turned back to Charles. Cornelia wondered if Jim and Henry were imagining their parents as children, like she was.

"Well, I wanted that ice-cream maker, and so did half a dozen other boys. But by Easter, it was pretty clear that only two of us were still in the running."

"You and Eddie Hoffmann." Eva laughed. "But there were at least eight of us girls still in. Sorry, you tell it."

Charles smiled. "You can go ahead and tell it, you know."

"Well, okay, if you insist." Eva scooted forward in her chair. "The elimination round was held two weeks before the picnic. We kids stood at the front of the church and recited Scripture as Mr. Jacob called out the reference for each passage."

"If you missed more than two words in any given passage, you were out," Charles added.

"By the end of the round, five contestants were still standing." Mrs. Roberts counted them off on her fingers. "Your father, your mother, Eddie Hoffmann, Elsie Jacob, and me. We worked like crazy for the next week. Competition got fierce. It wasn't so much about the ice-cream maker anymore."

"Speak for yourself." Charles laughed.

"By the day of the picnic, your mother and I were no longer helping each other. We weren't even speaking to each other! Here we were, best friends since infancy, and we were making an all-out war with a Sunday school contest."

"Girls." Jim rolled his eyes and Cornelia swatted his elbow.

"So who won?" Henry's question fell on deaf ears.

"The picnic day was glorious," his mother said. "The grown-ups decided to hold the contest outdoors so the little ones could run around. Parents sat on blankets in the shade, and we five lined up in a row."

Charles picked up the story again. "Eddie Hoffmann went out first, and boy, was he mad! Stomped off in a big huff, and nobody could keep from laughing because the verse he went out on was James 1:20—"

"'For the wrath of man worketh not the righteousness of God,'" Eva recited. "It started as a snicker, and then as people realized the irony, the laughter got louder and just made Eddie angrier."

"The next person to go out was Elsie Jacob. She never lost her dignity, just walked casually over to her mother with her nose in the air and plunked down as if she didn't have a care in the world, while her father fumed. It all proved quite entertaining."

"That left Mary, Eva, and me," Charles said. "I felt so nervous I thought I would be sick right on the spot. Ice cream had never seemed less appealing. I'd learned a lot of verses, but I figured those two girls were way smarter."

"Besides, you already had a little thing going for Mary," Eva teased.

"I won't deny it. I went out on the very next challenge. To this day, I don't recall the reference."

"Nor do I." Eva looked around to make certain she had everyone's attention. "I was just glad. Now it was down to Mary and me, and we'd gone from bosom friends to archrivals in the course of a week. I really wanted to show her up."

"Obviously, you won," Henry said. "You ended up with the prize."

"But she brought it here and called it ours," Jim protested. "So who won?"

Eva responded with a sly smile, and Charles took up the story with a twinkle in his eyes.

"The contest carried on. Both girls kept reciting Scripture after Scripture . . . from Proverbs, St. John, and Philippians. Neither of them made a single error. Old Man Jacob ran out of references from his required-learning list, so the parents started throwing out random verses. They assigned Eddie and me the task of looking them up and verifying the accuracy."

"The contest went on for what seemed like hours," Eva said.

"This story is going on for what seems like hours," Jim muttered. Cornelia smacked the back of her hand against her brother's shoulder.

"Especially to those of us who were waiting to enjoy some ice cream," Charles said. "The little children got cranky, and the men worried about getting home to milk their cows."

"At some point, Mr. Jacob declared the contest a tie, and when he finally did, the handful who still remained all cheered." Eva smiled at the memory.

"The adults produced cream and ice from I-don't-know-where," Charles said, "and for the rest of the afternoon, we cranked out ice cream. What no one had realized was how long it would take or how little ice cream the machine would make. I think everybody ate only a spoonful before it disappeared."

"Oh, no!" Jimmy wailed.

"At the end of the day, Mary's family took home the prize with the understanding that they would share it with Eva's family, passing it back and forth as often as they could."

"And you two were friends again?" Cornelia asked.

"Yes. But there's more to the story." Eva smiled at Charles.

Cornelia's father raised his eyebrows. "More?"

"It seems that while you had a thing for Mary, Eddie Hoffman had a little thing for *me.* While you were distracted, by Mary no doubt, he purposely had overlooked a mistake I made and pronounced it correct."

"Really?" Cornelia's eyes sparkled. "How romantic!"

"I should have gone out on the turn just before Mr. Jacob declared a tie. Your mother really did win."

"Did you ever tell her?" Henry asked.

"I never knew about it until years later when Eddie 'fessed up to me at my wedding. By then your mother was already married, the ice-cream maker had traveled between our homes on a regular basis, and we had grown up enough to laugh it off."

"That Eddie guy must have carried a torch for you the whole time," Jim said with a big grin.

"Oh, I don't know about that." Eva dismissed the notion with a wave of her hand. "I wouldn't have wanted someone so dishonest. He wound up marrying Elsie Jacob."

Everyone laughed.

"The best part? We all learned a lot of valuable Scripture," Charles said, "although we didn't see it that way at the time."

"True enough," Eva said.

"Now, Eva, if you aren't in too big a hurry, I think this calls for a celebration. Henry, if you'll be so kind as to drive that fancy car of yours, Corrie will be happy to show you the way to Tucker's General Store where you can pick up some ice."

Cornelia's head shot up from studying the ice-cream maker, but her father didn't seem to notice.

"We've got more cream than we know what to do with. Now, the sooner you're back, the sooner we can start cranking."

Cornelia's palms immediately began to sweat. She would be riding with Henry in the car, all the way to town and back? Alone? Part of her wanted to protest, but she didn't know how to do that without hurting Henry's feelings.

"Jim and I will do the milking while you're gone." Charles was already donning his coveralls.

"How come Corny gets to—?" Jim began, but a stern look from his father stopped him mid-complaint. He headed out the door and to the barn, craning his neck toward the fine car as he walked.

"And I'll wash these supper dishes," Eva offered. "Thank you for a lovely meal, Corrie."

And so it was decided.

CHAPTER 4

Cornelia grabbed a sweater and climbed into the Robertses' bright red car, and Henry hopped in behind the wheel. He headed down their driveway and turned right on the gravel road, toward town.

"Nice car," Cornelia said, to make conversation. She didn't care much about cars, but this one sure beat the rusty Ford Model T truck her family drove around in.

"Thanks. It's a '32 Pontiac five-window coupe. It's my dad's."

"I'm sure you could find the store on your own. There's not much in Roseburg."

"I'm glad for the company." Henry looked around at the freshly plowed fields. "Do you go to school in town?"

"Oh, no. I went to the one-room school just ahead, where Jim goes still. This will be his last year."

"What about high school?" Henry shifted gears as the car sped up.

"I didn't go. I was twelve when Mother died, and Daddy really needed me around the house. I finished my grade nine through correspondence, but by grade ten Daddy figured I'd had enough education."

When Henry didn't respond, she added, "It's more than a lot of the girls around here get."

"What about Jim?"

"Jim and Dad constantly discuss whether he should continue. He wants to quit school and help out on the farm. Dad thinks it would be good for Jim to take some high school, but he would need to board in town—which costs a lot. Plus, I'd be stuck helping Dad with the farmwork. So, I'd be fine with it if Jimmy stays home, even if he does get on my nerves sometimes. Nobody around here finishes high school if they're planning to farm. What about you?"

Henry hesitated. "I graduated last year."

Cornelia shouldn't have been surprised. Henry was a city boy, after all. But somehow knowing that she sat next to a high school graduate, especially one so close to her own age, felt intimidating and made her long for something more for herself.

"I've been working with my dad this past year, in his printing business. But to be honest, we haven't been getting along so well. Typesetting gets awfully tedious. Actually . . ." Henry paused. "That's the biggest reason for this trip out here. I'm going to stay with my cousins for the rest of the summer and help out on their farm."

"Wow!" Cornelia felt strangely pleased with this new information. "Do you even know anything about farming?"

"I've never done any, but it's always fascinated me. As far back as I can remember, I've loved to hear the stories my mother told about growing up on the farm. Besides a ball diamond, a farm is the only place I ever really wanted to be."

Cornelia recalled conversations around the kitchen table that she'd overheard through the years. The adults loved to discuss "the dirty thirties." They talked about how much harder the Great Depression was on city folk, many of whom were out of work, standing in long lines for soup to feed their families, or hoping for a few hours of work just to pay the rent.

"We may not have it so good, either," her father often repeated, "but even with the drought, we've always had potatoes and eggs to keep us going. And nobody's going to kick us off our land."

To her ears, the city sounded like a horrible place, and she was thankful to live in the country. She tried to picture Henry growing up in the noise and squalor and sadness she imagined Winnipeg to be.

Cornelia watched a jackrabbit bound across the road ahead of them. "I don't blame you for wanting to be out here."

"It sure is quieter."

"Is it true every house in the city has electric lights?" Cornelia found this hard to believe.

"Every house I've ever been in. I guess I'll miss that."

Feeling surprised by how quickly she'd become comfortable around Henry, Cornelia said, "I've even heard they have indoor bathrooms."

"Some do. We use an outhouse, but my parents hope to put in a bathroom soon. We already have running water in the kitchen. I'll miss that, too, I suppose. My cousins here have a pump in their kitchen, like yours. I guess that's just as good."

"What do you do for fun?"

"Baseball. All the way!" Henry's grin spread across his face.

"Really? Are you on a real team, with uniforms and everything?"

"I was. Even coached a kids' team for a while. Wesley Park is behind United College. It's home to the Winnipeg Amateur Senior Baseball League. In 1932, they built a new grandstand, bleachers, outfield fence, a public address system, and a cutting-edge lighting system." Henry's face glowed like the ballpark itself. "The park holds six thousand fans. They played the first night game in May of 1932, only one year after the first night game ever played at any level of baseball."

"So you're a history expert, too?" Cornelia grinned.

"Only baseball history. Osborne Stadium was opened in 1932 as well. It's another lighted facility. Football is usually played there, but it can also seat five thousand for baseball, and it hosts lots of tournaments and touring teams. Sherburne Park in the west end has dressing rooms and padded grandstand seats. It's home to the Winnipeg Maroons. I'd love to play for them someday."

Cornelia wasn't really taking in much of what Henry shared, but she sure loved how his eyes sparkled when he talked about baseball. And he wasn't through.

"Winnipeg now has three first-class baseball parks, two of them lighted and capable of hosting any level of baseball. They rival any facilities in baseball outside the major leagues. And that doesn't even count the community fields, where I play."

"You won't find any organized baseball around here, I'm afraid," Cornelia said. "But you'll definitely find guys who love to play if they're given the chance."

"Well, maybe I'll just do that." Henry grinned as he pulled up in front of Roseburg's only store, Tucker's General.

Mr. Tucker seemed happy to sell them two buckets of ice and insisted on carrying one to the car. "Fine automobile," he said, eyebrows raised.

Henry did not offer more than a simple "thanks," leaving an inquisitive-looking Mr. Tucker to watch them drive away.

On the ride home, Cornelia felt glad that her father had suggested the trip.

"It's your turn," Henry said. "Tell me what you like."

Cornelia grinned. "Well. Not baseball."

Henry reached one hand to the floor where one bucket of ice sat, picked up a chip of ice, and threw it at her, missing her nose by several inches.

"Strike one!" She laughed.

"Seriously, what do you do for fun?"

"Me?"

"Yes, you. Unless you want one of the folks in the backseat to go first." Now it was Cornelia's turn to toss an ice chip Henry's way, and she nailed his right ear.

"Hey!" Henry pretended he was going to throw the ice back at Cornelia, but then flung it out his open window instead. "The driver's off-limits."

"Well, I gotta admit, *that* was kind of fun."

"C'mon, you must do something for fun besides ice-chip wars."

Cornelia grew quiet. What *did* she do? She had so little time for anything but work. "Summer or winter?"

"Both."

"Well . . . in the summer, I go fishing with Jimmy sometimes."

"Really? Nearby?"

"Just down by the creek."

"Catch anything?"

"Oh, sure, all the time. I make Jimmy clean them, though."

"Meany."

"Hey, that's what little brothers are for. Besides, I do the cooking. And he doesn't mind."

Henry grinned. "Maybe you can show me your fishing hole sometime. So what do you do for fun in the winter? Skate?"

"No. Never owned a pair of my own. Winter evenings we listen to the radio. *Fibber McGee and Molly* is pretty funny. Jimmy likes *The Lone Ranger* and Daddy likes the *Grand Ole Opry*. Mother used to like listening to Guy Lombardo."

"Do you miss your mom a lot?"

Cornelia nodded. Was she ready to talk about her mother's passing with someone she'd just met?

"I like to read, too. I've read everything in our school library at least twice and everything on Aunt Miriam's shelves at least once. And . . ." She paused to gather her courage. "I write."

"Really? What do you write?"

"Oh, just stuff. In a diary. It helps. You know, with missing my mom and stuff."

Unsure why, Cornelia found herself telling Henry things she hadn't talked about with anyone else.

"It's been a lonely time," she admitted. "My best girlfriend from school days got married and moved away. Now I'm the oldest of the single girls at church. It's hard to know where I fit in. All the girls a few years older are settling into married life and having babies."

"Is that what you'd like to do?"

"Someday, I guess. I always thought I'd like to be a teacher, but I suppose that won't happen." Cornelia shrugged as though this didn't matter. They drove the last few miles in comfortable silence.

"It's nice to have someone my age to talk to," she said as they pulled back into her own yard.

"It was your dad's idea." Henry set the brake, then grinned at Cornelia. "Smart man."

They spent the rest of the evening cranking out delicious ice cream and eating it together, while their parents told more stories from their youth. When they finally said good-bye, Henry looked Cornelia in the eye and told her he'd be "seeing her around." Cornelia smiled back.

I'll have a lot to write in my diary tonight, she thought as she closed the door behind him.

CHAPTER 5

June 1939

Cornelia hung the last of her father's socks on the line and walked around the corner of the house, where she barely missed getting clobbered in the face with a large stick. Her brother was swinging it like a baseball bat.

"Whoa, Jim! Be careful." She swung her laundry basket at him, but he swerved out of the way.

"Sorry, Sis. Can I, Dad?" Jimmy begged.

"I don't see why not," Daddy said. "As long as it doesn't interfere with your chores and you don't hit anybody." He lifted his ax high over his head and split a piece of firewood with one blow.

"Can he what?" Cornelia asked.

"Never mind." Jimmy tossed a rock into the air and hit it with his stick. "It ain't for girls."

"Enough, Jim," Daddy said. "If you want to join in and be a team player, you'll need a more mature attitude than that." He turned to Cornelia. "That young Henry Roberts is recruiting players for baseball."

Cornelia looked at her brother's makeshift equipment. "Baseball *ain't* for boys who *ain't* got a ball or a bat."

"I figure if I get good with this rock and stick, then playing with the real thing will be a cinch." Jimmy ignored Cornelia's dig and puffed out his chest. "Henry's got a bat, a ball, *and* a glove. And we can use the school's, too. That's where we're going to play."

The next evening Cornelia, Jimmy, and their father walked the two miles to Jimmy's school. Henry and Walter Johnson were already choosing teams, and Jimmy eagerly made his presence known.

"I pick Jim," Henry said, as soon as he saw him. Jim strutted over to Henry's side, smiling like he'd just been handed a solid-gold trophy.

"We're never gonna be able to live with him now," Daddy said as he and Cornelia settled themselves on a blanket to watch the game. A handful of other spectators already dotted the schoolyard.

"Hi, Corrie." Cornelia looked up to see two former school chums, Angela Pendeski and Jean Little. The two were inseparable.

"Come to watch the game?" Angela asked, flopping on the blanket beside Cornelia.

"Or just the boys?" Jean whispered as she plopped down between them.

"Just my little brother." Cornelia sighed, glancing at her father.

"That's not what I heard." When Angela and Jean began giggling, Cornelia's father stood with a grunt and crossed to the fence where half a dozen other fathers sat or leaned on the top rail. Cornelia watched him walk away, then turned back to her friends.

"Word has it Henry's sweet on you, Corrie," Jean said.

"I wouldn't know." Cornelia could feel the heat in her cheeks.

"Wouldn't know or wouldn't say?" Angela tugged on Cornelia's hair as she and Jean burst into another fit of giggles.

By now the boys had finished forming their teams and Jimmy swaggered up to bat first. Jordy Jorgenson threw out the opening pitch, wide and high. Mr. Munson, who operated the gas station in town, was serving as umpire. He declared the pitch a ball, and Jordy threw out another. This time Jimmy swung, but missed.

"Stee-rike!" Mr. Munson sang out, like he'd been waiting for years to make such a proclamation.

On the next pitch, Jimmy managed to hit the ball and make it safely to first. One by one, batters followed suit until all three bases were loaded. Next, Henry was up to bat. He approached home plate and took a couple of practice swings.

"C'mon, Henry, hit 'em all home!" one of the other players called out. Henry glanced at the girls on the blanket long enough to catch Cornelia's eye. She gave him a shy smile, and he turned his focus back to the pitcher.

As though he'd been born to play ball, Henry hit the first pitch far into the outfield: a home run with bases loaded. Cheers went up as Henry circled the bases and ran home, and Cornelia saw Henry ruffle Jimmy's hair before sending him up to bat again.

As the game continued, the girls eventually lost interest and became absorbed in their own conversation. Angela and Jean caught Cornelia up on school news: who was staying or quitting, whether they'd have a new teacher in the fall, and which girls liked which boys. The girls almost missed it entirely when a foul ball came their way. At the last second, Cornelia stuck out one hand and caught the ball before it hit the ground. Without rising, she casually threw the ball back to the pitcher.

"Now how on earth do I call that one?" Mr. Munson spat on the ground and everybody laughed. The game resumed and the girls went back to their conversation.

After the game, Henry wandered over to Cornelia. "Walk you home?" he said. Cornelia nodded. With his bat slung across one shoulder and his glove hanging off the bat, Henry tossed the ball into the air with his free hand and caught it again as they headed down the gravel road. Jim quickly caught up and hopped in circles around Henry and Cornelia like an eager puppy in danger of wagging its tail clear off.

"Great game, Henry. Wow, you really know how to hit 'em!"

"You didn't do so bad yourself, slugger," Henry said. "Wouldn't surprise me a bit if you're the one hitting the homer next game."

"Jim!" Cornelia heard her father calling from about twenty feet behind them. "Give me a hand with this, would ya?" Charles Simpson fumbled with the blanket they'd brought along.

"Aw, Dad!"

"Jim."

"Okay." Jimmy scampered back to his father and together they folded the blanket. Cornelia could hear her father's soft voice, but couldn't make out what he said. For the rest of the walk, though, Jimmy and Daddy stayed several feet behind. She knew it had to be killing Jimmy.

"Thanks for your kindness to Jimmy," Cornelia said, smiling at Henry.

"He's a great kid. I wish he had the opportunities I had at his age."

"He does just fine." Corrie felt the need to defend her brother's supposed lack of opportunities.

"Oh, I know. In lots of ways, he has a lot I never did. So I guess it evens out," Henry said.

"Like what?"

"A beautiful sister, for one."

Cornelia felt the heat rising in her cheeks again and looked at her shoes. "And how exactly would that be an advantage?"

"If I had a pretty sister—or even an ugly one—maybe I wouldn't feel so shy around girls." Henry tossed his ball up and caught it again.

"You? Shy?"

Henry nodded. "Yep."

"Well, you hide it well."

"Some girls are easier to talk to than others. That was a nice catch tonight, by the way. No glove or anything." Henry's gentle smile made Cornelia feel warm everywhere.

"Why, thank you."

"Pretty decent throwing arm, too. You sure you don't play baseball?"

Cornelia laughed. "Probably comes from kneading bread."

"Well, you should consider it. Playing, I mean." Henry tossed the ball to Cornelia and she caught it. He ran ahead a few paces and walked backward so she could throw the ball back. They continued on this way, playing catch and making small talk, until they reached the Simpson farm. At his father's prompting, Jimmy ran on ahead, and Henry tossed him the ball as he passed.

When Cornelia, Henry, and Charles reached the front porch, Jimmy had glasses of cold water waiting. The four of them sat on the old chairs enjoying the cool June night, discussing the baseball game as the sun began its slow descent.

"C'mon, Jim," Daddy announced when their glasses were empty. "It's been a long day." He rose and headed for the door.

Jimmy tried to hand the baseball back to Henry, but instead of taking it, Henry handed Jimmy the bat. "Keep them till next week," he said. "But I'll expect you to be the most improved player by then."

Jimmy grinned. "Thanks, Henry. I'll practice."

"You best be headin' on home, too, young man. Got a long walk ahead of ya." Charles nodded in Henry's direction and then let the screen door slap behind him as he walked inside.

"Yes, sir," Henry called after him. He turned to Cornelia. "Thanks for coming to the game."

Cornelia looked up. "You're welcome. But I have a confession. I'm not really fond of baseball."

"I know. But hey, we all have our faults."

Cornelia swatted Henry's arm.

"That's why I appreciate you coming so much," he said. "And even if you're not . . . well . . . it's still a lot more fun when you're there."

Crickets chirped in the nearby grass. Henry took Cornelia's two hands into his own, and they stood facing each other quietly. She wished more than anything that the moment could last.

"Good night, Corrie," Henry said simply. "I'll see you soon."

"Good night."

Cornelia went inside, but stayed at the screen door, watching as Shep followed Henry off the porch and down the driveway. When Henry turned around for one last wave, she called the dog back and he obeyed, flopping into his usual spot on the porch.

"I don't blame you, boy," she whispered. "I want to be with him, too."

That night, Cornelia's diary entry was short but to the point:

If I never meet another boy for the rest of my life, I will be perfectly happy with this one.

CHAPTER 6

July 1939

The rising sun awakened Cornelia and brought a smile to her face as she realized what day it was—Sunday! For the past four weeks, ever since Henry Roberts's initial visit to her family's farm, he had attended her church with his cousins. Each week he sought Cornelia out after the service, and they chatted until one of them needed to leave—usually Henry, since Cornelia's father was in charge of closing up the church and her family always hung around "till the last dog was hung," as her aunt Miriam put it. They usually went to Miriam's for Sunday dinner. Her father's spinster sister was not afraid to say what she thought.

For the first time since childhood, Cornelia had begun to look forward to going to church. She sat gladly through the boring sermon and read along with the Scriptures she no longer believed. With the rest of the congregation, she sang what she deemed unsingable hymns to a cranky old pump organ pumped by an even crankier Mrs. Borthistle. She made sure to sit where she could see Henry, at least in her peripheral vision, and each week without fail, he approached her after the service as they all stood around socializing outside. They both knew people watched with interest, and they didn't care.

Throwing back the covers, Cornelia began the careful process of preparing to look her finest, putting on the outfit she had meticulously ironed the day before: a navy blue and white patterned dress with a wide white collar, large white buttons down the front, and a white belt that cinched neatly at her waist. Not that she owned many clothes from which to choose. She alternated between the same two "church" dresses each Sunday, pairing each one with the same hat, gloves, and bag. *Still. That's no reason not to look my prettiest,* she told herself.

"Justification. It's *just as if* I'd never sinned." Pastor Johnson paused to let the words sink in. "That's what Jesus did for us when he died on the cross. He took the punishment so we can be justified and have eternal life."

Cornelia had been hearing this teaching since toddlerhood. She'd embraced it back then. When she was young and naïve, she easily accepted a good God who loved her. At the time, life was secure and the word *depression,* though she heard it daily from the adults around her, held little meaning. Sure, her family had lived through tough times. So had everyone. Cornelia could remember only one time that she'd gone to bed hungry because the family ran out of food. For some of her friends from school, hunger was a regular occurrence, and she felt blessed in comparison. When your world is small, you don't want much. Her parents filled their home with laughter, and she knew she was loved. That was enough.

But that all changed when her mother took sick. Cornelia was only eleven at the time. Old enough to understand what her mother told her: that the only thing that would save her was a lot of prayer. Young enough to feel engulfed by confusion when she prayed nonstop for months and her mother died anyway.

Jesus's words in Mark 11:24 had been burned into her heart: "Therefore I say unto you, 'What things soever ye desire, when ye pray, believe that ye receive them, and ye shall have them.'" Cornelia had come to the only reasonable conclusion: If that was the kind of lying God she served, she would stop serving him.

No one knew about the change within her, of course, except for her diary. She continued to attend church and family prayers like always. She memorized the required Scriptures and answered questions in Sunday school. She smiled and sang and brought casseroles to church potluck suppers. After all, she was the lady of the house now. But on the inside, she held firm. A God who robs you of your mother on your twelfth birthday is *not* a good God. End of discussion. She had reached her conclusion before the funeral began and sat through it without a tear. In the following months, her mother's sisters, Nonie and Margaret, commended her for her courage and marveled at what they took to be her maturity.

"You're doing so well, Corrie," Aunt Nonie had said with a tear in her eye. "What a strong girl you are. We're all so proud of you, and we know your mother would be, too."

The words made Cornelia feel like a fraud at first, but as time went by and she continued her charade, the act became second nature.

Pastor Johnson wrapped up his message and introduced the closing hymn. Cornelia stood and smoothed out her dress as the pump organ started cranking out the melody of "More Secure Is No One Ever." Together they sang:

Neither life nor death can ever from
the Lord His children sever;
For His love and deep compassion
comforts them in tribulation.

Cornelia loved this part of the service because her precious moments with Henry were only minutes away, and she smiled in anticipation like a little girl on Christmas morning. She felt herself beaming, and Pastor Johnson smiled back as he led the congregation. *He's probably impressed with my spiritual devotion*, Cornelia mused, and kept smiling right back.

After the pastor's benediction, the music started up one last time for the doxology and the dragging out of the last "Aaaaah-men" while ladies gathered their purses from the pews and men dropped the hymnbooks back into their slots for next time. Thoughts had already turned to dinner or to conversations anticipated with fellow parishioners. Someone needed a neighbor's advice on how to treat a sick pig, while another person needed a recipe for dumpling stew. And someone needed to spend a few cherished minutes with the man of her dreams.

Cornelia shook Pastor Johnson's hand on the way out of the church without really hearing his comments to her. She spotted Angela Pendeski and Jean Little already standing together in the sunshine, and she approached them, feeling confident that Henry would soon approach *her*.

"Hello, girls," she called out, glancing back over her shoulder to see whether Henry had exited the building yet.

Angela smiled. "Hi, Corrie. Did you hear the latest? Becky's engaged."

Cornelia had not heard, but she wasn't surprised. Becky Tarr had been going out with Robert Mitchner for nearly a year. For the next several minutes, she feigned great interest in what the other girls said about how, when, and where the proposal had happened, who heard about it first, when the wedding would take place, and who would be in the wedding party.

Wondering what was taking Henry so long, Cornelia turned just in time to see him getting into his cousins' car. Within seconds, the vehicle filled with the other members of the household and they drove away.

Cornelia could not believe her eyes. How could he leave without even saying hello? Was it something she'd said? She tried to remember the details of their conversation from the previous Sunday. Had she been too aloof? Did he not realize how much she liked him? Was it the way she looked? *If only I had something new to wear!* she thought for one shallow moment. Feeling despondent, she took a seat on the platform surrounding the water pump and waited. Maybe they'd had some kind of emergency and had to rush away, she consoled herself.

Eventually the little congregation finished dispersing and her father closed up the church. Cornelia climbed into the pickup truck between her father and her brother, and they rode in silence the six miles north to Aunt Miriam's for their regular Sunday dinner. Cornelia blinked back tears. How could she wait another week to see Henry? Especially when summer was already so short, and she didn't know how much longer he might stay.

Maybe that was it. Maybe he knew he must leave soon and didn't want to get more deeply involved with her. Maybe he had a girl waiting back in the city.

Quit torturing yourself, she thought as they rounded the last corner to Aunt Miriam's neat farmyard with its white picket fence lined with red geraniums. There was sure to be a perfectly reasonable explanation.

Cornelia helped her aunt with lunch preparations and listened to her diatribes. Miriam had been a schoolteacher for twenty-five years at the same one-room school she had attended as a girl with her brothers. Cornelia and Jim were glad she hadn't been the teacher at their school. Aunt Miriam treated them generously, but she was also free with her opinions and had one about everything.

"Stand up straight, Jimmy," Miriam launched into her lecture on good posture as they took their seats. "And no slouching at the table."

Their meal of roast chicken, potatoes, and carrots passed while Miriam delivered her usual litany of comments about the economy, politics, and "young people these days." After they finished eating, the adults took their coffee onto the porch while Cornelia and Jim washed the dishes, as was their custom.

Once the dishpan had been hung back on its hook, Jim went to the living room to listen to his aunt's gramophone while Cornelia poured a cup of coffee for herself and headed out to the porch to join the adults. Perhaps she could hurry her father along and they could head back home, where Cornelia would pour her heart out in her diary. She stopped short, however, when she reached the screen door and overheard her aunt's words.

"You did the right thing, Charles." Aunt Miriam spoke from an old wooden rocking chair, where she sat holding a dainty teacup with both hands. "I'm sure Henry is a fine young man as city boys go, but he'll never last on the farm, and you can't have him breaking her heart. Or worse yet, carting Corrie off to Winnipeg when you need her here."

"Well, now," Cornelia's father argued from where he half-stood, half-sat on the railing. He stared into his coffee cup. "I hear what you're saying, but I don't know. Sooner or later, she'll find herself a husband and I'll lose her anyway."

"Not necessarily. I didn't find one and I've done just fine. Besides, there are plenty of local boys." Miriam plunked her cup down on a side table for emphasis. "If she settles down here, she'll live nearby and it will be far better for everyone. Trust me."

"I do trust you, Miriam. That's why I took your advice and talked to the boy. You should have seen his face." From his perch on the railing, Daddy gazed out over the neighboring fields. "Oh, don't get me wrong. It's not like I outright forbade him to talk to her. I just suggested since he wouldn't be around much longer, perhaps it wasn't in Corrie's best interest for him to continue pursuing her." Daddy turned around again. "You'd have thought the sky fell in. I think he really cares about her."

"He'll get over it—" But Miriam's words were cut short by the sharp slap of the screen door.

Her heart racing and her face hot, Cornelia marched right past them without a word, straight to the truck.

"Corrie, what on earth—?!" her father called after her, but it was too late.

"Cornelia, what's the meaning of this?" Miriam croaked. "You come back here right now!"

"You are not my mother!" Cornelia hurled the words over her shoulder and then jumped into the truck, started it, and drove off. She headed down the road toward the Roberts family farm, not knowing for sure what she'd say when she arrived. She had only driven the truck a few times, but she didn't care. She drove well enough to get there in one piece, and she was clear about her mission.

How dare they plan my life? Her thoughts raced as the truck bumped down the gravel road. Just when she finally found a little happiness in her dismal existence, her father and his miserable sister had had the nerve to take it away, without even asking her opinion!

The five-mile drive was not nearly long enough to give Cornelia time to cool off. She was still driving much too fast when she pulled into the Robertses' farmyard. As she pulled up, chickens scattered in a flurry of feathers and squawks. Cornelia began to wonder how she would maintain her dignity.

Henry, his cousins, and an assortment of neighbors were playing a ball game on the lawn, a game that Henry had no doubt organized himself. Every eye turned toward the Ford truck. Cornelia thought she saw one of the Morgan twins among the ballplayers. The Morgan twins were the biggest gossips in the whole community, and that was saying a lot. Perhaps it was their presence that caused Cornelia to stop and catch her breath before getting out of the truck. No point turning this into the ultimate humiliation if she could help it.

She held her head high and walked with deliberation toward Henry.

"Henry, would you like to go for a drive with me?" Her tone told him and everyone within earshot that Henry had better go with her if he knew what was good for him.

"Uh—" Henry looked around. "Sure."

Ignoring the snickers, Cornelia turned on her heel, marched back to the truck, and climbed back into the driver's seat. She waited for Henry, still clutching his catcher's mitt, to climb in beside her before starting the truck. A half mile down the road, she took a right turn, which she knew would lead them to the edge of a creek bank, away from prying eyes and ears. She and Jim fished there regularly and she knew the place well. When she reached the end of the road, she stopped the truck and set the brake. From there they could look out over the creek. Cornelia was relieved to see that no one was fishing here today.

Neither of them had spoken a word.

"You're quite the Sunday driver." Henry stared straight ahead, a wry grin on his face.

"I want to know what my father said to you." Cornelia continued to stare out the windshield, her hands still gripping the steering wheel lest Henry see them trembling.

"Oh. That." Henry sighed. "Your father suggested to me that since I don't plan to stick around beyond the end of the summer, it might be better for you if . . . you and I . . . didn't get . . . you know, too interested in each other."

Cornelia blinked twice. "And do you agree with his suggestion?"

"I'm not sure what to think, Corrie." Henry shrugged. "I thought maybe you asked your dad to talk to me."

"Asked him? Why would I . . . ?" It suddenly dawned on Cornelia that Henry had no idea how she felt about him.

"I did not ask him. And I don't agree with him. Unless . . . unless you have a girl waiting back home."

"No! Nothing like that. Here's the thing, Corrie. I don't want to go back to the city. I love it here. I think I'm catching on quickly to the work, and my family here needs me. Uncle Ben's health is getting worse. Plus . . . I like you. A lot. I planned to ask my family if I could stay on even after harvest, but after your father spoke to me . . . well, now I don't know what to do. If you're not interested in me, it's just as well if I go back home."

Cornelia's heart raced. Henry might actually stay? She knew she shouldn't get her hopes up, but she knew what she had to do.

"Henry? Would you please come to our house for dinner next Sunday?" The proposal breached everything sacred: her family's Sunday dinners with Aunt Miriam, the general practice of company visits including an entire household, the fact that she—and not her father—had extended the invitation. Cornelia didn't care. She had a point to make, and Aunt Miriam was going to get that point.

Henry smiled. "Yes, I believe I would love to come. And now, since we're here, would you care to take a walk down by the creek?"

For the next hour, they sat by the edge of the creek, tossing in pebbles, watching tiny frogs, and listening to birds. They talked about their favorite books, which countries they would most like to visit if they could travel, how to feed calves whose mothers died, and which vegetables would be ready for picking that week. Neither mentioned Cornelia's father or aunt again.

"My cousin told me you were only twelve when you lost your mother." Henry pushed a strand of loose hair away from Cornelia's face. "That must have been really hard."

Cornelia nodded. When she looked up into Henry's eyes, she saw warmth and compassion. For once, no one was telling her how brave or how responsible she was; he was merely acknowledging her pain. It felt good—as good as his calloused hand around her soft one.

When the sky began to cloud over, Henry slipped an arm around Cornelia and pulled her closer to him. She thought her heart skipped three beats when he pressed his face closer to her hair.

"Mmm," he murmured directly into her ear. "You smell so good." He lightly kissed her temple, then her cheek. Cornelia's heart raced even faster, and she wanted to stay this way forever.

When she turned her face toward him, Henry's lips brushed hers lightly. Their eyes met, and she returned the kiss, pressing harder and breathing in the warmth of him until she thought she'd pass right out.

When a massive wet drop landed on her nose, Cornelia opened her eyes wide. Rain! And not just a light sprinkle. Laughing, Henry jumped up and took Cornelia's hand. They climbed back into the truck.

"Sometimes the good Lord sends the rain to keep us out of trouble," Henry said, laughing.

Cornelia could feel her cheeks turn red as she started the engine and switched on the windshield wipers. The rain and the wipers created too much noise for them to engage in further conversation, but they rode in comfortable silence back to Henry's now-deserted farmyard. Cornelia dropped him off and headed back to Aunt Miriam's to face her family.

Her hands shook. No one had ever witnessed her behave so impulsively before, and she had no idea how to behave now. *You can do this, Corrie,* she told herself. She took a deep breath and walked to the house, where she found her father, aunt, and brother seated around the kitchen table, worried frowns on their faces. They looked up in unison and Cornelia was shocked by the sight of Aunt Miriam's red-rimmed eyes.

"Corrie—" her father began, his voice registering relief.

Cornelia cut him off. "I apologize for my abrupt departure and for taking the truck without your permission," she said, keeping her head held high. "Now it's time for us to go home. Thank you for dinner, Aunt Miriam. Please do not expect us next Sunday. We will have a guest of our own. See you in two weeks."

Just like before, she turned on her heel and headed back to the truck, but this time she climbed in the passenger side and took her usual spot in the middle of the seat. After her father and Jim got in, they drove all the way home in silence, though Cornelia felt certain she detected a satisfied smirk on her brother's face.

CHAPTER 7

October 1939

A soft breeze played with strands of Cornelia's bobbed hair as she sat next to Henry on the blanket. The spot along the creek had become their favorite, but now fall hung in the air with a nip that told them frost would come soon. With harvest under way, the two had not seen nearly enough of each other to suit them.

"Thank God for Sunday." Henry smiled at her.

"Yes. Thank God."

They lay gazing at the clear sky, an occasional leaf breaking free from its birthplace and falling across the blue canvas in a lazy twirl. Cornelia *was* thankful, though not to God. She was thankful for her time with Henry on Sundays, for the break from work, and for the good harvest. She was also increasingly thankful to be living in Canada.

During the harvest, her father discontinued his regular weekday naps and ritual of listening to the radio, but Cornelia listened enough to know that Herr Hitler made the news daily. Ever since his invasion of Poland on September 1, things had been happening quickly in Europe. Two days after the invasion, Britain and France had declared war on Germany. On September 9, it had been announced that several Canadians, including children, were on board an unarmed ocean liner, the SS *Athenia,* which had been sunk by German U-boats. On the tenth, Canada had declared war on Germany.

Prime Minister William Lyon Mackenzie King had assured Canadians that the country's war efforts would be voluntary, and thousands of men began flooding the recruiting offices to enlist, including many of Henry's friends. Cornelia feared that Henry was considering doing the same. To her, it seemed the war was happening a million miles away, and enlisting struck her as a ridiculous thing to consider, even for a minute. Surely things would settle down soon and Europe would resolve its own problems. Meanwhile, she and Henry could enjoy each other's company in peace.

"I've got a little present for ya." Henry reached into his knapsack.

"You do?" Cornelia's eyes brightened. "What is it?"

Henry pulled out a book and, grinning, placed it in her hands. Cornelia looked down to see a green hymnbook. *What an odd gift,* she thought. *I guess I've fooled Henry, too, if he really thinks I'd appreciate this.*

"Thank you, but . . . you obviously haven't heard me sing." She looked up for some explanation.

"Not up close, no. But I've watched you sing. You smile. I brought this hymnbook with me from home. I usually read the words of one hymn a day along with my Bible reading. I don't know . . . I find them inspiring and encouraging. I thought you might, too."

Cornelia thumbed through parts of the book, glancing at words both familiar and new, written years before by men and women of faith. Inside the front cover, Henry had written: "To Corrie, with love from Henry. Sing one a day for me."

"It's good some people can find hope and strength like this, I guess." She closed the book.

"Don't you?"

Cornelia hesitated. "What would you think if I said no?" She played with the blanket's frayed edge.

Henry shrugged. "I guess I'd think . . . you'll come around eventually."

They let the matter drop. Henry gazed across the creek, where a field of wheat ready for harvest waved at them as though it hadn't a care in the world. "Hard to believe there's a war going on, isn't it?"

"There's almost always a war going on somewhere, isn't there?" Cornelia shrugged.

"Not for Canada."

Cornelia looked at him. "You're not thinking of enlisting, are you?"

When Henry didn't reply, she had her answer. Tears immediately began to form, and she blinked hard to maintain her composure.

How could I be so stupid, she thought. *How could I let myself grow close to somebody when I knew one way or the other, he'd be taken away from me?*

"Henry, please don't do this. I need you here. Your aunt and uncle need you. I'll just die if anything happens to you—"

But Henry was already kissing her, pulling her tightly to his side. She kissed him back but then pulled away.

"I'm serious, Henry. Why would you abandon your uncle and aunt?"

"Abandon them? Is that what you think?"

"What do you call it?"

Henry stood. "If a bear jumped out of that bush right now intending to attack you, and I stepped in and fought it off, would you think I abandoned you?"

She considered his argument, understanding the theory but rejecting the story. "The bear would kill you first and then come after me. So what good would that do? Besides, we don't have bears around here."

"The bears will eventually move in if there's no threat to them here."

Cornelia dragged her fingers through her hair in frustration. "Henry, you've got your whole life ahead of you! Why would you risk it like this?"

"Maybe this is just something I have to do."

She could tell Henry's mind was made up, but she wasn't ready to give up that easily. "You think this is some game, some big adventure you're missing out on?"

"Of course not. What do you think I am, a little kid? I've thought about this."

"Don't you know anybody who fought in the last war—'the war to end all wars'? Ask one of them to tell you how effective it was."

Henry sighed, but said nothing for several long seconds. His face grew solemn.

"My father fought in that war," he said through gritted teeth. "He sacrificed an arm for this country. Don't you tell me I don't know."

This was news to Cornelia. Henry had never mentioned his father was an amputee, or even that he was a veteran. She got up from the blanket and walked to the edge of the creek. "Well, that proves my point. That's terrible! What possible good can come from it? You of all people should know firsthand how futile—"

"I of all people should be grateful and filled with respect for my father, who gave so much. Who am I to offer any less? You don't get it. Where's your patriotism? You think this country was handed over freely? How can I *not* enlist, Corrie?"

Cornelia turned around to face him.

"No, *you* don't get it! Your father sacrificed to free you from all that!" she shouted. "It will all have been for nothing if he loses you, too!"

Instead of shouting back, Henry's voice became strangely quiet. "Or maybe for once in my life I'd do something to make him proud of me."

Cornelia knew it would be better to say nothing, but she couldn't risk having him think she was changing her mind. "Well, I won't be proud of you. Not for a minute!"

Henry simply dusted off his cap, replaced it on his head, and walked away.

"Where are you going?"

"Home." And he continued walking down the road without a word.

Resisting the urge to scream his name, Cornelia watched him leave and stifled her sobs until he was out of earshot. She picked up the hymnbook and threw it as hard as she could in the direction Henry had gone, but it only landed in the dust with a thud.

She sat on the blanket and cried until she could cry no more.

CHAPTER 8

Cornelia dug up the last of the potatoes, shook off the dirt, and placed them in a bulging gunnysack, tossing their shriveled leaves aside. She tied the sack shut with a sigh and dragged the heavy load to the root cellar door, leaving it there for Jim to haul down later. Stopping at the well, she pumped herself a cup of water and sat down to drink it as she thought back to the afternoon nearly five months ago when she'd planted these same potatoes. Who would have guessed on that May morning that by evening she would have met the love of her life? A lot can happen in a short time.

She and Henry had made up, although she still felt heartbroken about his decision. The community seemed deeply proud of its boys, and last Sunday all the newly enlisted men had stood at the front of the church while the pastor and congregation offered up a prayer of blessing and protection. Cornelia had studied the other women during the prayer: mothers smiling through their tears, girlfriends and young brides beaming with pride. *Are they all pretending or is it just me?* she wondered. *What's wrong with me? I'm supposed to feel proud. I only feel confused and disgusted.* She recalled her father's words the night she returned home and told him of Henry's decision.

"Sounds like his mind's made up," Charles said. "You might want to think about respecting his choice, even if you don't understand it. Who will there be for Henry to come home to if not you? Is that what you want?"

Her father's wise words had been enough to soften Cornelia's heart, and before the week ended, she initiated a conversation with Henry that began with an apology and ended in a lot of hugging and kissing.

Tonight would be their last evening together before he boarded the train in the morning with nearly a dozen other local boys. His parents would meet him in Winnipeg for a brief reunion before sending him on the next leg of his journey, toward a training base outside Vancouver.

Cornelia took her bath with care and put on her navy skirt and Henry's favorite soft pink sweater set. Her aunt Nonie had graciously offered to take supper out to the field for the harvest crew tonight so Cornelia could prepare for an evening with "her fella."

Roseburg was throwing a farewell dance, and Cornelia knew she and Henry would at least make an appearance. She hoped they'd leave early and spend a lot of time alone, though. She was certainly not in the mood for celebration or chitchat.

Cornelia was surprised when Henry pulled up in his uncle's truck. Until that point, his uncle Ben had allowed him to drive it only for farm purposes. When Henry came to see her, he trekked to her place on horseback or bicycle, or was occasionally chauffeured by Cornelia herself, much to his humiliation.

When he stepped out of the truck, Cornelia felt her breath get sucked away, and her knees almost buckled. Dressed in his newly issued uniform, Henry stood before her as an official member of the Royal Canadian Army. She had known that the new recruits were to wear their uniforms to the dance tonight and on the train tomorrow, but she hadn't prepared herself for the picture now before her. Henry, a soldier. He looked taller.

"Hello, beautiful." He took her hand and kissed it lightly.

She couldn't choke out so much as a hello. Henry led her by the hand to the truck and opened her door with a grand flourish. "M'lady."

As she climbed in, Cornelia smiled back. She felt like a princess. *Maybe I should just relax and enjoy it,* she told herself. *This is Henry's night, after all. Be there for him, Corrie. You can do this. Give him a reason to want to come back.*

As she walked into the town hall, Cornelia couldn't believe the efforts the ladies of the Women's Institute had made to create a festive atmosphere. The aroma of freshly brewing coffee and fall flowers masked the usual musty smell of the building. Red, white, and blue streamers created a glorious canopy above their heads, while miniature Union Jacks graced every table. The room was filled with her former schoolmates—the boys in their new uniforms, the girls wearing their finest.

Onstage, the Brewster Brothers band was already taking requests, playing each one with their enthusiastic blend of toe-tapping guitar, fiddle, and accordion music. The three of them were also in uniform, and Cornelia wondered if they would have opportunities to use their talents once they shipped out.

It was not considered good etiquette to dance every song with the same man, so Cornelia dutifully accepted each invitation extended to her and made the rounds of the boys in the group. She chatted briefly with each one, wishing him well and doing her best to bolster her own courage and patriotism even though her heart ached. During every dance, she managed to spot Henry and make eye contact across the room, whether he was dancing with another girl or taking a break at one of the tables. Each time, her heart soared with longing for him, and she refused to let herself think of what the next day would bring.

The older women kept the punch and sandwiches coming, and the young people danced the night away. It was midnight when Henry and Cornelia finally stole away and drove his uncle's precious truck to their favorite spot down by the creek.

"Awfully chilly for sitting here tonight." Cornelia rubbed her arms. Henry reached behind the seat and pulled out a thick quilt. She smiled at him and begged time to stop as they snuggled together, watching the stars into the wee hours of the morning.

CHAPTER 9

November 1939

Cornelia placed a towel over her bread dough and carried it to the wood stove. After she'd opened the oven, she set the bowl on the oven door, allowing the comforting warmth to fill the room and raise the dough. She paused in her work long enough to watch out the window for a while. Harvest was over. The last of the fall leaves blanketed the ground. Gray clouds filled the sky and Cornelia wondered if it might snow. She spotted her brother letting the cows out of the barn and knew he would soon bring in the morning's milk.

Another gloomy day. She sighed. The same mundane chores and the same endless thoughts about the same absent person filled her days. Three weeks had passed since she'd said good-bye to Henry, and already she had trouble picturing his face.

Just as she turned back to the kitchen, Shep began to bark and Cornelia looked toward the road. An old gray truck bumped down their driveway, and she strained to figure out who was driving, to no avail. It wasn't until the driver got out that she recognized her friend Agnes.

How unusual, she thought as she pushed the coffeepot to the hottest part of the stove and went to open the front door.

Agnes held her eight-month-old son, Wayne. Both smiled at Cornelia.

"Corrie!" Agnes was out of breath as she came in. "I went to town this morning and decided to stop by. We've hardly seen each other, except at church. How are you?" Her words all seemed to come out in one big gush.

Cornelia reached out and took the baby, who immediately began to wail for his mother as she took off her coat. Cornelia gave him back quickly and poured Agnes some coffee. Agnes's husband, George, was one of the men who'd enlisted and boarded the train at the same time as Henry. George and Agnes had been schoolmates of Cornelia's long before they became a couple, and while she and Agnes had once been close, they hadn't socialized much since Agnes had married. Although the girls were the same age, marriage and motherhood set them worlds apart, at least in Cornelia's mind. Now, however, they had much in common once more.

"Did you hear?" Agnes's eyes sparkled. "Betsy Miller got her first letter."

Cornelia looked up, feeling instantly flooded with jealousy.

"When?" As if it were some sort of race.

"Yesterday. William wrote it on the train to Vancouver and mailed it from there, so she'd be the first wife to receive a letter. It didn't contain much new information, but he described the Rocky Mountains to her. 'You've never seen anything like it,' he said. 'I wish I could send pictures. They're breathtaking!' That's about all she shared with me, of course. I just came from her place."

Cornelia longed to simply catch a glimpse of Betsy's letter, knowing that Henry might have sat within William's sight as he wrote it.

"Did he mention the other men?"

"I was getting to that." Agnes placed little Wayne on the blanket she had spread on the floor. "The letter contains greetings for each of us. She's bringing it to church on Sunday, and she'll read that part aloud. There's just one thing." She looked Cornelia in the eyes. "Henry isn't with them."

"What?" For a brief moment, Cornelia hoped Henry had changed his mind and was still in Winnipeg or, better yet, on his way back to Roseburg.

"He got separated from the rest of our boys in Winnipeg and sent to another division. William thinks Henry's group headed in the opposite direction, to a training base in Ontario."

Cornelia stared at her shoes, determined to keep the tears inside. Somehow this news made Henry seem even farther away, and she wondered how long it would be before she received a letter of her own. It wouldn't seem right, she supposed, for her to receive one before any of the married girls. She and Henry had discussed the possibility of marriage when he returned, but it was not a formal engagement. Tucked away in her diary were two short notes in Henry's handwriting: one he'd left on their front porch one day when nobody was home, simply saying he'd stopped by. The other was for her eyes only, and Cornelia had memorized it backward and forward:

"Dear Corrie, I'm sorry about our spat. Thank you for returning my affection even though you don't completely understand why I'm enlisting. It's just something I have to do, but I don't want this to come between us. I've never met a girl like you and I really hope you will wait for me. I love you, Corrie."

At the bottom, he drew a heart with both their full names inside it: "Cornelia Faith Simpson + Henry Wallace Roberts."

The two young women spent the next hour visiting and playing with the baby. By the time Jim came in the back door, milk buckets in both hands, little Wayne was starting to fuss and Agnes decided it was time to leave. Cornelia thanked her for stopping by and then watched from the door as Agnes tucked her baby into a basket on the seat of the truck, walked around to the driver's side, and drove away.

Turning to the pails with a sigh, she began the daily chore of pouring milk through the cream separator and hauling the cream down to the cellar. It would be picked up the next day by the cream man, Mr. Bentley, who paid ten cents a quart.

Later that evening, Cornelia's father cleared his throat and asked about Agnes's visit. "Any news from your young man?"

"If you mean Henry"—Cornelia hesitated—"no." She was in no mood to go into explanations.

"Who else would Daddy mean, silly?" Jim teased. "You got another fella besides Henry?"

"No, of course not. But you both talk about him like he's my property or something."

"Well, ain't he? He's practically your husband." Jim grinned. "And when he is, he's gonna take me fishin' every day and teach me how to drive his car, and we're gonna go all the way to Winnipeg, watch ball games, and eat all the ice cream we want!"

His father cut Jim off before the list could grow any longer. "That fancy car belongs to Henry's father, Jim, don't forget. Now there's a newspaper on the seat of the truck. Could you go fetch it for me, please? And make sure Shep's got fresh water."

Jim left the house and Charles turned to his only daughter.

"Corrie, did Henry pop the question before he left?"

Cornelia wasn't sure what to say. "No-o . . . not exactly. Nothing's official. He would need to talk to you first anyway, right?

"He did, honey."

Cornelia looked up in surprise. She studied her father's blue eyes to make sure he wasn't teasing, but she couldn't speak.

"He did it just a few days before he left. I thought he planned to propose before they shipped out, but I guess he decided to take my advice."

"Your advice?" Cornelia could feel the blood rushing to her head. "You told him not to propose?"

Her father raised his palms toward her. "No, no, no. I gave him my blessing to ask you, Corrie. He's a good man, and I can see how much the two of you care for each other."

Cornelia studied her father's face. "Then what did you mean?"

"I told him I thought it might be better to wait until he returns before making things official, that's all."

Cornelia looked at her hands, which trembled in her lap as a result of emotions she could neither contain nor identify. *You mean* if *he returns*, she thought. She found herself feeling mildly annoyed at her father, both for withholding this information and for suggesting that Henry delay his proposal. Her stomach churned if she allowed herself to think about her father's reasons for doing so, and she pictured Henry's father returning home from war with a missing arm. Did Daddy think she would change her mind if Henry came home wounded? More than the worry, though, her heart flooded with joy to know Henry had asked for her hand in marriage, and that her father had agreed.

That night as he prepared for bed, Charles Simpson smiled at the unfamiliar sound of his daughter humming contentedly.

CHAPTER 10

December 1939

Saturdays always held plenty to do. Today Cornelia was carrying clean clothes in from the frozen outdoors and heating irons to press shirts for her father and brother to wear to church the next day. She sighed, dreading another Sunday dinner at Aunt Miriam's. The tension had never really cleared between them since that day back in July when Cornelia had given her aunt a piece of her mind. Cornelia carried no regrets, however, except for the angst the situation caused her father.

"Mary would never let her get away with that kind of disrespect, Charles," Miriam had told her brother while Cornelia was within earshot. "And you shouldn't, either. It's going to come back to haunt you, mark my words. There's a wild and willful streak in that girl."

To Cornelia's relief, her father had never mentioned the incident to her. She suspected that on some level he even admired her for doing what he could not do: stand up to his older sister. He hadn't backed down to Miriam, though. He'd merely listened and made no reply, although Cornelia did once hear him mutter something about "those who can't do, teach."

Cornelia knew her aunt meant well. She had been good to them over the years, and she led a lonely life. But there were some Sundays when Cornelia would just as soon be relieved of the endless opinions, go straight home from church, and spend her one free afternoon dreaming of Henry and the life they would make together as soon as he returned. *If I believed in prayer, I'd ask God to bring him home quickly*, she thought, pushing an iron between the buttons on Jimmy's shirt. *Today would be a really good day to bring him home. Yesterday would have been even better.* When she heard a vehicle pulling into the yard and Shep barking, Cornelia put the heavy iron on the stove top with a thud and went to the window.

When she spotted the red Pontiac, Cornelia's heart began to pound furiously. For one fleeting second her mind even allowed her to consider the "prayer" she had almost prayed for Henry's return. Maybe God would finally prove himself—make it up to her after all she'd been through. Maybe God knew how desperately she needed Henry. Maybe God had come to his senses and brought Henry back to her. She didn't even bother to grab a sweater, but charged out onto the icy walkway so carelessly she almost landed in a snowbank.

When a one-armed stranger stepped out of the car, Cornelia stopped in her tracks. Slowly a light began to dawn on her, and Eva Roberts climbed out of the car as her husband opened the passenger-side door. Cornelia strained to see into the backseat, looking for some sign of a third person, but to no avail. Why had Henry's parents driven all the way from Winnipeg in the middle of winter?

Mr. and Mrs. Roberts trudged toward Cornelia with somber faces, and Eva enveloped her in a long embrace. Cornelia's head began to spin. What was going on?

"Corrie, dear, this is Henry's father." Eva stroked Cornelia's hair. "I'm afraid we've come with some awful news."

Cornelia looked up at Samuel Roberts. His eyes reminded her of Henry's, but whereas his son's eyes always held a teasing twinkle, Samuel's reflected only sadness. He remained silent.

"We've lost Henry," Eva whispered. "We've lost our boy."

Cornelia took a step backward. "What do you mean, lost him?"

"We wanted to come tell you ourselves, before you heard it some other way," Samuel said. "May we come inside?"

Suddenly Cornelia felt like she was twelve years old again, as if her father was crying and trying to explain to her that her mother was dead.

"No. Don't come inside. Don't—"

Suddenly she realized that her father was behind her. He wrapped one arm around Cornelia and reached his other toward Henry's father.

"Charles Simpson," he said. Cornelia watched the awkward handshake as her father put out his right hand to shake Mr. Roberts's left, the only hand the man had. "Please come inside and warm up."

When she looked back later, the next thing Cornelia would remember from that day was sitting at the kitchen table as her father and brother hovered nearby. Someone placed a blanket around her shoulders. Cornelia felt faintly aware of a kettle whistling on the stove, and of her father pushing a hot cup of tea into her hands. She stared at the cup, as if trying to recall what one did with tea. Something inside her head screamed at her to wake up. Surely this was the most horrible dream of her life.

But it was not. Henry's parents were standing there, in her kitchen, and they had driven a hundred miles to tell her the news in person. On December 10, aboard a train bound for Halifax—from which he had been scheduled to set sail for England with the First Canadian Division—Henry had been killed in a train wreck.

A train wreck! How was this possible? To join the army and go to war was one thing, but to not even make it to that war was unthinkable.

What valor was there in that? Cornelia closed her eyes, and all she could see was Henry, smiling so proudly in his uniform the night before he shipped out. The best and worst night of her life.

And now she sat alone, left with her own train wreck. Henry's parents were kind to come tell her in person. "We know you two loved each other," Eva said. "And we wanted to be near the girl who captured our son's heart."

They offered to take Cornelia back to the city with them, where there would be a funeral for Henry in two days. Cornelia heard the pain and loss in their voices, saw the agony on their faces. She appreciated them involving her, but felt certain their compassion would be short-lived when they learned what only she knew.

Because, for this moment at least, she was the only person on the planet aware that she carried Henry's child.

PART 2

Benita

The Lord will fulfill his purpose for me . . .

Psalm 138:8

CHAPTER 11

Winnipeg, Manitoba
March 2006

Sunlight caught the prisms Benita Watson had hung in her kitchen window, creating tiny rainbows that danced around the walls and appliances. She gathered after-school snack dishes left on the kitchen table by Katie-Lynn and James. Doing the work herself was less bother than calling her nine- and seven-year-olds back to the kitchen and making them clean up their own mess. She loaded the plates into the dishwasher with a sigh.

"So what do we do now?" she muttered, closing the door of the machine and picking up the unpaid bills that were piled on the counter. The last of Ken's severance paychecks had been deposited, and no new work had presented itself. Benita's part-time earnings from her job at the corner store helped the family, but if Ken's employment situation didn't change soon, they were going to be in deep trouble. The theme song from an old sitcom drifted in from the living room where her husband and children were lounging on the couch and floor.

I hate him.

She tried to shake the thought, but since Ken's layoff, it had popped into her mind more frequently with each passing day. Why wasn't he making more effort to find work? Couldn't he see how hard she struggled, how she dreaded becoming the family's sole provider?

When the phone jangled, Benita called to the kids to turn down the TV.

"Hello? Oh, hi, Mom." The laugh track from the television still overpowered her mother's voice. "Can you hang on a minute?"

Benita held the receiver against her shoulder and called into the living room again. "James! Katie-Lynn! I asked you to turn down the TV!" She waited for the volume to subside before putting the phone back to her ear.

Grace Gladstone's voice sounded unusually weak. "Benita, honey, I've got bad news. It's your grandma Cornelia. She's suffered a stroke."

Benita sat on the nearest chair and gripped the edge of the table with her free hand. "A stroke? How bad is it?"

"She might not pull through, honey. In fact, her doctor seems fairly certain she won't. I thought you might want to see her . . ."

The tiny rainbows circling the room seemed to grow and wrap Benita in a confusing matrix of color and light. She squeezed her eyes shut, trying to focus on what she'd been told. *Breathe*, she reminded herself.

"Benita?" Grace said.

"Yeah, I'm here." Benita tried to steady her voice.

"We knew this would happen sooner or later, honey."

"But Mom, I just saw her yesterday. She was fine. We're working together on a quilt for Katie-Lynn." She fiddled with the dish towel hanging from one shoulder.

"I know, she told me. This is how it goes sometimes, sweetie."

"She can recover, right? Lots of people do. I mean, she's only—"

"She's eighty-four, Benita."

"—yeah, she's only eighty-four. Lots of people live to ninety-five or even older these days." Benita tucked the phone into the crook of her neck and started to vigorously polish the toaster with her towel. Anything to hold back the panic that threatened to erupt.

"Yes. Lots of people do. Do you want to see her? We're on our way to the hospital now."

"We? Who's with you?" Benita's parents had divorced when she was only three, and her mother never remarried. Never even dated anyone, as far as Benita knew.

"I've picked up Uncle Jim and we're en route. I can swing by your place if you want to come with us."

Benita took a deep breath before answering. "Yes. Okay. Should the kids come?"

"Not if Ken's there to stay with them. They won't let the kids in anyway, and even if they did, I'm not sure they should see her like this. It won't be the Gram they know."

Suddenly it dawned on Benita that her mother could be losing *her* mother. "Are you okay, Mom?"

A short pause. "We do what we have to do. We'll be there in five minutes." The phone went dead.

Ken wandered into the kitchen, and when Benita explained the situation, she was surprised to see his eyes well with tears.

"I don't know when I'll get back. Can you cook a frozen pizza for yourself and the kids, please? And there are carrot sticks and apples in the fridge. Where's my jacket? And James has to finish his reading practice. I need my purse. Katie-Lynn's grounded from the phone and the computer—"

Ken took Benita in his arms. "Just go, we'll be fine. Tell Gram we love her, and we'll come see her as soon as we can."

She gave Ken's back a quick pat and pushed free of his embrace, reaching for her purse.

Benita silently walked the hospital corridor with her mother and her great-uncle. What would she see when she reached her grandmother's room? Grandma Cornelia had been like a second parent to Benita, only better. After her parents' divorce, Benita and her mother had moved in with Gram until Benita started grade one. For the next six years, she'd gone straight to Gram's house every day after school and stayed there until her mother finished work. A retired schoolteacher, Gram had tutored Benita with her schoolwork, but she'd also done so much more. She'd become a friend and true confidante, and Benita couldn't imagine saying good-bye to her.

"Only two visitors at a time," a nurse informed them when they reached the intensive care unit.

Benita volunteered to hang back. She took a chair in the waiting room and sat watching patients, staff, and visitors come and go while her mother and Uncle Jim were in Gram's room. She examined her fingernails, her rings, the wallpaper—anything to keep from thinking too hard about where she was sitting or why she was there.

When Grace came out wiping her eyes, Benita's heart sank. "Is she gone?"

"No, she's still with us. Go on in."

As soon as Benita did, she understood her mother's tears. Gram looked as pale as the sheets she lay on. Oxygen tubes, feeding tubes, heart monitors, and equipment Benita couldn't identify all competed for attention. The woman on the bed bore little resemblance to her Gram. Benita sat in the chair beside the bed and then restlessly stood again. Gram's eyes were shut, and she gave no response when Benita took her hand.

"Gram." She spoke softly. "It's Benita."

She looked out the window, wondering what she could possibly say. "I'm so sorry this happened to you."

A kaleidoscope of memories whirled through her mind . . . playing crazy eights at Gram's table, dunking homemade gingersnap cookies into her milk after school, helping Gram pick tomatoes and beans and flowers. Countless books read together. Gram sewing Benita's prom dress and, later, the little flower girl's dress for Benita's wedding. If this was good-bye, how did one wrap up an entire lifetime of love? Could Gram even hear her? *What would I want someone to say to me if I were lying on that bed?*

"Gram, I want you to know I love you very much. You've been such a good friend to me all my life." Benita's voice caught. She wasn't sure she could say more, yet she knew she must. She took a deep breath and tried again.

"I deeply admire you, Gram. I know so little about your early life . . . whenever we were together, you were content to make everything all about me. And I guess I was selfish enough to let you do it." Benita lifted a sleeve and wiped a tear from each cheek, wondering whether Gram was hearing her words.

"Thank you for speaking words of wisdom into my life. Thank you for teaching me so many things—how to sew and crochet and bake. How to stand up for myself. You always showed so much spunk and good common sense."

Benita wandered over to the window and looked out at the early winter dusk settling in. She longed to pour her heart out, to tell Gram how frightened she was about the future. How unfair it all was, what an unambitious disappointment her husband had turned out to be. Until now, she had wanted to spare her grandmother the worry, but now she regretted not opening up to her. Gram would know what to do. She turned and looked at the still form on the bed.

"Please don't go yet, Gram. I want you in my life. I still need you. I want Katie-Lynn and James to have you in their lives for a long time."

Benita sat for a few more minutes until a nurse came in, then quietly kissed her grandmother's forehead and whispered, "Good-bye, Gram. I love you."

Benita left the room and rejoined her mother and Uncle Jim. They rode all the way home in silence. As her mother drove, Benita wondered: *How many untold stories remained locked in her grandmother's heart? What secrets might go with her when she left this world? What made this woman so strong; what had enabled her to survive the losses of her life without surrendering to bitterness?* As they rounded the corner to Benita's home, a tear finally found its way down her cheek, and she let it fall unchecked.

CHAPTER 12

April 2006

Benita held the hands of both her children as they stood by the graveside, Ken maintaining a stiff presence behind her. As Pastor Gray prayed, Benita glanced at the flowers in Katie-Lynn's hand and wondered how long they would stay fresh on the grave. She brushed lint off James's shoulder and smoothed his hair. She looked at her shoes and thought about the good price she'd paid for them. She tried everything she could think of to keep from hearing the words of farewell and watching the casket's slow descent. She had another couple of hours yet to endure: people paying their respects, expressing their sympathy, the endless rounds of "I'm so sorry for your loss." Then she could be alone for a while.

Once they were back at her mother's house, Benita kept herself busy in the kitchen arranging food on plates and making coffee. A vague sense of guilt hovered over her, and she felt as though she should be more appreciative of the condolences and simply be thankful she'd had a grandmother for the first thirty-five years of her life. Few people could say the same. *Sooner or later, we all experience loss like this*, she chided herself. Why should she be immune? She heard laughter coming from the living room and ventured as far as the doorway. Friends and family were sharing their memories of Gram, and now it was Ken's turn.

"Benita and I were taking Gram for her eye doctor appointment in our little Jetta." Ken's eyes were glistening. "She could walk, but we took along a wheelchair to speed things up. It was quite the ordeal, helping her out of her wheelchair, getting her buckled into the front seat, and then loading the chair into the trunk. Gram submitted to the whole thing without a word. But as I climbed into the backseat and started complaining about how hard it was to get in and out of such a little car, she spoke up.

"'Huh,' she said. '*I* didn't have any trouble.'"

Everyone chuckled and Benita smiled as she remembered the day. Gram's sharp wit never left her, even throughout her pain and dependence on others. Benita spotted her mother, seated on the sofa next to Uncle Jim. Gram's brother hadn't been as fortunate. Although he was four years younger, some form of dementia had slowly closed in and he seldom spoke now. He still had as many good days as bad ones, but it was never easy to tell how much he grasped about what was going on around him. His wife, Judith, had died from cancer ten years earlier, and Uncle Jim hadn't been the same since. His only son, Andy, hadn't made it to Gram's funeral. Since Andy had no children of his own, it seemed the Simpson line was dying out.

By five o'clock, the crowd had dispersed and Ken took the children home, promising to return for Benita later. She helped her mother clean up and put away the abundance of food, packing up some for Uncle Jim and some to take home herself.

As she was putting away a heavy glass serving plate, Grace stopped to stare at it. "This was hers," she said softly.

"What's that, Mom?"

"Oh, this plate. I've been using it so long I almost forgot it belonged to your grandmother. I should set it aside for you before it gets broken."

"You don't have to do that, Mom. You can still use it for years. Decades!" A sudden panic set in at the thought of losing her mother one day.

Grace wrapped the plate in a clean towel. "It was a wedding gift to my parents, and believe me, a precious one in those days. I think I'll add it to the silver suitcase."

"What silver suitcase?"

Grace looked up, surprised. "At Gram's. In the attic, there's a big silver suitcase. Surely you've seen it."

Benita hadn't been in Gram's attic since childhood. She remembered a trunk of old dress-up clothes Gram had let her play with, but a silver suitcase?

"I don't remember."

"Well, it was Gram's treasure box, and she rarely allowed me to touch it, much less explore its contents. I'll need to go over there and sort through all her stuff soon, including the silver suitcase. Can you help me?"

They scheduled the next Wednesday to get started. Benita returned home, exhausted. She lay awake far too long, trying in vain to push waves of grief back into the vast ocean called Sorrow.

CHAPTER 13

Benita squinted into the sun as she pinned jeans to the clothesline, feeling thankful the weather was warm enough for her to dry the clothes this way. Anything to save money. She had started making oatmeal every morning for breakfast, which no one enjoyed much, including her. But given the mere pennies each serving cost, she knew it made good economic sense. Besides, it was healthier for everybody. So what if Ken complained? If he didn't like it, he could go out and get work, any work that was available. Why was he so fussy? One thing was clear to her, if they were going to survive, it would be up to her. She had stopped buying her treasured home-decorating magazines long before and had recently canceled their cable subscription, although the company had yet to turn off their service. She dreaded the complaints she would hear from James and Katie-Lynn when it finally happened. Funny, they hadn't fussed a bit when she canceled their hated piano lessons, though it broke her heart to think her children might never learn to play.

As she carried the empty basket inside, Benita checked the clock. Time to leave for work. In theory, Ken spent the school hours of each day job hunting, then caring for the children so Benita could put in as many hours at the store as she could get. She suspected, though, that he spent far more hours playing games on the computer than he did looking for jobs these days. She ran a brush through her hair, grabbed a purse and jacket, and headed out the door for the six-block walk.

As she passed the playground, she spotted an older woman and a curly-haired toddler laughing together in the sandbox. A lump caught in Benita's throat. Had they really buried Gram yesterday? And now life was supposed to return to normal, with breakfasts and laundry, and grandmothers with grandchildren. Benita swallowed hard. *I can't think about this now*, she reasoned. *I have to get to work and be pleasant to people. Besides, everybody's carrying their own load; we've all got our stuff.*

After she'd entered through the back door of Schneiders' Corner Store, she hung her coat and placed her purse in her "locker"—a simple wooden crate nailed to the wall. Inside lay a card-size lavender envelope with her name on it. *How nice,* she thought, tucking it into her purse for later. She stepped into the storefront where her employers, Brian and Pamela, were preparing for their lunch break.

"Benita." Pamela's warm hug touched a wounded spot in Benita's heart, and she swallowed hard. "We're so sorry about your grandmother. I know you two were close. How are you? How are Ken and the kids?"

"We're fine. Thank you for the time off; it felt good to help Mom with the arrangements. And thanks for the card . . . I'll open it later, when I don't need to worry about smudging mascara with tears. Been busy this morning?"

"About normal." Pamela returned to business. "Brian and I have errands to run. There's a shipment coming in at three o'clock, so we'll definitely be back by then."

"Sounds good. Anything else I need to know?"

"Mrs. Krause's order will be picked up around one. It's all packed in that box right there, plus a clearly marked bag in the cooler. We didn't receive any oranges this week, so if anyone's asking for oranges, tell them sorry, but it'll be next week at the earliest."

"Okay. Um—Pamela?" Benita said.

"Yeah?"

"I just wondered . . . if there's any chance you could use me for a few more hours, I'd be happy to take them. Ken's home now, so I can pretty much work anytime—evenings, weekends, whatever you need."

"Aw, honey, I know. But nothing's really changed since we had this conversation a few weeks ago. It's getting nearly impossible to compete with the big grocery stores, and our only customers are senior citizens, dying off like flies. I thought you understood."

"I do. I just thought I'd check. It's okay."

As Benita stepped behind the counter, Pamela and Brian walked out the front door. Brian, who had remained silent since Benita's arrival, spoke before the door shut behind them.

"She doesn't understand we wouldn't keep her on at all if we didn't feel so sorry for her."

"Sh-h-h!" Pamela glanced back over her shoulder as the door closed with a clang of its overhead bell.

Benita froze as Brian's words sunk in. *I will not cry, I will not cry,* she told herself. *Easier to be angry. Customers dying off like flies, eh? Well, whose fault is that? Maybe if they'd fix this place up, offer what the younger people wanted, and get with the times, they could gain a whole new clientele. Maybe if they'd split up for half an hour to run their stupid errands instead of insisting on being together twenty-four-seven. How ridiculously inefficient.*

In her heart, though, Benita knew that if Brian and Pamela were more efficient businesspeople, they wouldn't need her. One of them could mind the store while the other ran errands. Their codependency, if that's what it was, worked in Benita's favor. As long as they didn't go bankrupt.

The bell over the door clanged again, and Benita was glad for the diversion. But it was only the paperboy. After he left, she spread the *Winnipeg Free Press* out on the counter and went straight for the job ads. Surely someplace in this city could provide more job security. An insurance company needed an administrative assistant. Why hadn't she finished those community college courses? The *Free Press* wanted freelance reporters. She liked to write, but couldn't imagine asking questions of perfect strangers and then writing about what they told her, at least not in a way anyone would want to read, let alone pay for. Every health-care facility in town needed nurses. *No kidding.* Benita could feel the cynicism rising from her heart to her brain. Maybe better health care could have saved Gram.

Benita wrote her own fantasy ad in her mind. "Wanted: a mildly depressed mother of two with little education or experience, to redecorate homes for clients we will find for you. Name your salary. Unemployed husband preferred. Vehicle provided."

"Now *that*, I'd apply for," she muttered as a customer walked in. She folded the paper and slid it under the counter.

For the rest of the afternoon, Benita kept busy serving customers, and stocking and dusting shelves. When the delivery truck arrived, she allowed the driver to unload everything, signed his papers, and then ran to answer the phone. Expecting it to be Brian or Pamela calling to explain their delay, she was surprised to hear Ken's voice on the line instead.

"Hi, honey. How's it going?" He sounded cheerful.

"Well, a bit crazy at the moment. For some reason Brian and Pamela didn't come back in time for the delivery guy, and I've got all these boxes sitting here waiting to be unpacked . . . and the after-school crowd arrives shortly."

"Want me to pick up the kids?"

"Yes, please. I'm not sure how long I'll be here, but every extra minute I can stay helps, even if this job pays only minimum wage."

Ken's silence told Benita she'd hurt his feelings again. He would take her words as another dig about him not providing for the family.

But darn it! I can't walk on eggshells all the time, she thought. Why did he have to be so sensitive? Besides, if the shoe fits . . .

"Please have James and Katie-Lynn bring the laundry in off the line," she said. "Give the jeans and towels a quick fluff in the dryer, but make sure it's set on 'air fluff.' I'll call you later."

The next two hours passed in a blur as Benita sold candy, chips, and comic books to children who, in her opinion, possessed more money than brains. Between customers, she unpacked tins of beans, boxes of macaroni, and cartons of cigarettes. At least none of the stuff was perishable. After breaking down the last box and adding it to the recycling pile, she looked at the clock and was shocked to see that it read nearly six. Closing time. *Where are they and why haven't they called?* Panic was setting in when the phone rang again. *Thank God.*

"Schneiders' Corner Store, Benita speaking."

Ken again. "Hey. You still at it?"

"Ken, I'm really getting worried. Brian and Pamela said they'd return by three, and I haven't heard from them. It's closing time."

"Have you tried their cell phone?"

"Yes, several times. It just keeps giving me a message. I don't know what to do." She looked out the big storefront windows.

Ken sighed. "Well, for now I think you should probably close the store and—"

"Oh my gosh, two police officers just walked in the door. Something's happened, Ken."

"I'm coming. Be there in a minute." And the line went dead.

CHAPTER 14

Benita waited behind the counter while the two police officers entered the store. The first was a blonde woman with a tight knot of hair at the back of her neck, below her hat. A black male officer followed her in.

"Good afternoon, ma'am," the female officer said. "Are you on duty alone today?"

Still exhausted from the loss of Gram, Benita thought she must be hallucinating. Too many sleepless nights were taking their toll. "Yes."

"Any customers in the store right now?"

"N-no," Benita glanced from one officer to the other. "What's happened?"

"It's almost closing time, right?" the male asked. Benita nodded. "Mind if I go ahead and lock this?" He proceeded to lock the door, and Benita didn't bother to respond.

"This store belongs to Brian and Pamela Schneider, correct?" the female officer asked, notebook in hand. "They live upstairs?"

"Yes! Please tell me what's going on."

Benita stared at the officers as they exchanged a sad glance. "Ma'am, I hate to have to tell you this, but your employers were in a horrible car accident this afternoon. Can you help us contact their next of kin? Do you know the family?"

Benita swallowed. "Rod and Stacey are the Schneiders' adult children. They both live in other cities," she said. "Are they—badly hurt?"

The two looked at each other. The male nodded. "They were both pronounced dead on arrival at the hospital," the female officer said. "I'm so sorry."

Benita sank to the stool behind the counter. *Brian and Pamela, dead?* Somehow, she found the presence of mind to guide the police to a notebook beside the phone, which included a handwritten list of important phone numbers.

Benita watched absently as the male officer wrote down the phone numbers of Brian and Pamela's children.

"Thanks for your help, ma'am," he said. "And again—I'm sorry. Please don't say anything about this until we've had a chance to contact the Schneiders' family. They'll be visited in person by officers in their own cities."

Ken arrived at the store just as the police left. Benita let him in and promptly collapsed in his arms, sobbing as she told him the story. It was too much.

"What's going to happen, Ken? The store will close. I'm going to be unemployed, too. What are we going to do?"

Ken said nothing. He held Benita and let her cry, stroking her hair. When she stopped, he simply said, "Let's lock the place up. Show me what all needs to be done."

Together, they closed the store for the night, Benita wondering whether it might be for good.

CHAPTER 15

"Hi, sweetheart, it's Mom," Grace Gladstone's voice rang out over the phone.

Today was the day they'd planned to sort through Gram's things, and Benita felt no reason not to follow through, in spite of the additional drama going on in her world.

"I'll meet you there in an hour, Mom." There would be plenty of time to tell the story while they worked. Besides, if she explained now, her mother would most likely insist that they call off the day's plans. But Benita welcomed the diversion. She quickly showered, dressed, and headed out the door.

When she arrived at Gram's house, her mother was waiting on the front step.

"I couldn't go in by myself," Grace said. "It's just too hard."

Benita put an arm around her mother and they went in together. The familiar apple-cinnamon smell instantly overwhelmed them both, and they sank to the hardwood floor and cried. Grace pulled a packet of tissues from her purse, and together they created an ugly pile of used tissues that grew so big, Benita's tears finally gave way to a soft chuckle at the sight of it. She reached out and nudged the foot of a cast-iron doorstop that looked like a silly butler holding out a tray. His paint was badly chipped, and both tips of his handlebar mustache had broken off. Gram had used the doorstop as a catchall for mail, keys, and purses for as long as Benita could remember.

"Whatever should we do with this hideous thing?"

Her mother grinned. "I have no idea! You want it?"

Benita dissolved into giggles, and her mother joined her until their laughter turned back into crying. Once their tears were finally spent, the two of them wiped their eyes and looked at each other.

"I'll go make us some coffee." Grace got to her feet. "Then we really do need to get busy."

Over coffee, Benita told her mother of the previous day's events.

"Oh, you poor thing. I can't believe it." Grace covered Benita's hand with her own. "When it rains, it pours! What will you do? Are you out of work?"

"I don't know, Mom. Wait and see, I guess. Look for a new job in the meantime."

"Does Ken have any leads on a new job?"

"Not really. I don't think he's trying hard enough, Mom." Benita wrapped her hands around her mug. "I think he'd be perfectly content to let me bring home the bacon. And everything else. Only now I might not be bringing home anything."

"Well, I didn't have a man bringing home any bacon, and we made it through just fine, you and me." Grace carried her mug over to the sink and rinsed it.

"I really can't think about it right now." Benita sighed. "So, what shall we tackle first?"

They spent the rest of the day sorting and packing. Gram had been downsizing for a while. Most of her remaining belongings were destined for the local Goodwill; a few choice items were set aside for sentimental reasons. The two of them tended to think alike and had little trouble coming to quick decisions. By five o'clock, they'd reduced every room in the house to its furniture pieces and stacks of clearly labeled boxes. Grace had discovered her mother's Bible, and she placed it lovingly on the seat of her car to take home.

"I am way too pooped to start on the attic, honey. Can we schedule another day?" Benita's mother brushed dust from her jeans and sweatshirt. "After we haul all this away, we'll need to spend time cleaning, too. Probably even painting, if we decide to sell."

"What about tomorrow? Rod told me the store was to stay closed till further notice, and his parents' funeral isn't until Friday."

They agreed to meet again the next morning. Benita's mother helped her load her car with food items from Gram's pantry and some of the special things Benita had chosen as keepsakes for herself and her children.

"I'll sure sleep well tonight," Benita muttered with a yawn on the drive home. She arrived to find Ken and the children finishing a meal of canned soup and toast.

"Just enough left for you." Ken ladled soup into a bowl and dropped two slices of fresh bread into the toaster for Benita as she sank gratefully into a kitchen chair. Ken put the children to work hauling in the groceries and putting them away.

Sometimes he can be such a good man, she mused. It was easy to love and respect him when he was kind and sweet.

Why did those moments have to be so few and far between?

CHAPTER 16

Benita was attending her second funeral within a single week. While Gram's had been difficult because of her grief, this one felt difficult because of both grief and fear for her future. Ken had suggested that he attend with her.

"Why? You barely knew them," she'd said.

"I know. It just seems like the respectful thing to do."

"If you respect your family, then you'll spend that time looking for another job." She had closed the door behind her without saying good-bye, and now sat in the service regretting her words. Why was it so hard for her to contain her anger? All her badgering didn't motivate Ken one bit. If anything, it worked against her. She tried to focus on the two flower-covered caskets at the front of the church and listen to the tribute Rod and Stacey were giving their parents.

"Most of you know we grew up living over a store," Stacey began. "As a young couple, Mom and Dad took a huge risk in buying that place and making a go of it. I have such admiration for them, for the courage and determination they showed."

Benita recalled the last thing she had heard Brian say, about how they kept her on staff only out of sympathy. Did Stacey and Rod have any idea how challenging it had been in recent months for their parents to keep the business afloat?

Rod spoke now, reading from his notes. "It may come as a surprise to many of you that Mom and Dad were also working hard on their marriage. They celebrated their twenty-fifth anniversary three years ago and began seeing a counselor around the same time."

Benita looked up in surprise. A marriage counselor?

"Yes, it was costly, in lots of ways. But it helped them a great deal, and they shared freely with us about why they'd sought help. They knew it was important to Stacey and me that they not only stay together, but set an example of what a good marriage can look like. We sensed the atmosphere in their home change, and saw more relaxed and loving expressions on their faces whenever we were around them. I'll always be grateful to them for this.

"My sister and I agreed to share this with you today because it's important. Life is too short to give up on relationships. Although this is a sad day for Stacey and me, it would be far sadder if Mom and Dad had given up on each other. Instead, they left this earth with no regrets, even though they weren't given the chance to tell us good-bye. Stacey and I have a legacy we can be proud of. When we find ourselves hitting the inevitable bumps in the road of life, we'll seek outside help because our parents taught us that that's what you do. I hope you'll remember their example. Thank you so much for coming today. It means a lot."

He tucked the note card into his pocket and quietly left the platform with one hand on his sister's shoulder. Benita felt sure there was not a dry eye in the place. She wondered what troubles had led her employers to seek counsel. She and Ken had never before experienced the kind of tension they'd felt in their own marriage this year. The ongoing unemployment situation was enough to drive anybody a little nutty. Add to that the loss of Gram, which Benita knew she had barely begun to grieve. And now this. It probably would be helpful to talk with a professional, but how on earth could she pay for something like that now?

The pastor closed in prayer. With tear-stained faces, Brian and Pamela's family members followed the two caskets up the aisle and out the door. Benita found it too painful to keep looking at their hurting faces. Instead, she focused on a stained glass window and tried to pick out the words of the song being sung, which struck her as an unusual choice:

All the way, my Savior leads me,
what have I to ask beside?
Can I doubt his tender mercy, who
through life has been my guide?
Heavenly peace, divinest comfort, here
by faith in Him to dwell
For I know, whate'er befall me, Jesus
doeth all things well.

All the way my Savior leads me, O
the fullness of His love
Perfect rest to me is promised in my
Father's house above.
When my spirit, clothed immortal, wings
its flight to realms of day,
This my song through endless ages:
Jesus led me all the way.

The song was still running through Benita's head hours later, toward the end of the long day. Once the children were asleep, she and Ken sat down with cups of decaf, their feet sharing a footstool in front of the couch. They simply enjoyed the silence for several minutes before Ken spoke.

"How was the funeral?"

"Sad. I did learn something surprising." She told Ken about the marriage counseling. "I always thought it funny how they 'ran errands' together, for things one person could easily do. I figured it was some kind of unhealthy attachment. They were probably going to their counseling sessions."

Ken pulled off one sock, then the other. "So they didn't just have to pay the cost of seeing the counselor, they also had to pay you."

"Yeah, I guess. That's quite a commitment when you think about it."

Neither said more about counselors, money, or work for the rest of the evening. Later, as they prepared for bed, Benita hummed "All the Way My Savior Leads Me."

"I remember that hymn from when I was a kid," Ken said around his toothbrush.

"Me, too. I remember Gram singing it while she worked. Off-key, of course. I wish I'd thought of it last week; we could have used it at her funeral, too. I think it was one of her favorites."

Ken rinsed his mouth and spit the water out in the sink. "What would you think about going back to church sometime? The kids aren't learning anything about God or faith." He tapped his toothbrush on the edge of the sink.

"Well, I wouldn't say they aren't learning *anything*. We've read to them from that children's Bible that Gram gave them. At least I have."

"Kind of defensive, aren't we?" Ken placed his toothbrush back in its holder.

Benita sighed. "Faith must have been so much simpler in Gram's day. It was her middle name, you know—Cornelia Faith. In her day, you grew up surrounded with it and never questioned. I bet she never knew a moment of doubt in her life."

CHAPTER 17

Today's the day, Benita decided. She eyed the silver suitcase in the corner of her bedroom.

"Mom gave me specific instructions to give this to you, Benita." Grace had handed Benita the treasured item the previous Thursday, when the entire family had descended on Gram's house for the final clearing out of her effects. "Why don't you take it home with you now? You can go through it in a relaxed fashion, little by little. As time allows."

"You mean, as my heart can handle it?"

"That, too." Grace had smiled.

Benita felt honored to be entrusted with the curious box. *I'll at least see what's on top.*

She made a pot of coffee while the oatmeal bubbled on the stove. Back in the bedroom, she pulled on some jeans and a sweatshirt, keeping an eye on the silver suitcase the entire time, wondering what she was about to discover. By the time she returned to the kitchen, the rest of the family was up and ready for breakfast.

Half an hour later, Ken was searching for career opportunities in the *Winnipeg Free Press* and the kids were engrossed in the comics. Benita poured herself a second cup of coffee and ventured back to the bedroom, where she stood eyeing the silver suitcase for a full two minutes. Finally she picked it up and carried it to the back porch, where the morning sun bathed the closed-in space with comforting warmth. Benita figured this was the ideal place to tackle what she sensed would be a most private journey.

She sat in her favorite wicker chair and pulled a small matching table close. With the trunk in front of her and her coffee mug off to the side, she got ready to begin, but then paused. This seemed like a sacred moment, and Benita felt that something more was in order. She remembered the hymn that had played in her head last night. *Music*, she decided. She fetched a small CD player from the living room and looked through the family's stack of music options for the perfect selection. She flipped through *Oldies of the '70s*, Ken's country collection, Strauss waltzes, and Tchaikovsky's piano concertos. She finally settled on her favorite *Solitudes* collection, which featured mellow music combined with bird sounds. Gram had loved birds. *You're procrastinating, Benita*, she told herself. *Let's get to it already.*

Once the CD was playing, Benita took one last swallow of coffee and ceremoniously opened the little trunk her mother insisted on calling a suitcase. Instantly, the apple-cinnamon smell of Gram's house wafted up. She felt the weight of memory push her against the back of the chair and she leaned back, simply looking at the top layer of the suitcase's contents.

"I don't know what I expected," she muttered. "Bats to come flying out, maybe? Something magical, maybe a genie? Wouldn't that be great? I'd wish for a million dollars and all our problems would end. Plus, I'd still have two more wishes."

She was procrastinating again. *Why was this so hard?*

One item at a time, she told herself. The only visible item was a neatly folded quilt, so Benita gently pulled it out and spread it across her lap. It wasn't the prettiest quilt she'd ever seen, and she could tell that it had been made the old-fashioned way—using old clothing for material, as a money-saving measure. Today's quilts, although gorgeous, always made Benita laugh. Quilters chose brand-new, color-coordinated fabrics, often precut into little pieces, and sewed them together into intricate and flawless patterns that were designed to be the focal point of a room. There was nothing cost-efficient about them.

This, the real McCoy, would have been a much greater challenge, with its unmatched bits of fabric in varying weights. In one corner, a note was pinned. Benita recognized her grandmother's handwriting:

> *This quilt was made for me by my mother, out of scraps left over from all the clothing she sewed for our family before she fell ill.*

Benita wished Gram were here to tell her about each piece. The quilt was much smaller than those made today. No doubt it had been designed for a double bed. It would fit nicely on Katie-Lynn's twin bed. *Why hasn't this been used?* She decided it was not going back into the suitcase.

Setting the quilt aside, Benita took a deep breath and looked into the suitcase again. An odd bucket contraption took up one entire side, but when she pulled it out, Benita knew immediately what it was. Although she hadn't thought of the thing in years, she remembered Gram cranking out homemade ice cream on it when she was a tiny girl. This had been their Sunday night ritual, each person taking a turn managing the crank until at last the ice cream was done, and they could enjoy the creamy sweetness.

One Christmas when Benita was eleven or twelve, Grace had presented Gram with a brand-new electric ice-cream maker to make the job easier. Oddly enough, the ritual seemed to fade and die shortly after that, and Benita remembered nothing of the new appliance beyond watching Gram open it on Christmas morning. She was thrilled now, however, to discover the original and wondered if it still worked. *Even if it doesn't,* she decided, *it's going to look fantastic in my kitchen corner with the other antiques.* The writing on the side was faded and unreadable, but *1910* was etched into the handle and still clearly visible, making the machine ninety-six years old.

The next item was a tattered old green hymnbook with *Tabernacle Hymns* printed on the front cover; its back cover was missing altogether. It still held together, though, and when Benita thumbed through it, she discovered that only one page was missing. Some pages had lyrics circled or notes in the side margins, much like the ones Benita had seen Gram write in her Bible. She took her time browsing through its pages, remembering Gram's off-key but joyful singing.

The remainder of the silver suitcase was filled with old notebooks of various kinds, some tied together with string, some holding their own; all of them carefully labeled on the front in Gram's familiar handwriting with the word *Diary,* followed by the year. The top few were from the mid-1950s, and as Benita gently lifted them out, she discovered that the diaries went backward in time from there, all the way to 1934. A quick calculation told Benita that Gram had begun diary keeping at the age of twelve. Most of the notebooks had been written with a fountain pen, the ink bleeding ever so slightly on the brittle covers.

Benita sat back in her chair again, her heart pounding. *Oh my gosh. This really is a treasure,* she thought. *Where do I start?* But even as she asked the question, she knew the answer. She would start at the beginning, and read every word her grandmother had written, in chronological order.

PART 3

The Suitcase

For he will command his angels concerning you to guard you in all your ways.

Psalm 91:11

CHAPTER 18

Carefully, Benita picked up the earliest of the diaries, dated 1934. The words, written in bleeding ink on yellowed pages, were difficult to read. The handwriting of a twelve-year-old girl bore little resemblance to Gram's penmanship, which Benita knew well. She noticed her heartbeat pick up its pace and felt a mild sense of guilty intrusion as she opened the diary to its first page, dated January 1. With shock, she read the first words:

> *Dear God. I hate you with all the hatred I can hate. There, I said it. Strike me with lightning if you want, I don't care. Daddy gave me this diary for Christmas because he thought it might help me with missing my mother. You took her from us five months ago today, on my twelfth birthday, and I will never forgive you, never ever ever. So this is the last letter you will get from me. From now on, I shall write in my diary but it will not be addressed to you. Yours truly, Cornelia Faith Simpson.*

Benita didn't know whether to laugh or cry. Her heart ached for this poor, motherless girl who felt so abandoned by God. Yet this girl bore little resemblance to the person she'd known as her faith-filled Gram. Benita couldn't help wondering how and when Gram had come to terms with God. The next entry, dated February 14, was a letter to Gram's late mother.

> *Dearest Mother: I think you would have been proud of me today. I finally got the bread just right, the way you used to. Daddy said it tasted as good as yours and I cried a little. Jimmy looked sad. He misses you. Agnes and Becky brought heart-shaped cookies to school today for Valentines and we all ate one. We don't have sugar and things to make cookies. Daddy says it's because Agnes and Becky's father runs the store and we'll have cookies again when the depression ends. What's a depression and how long does it take to be over? I need to go to bed now. Tomorrow is laundry day. I sure hope it's not too cold out. I love you and miss you. Your darling daughter, Corrie.*

Benita tried to picture Gram as a young girl, but managed only to picture herself at that age. Benita hadn't hated God, though. If she'd hated anyone, it was the unseen father of whom she had no memory. By his absence, he'd taught her she must depend only on herself if she was to make it in life. Gram had tried to teach her otherwise. Grace, on the other hand, had taught her through example that maybe God and her father were one and the same.

The sound of a motor starting and stopping in the garage told Benita that Ken had taken a break from job hunting to tinker with his lawn mower. She decided to keep reading.

May 12. It's Jimmy's birthday and he is 8 years old today. Aunty Nonie and Aunt Miriam came by with a little cake and a new pair of overalls for him. They cooked potatoes and eggs and stayed to eat with us.

Mr. Halston says Shep was the daddy to his last bunch of puppies and so we need to keep Shep tied up for a week or so because they don't want Gypsy to have another batch. I overheard him discussing it with Daddy, all hush-hush like I don't know what that stuff's all about. But I do, Mama. I know about that stuff. It's not hard to figure out.

Angela and Becky were bragging about how they are women now. They think they're so smart. I've been a woman for months already. Stupid girls. Just because I don't feel like talking about it. Aunty Nonie helped me when my time came.

Poor Shep.

An hour passed, and Benita remained engrossed in her grandmother's story. Details of her friends, the secrets they shared, the squabbles they fought, and the clothes they wore filled the pages of the ratty old notebook. Several entries included threats of what she would do to Jimmy if he called her "Corny" one more time. After each entry, Benita told herself *I'll read one more, then I'll go get some work done.*

June 30. School is out and I passed Grade 7. One more year and I will be done with school. It's a beautiful day and I'm looking forward to the summer even with all the work to do around here. The Sunday School picnic is this Sunday and I hope to win new hair ribbons for perfect attendance. Plus, we won't have to go to Aunt Miriam's for Sunday dinner on account of the picnic. Jimmy and I don't mind at all. She's completely unbearable sometimes and I don't know how

Daddy puts up with her constantly telling him how he should raise his own children.

"Mom?" Katie-Lynn called from the kitchen. "The phone's for you."

Benita hadn't even heard it ring. She set the diary down carefully and took the cordless phone from her daughter. She looked at Katie-Lynn, now nine, and tried to imagine her losing either of her parents and taking on household responsibilities as her grandmother had. Unfathomable. Benita put the phone to her ear.

"Hello?"

It was Stacey, her employers' daughter, and Benita instinctively knew this would not be a call back to work. Instead, Stacey wanted to set up a meeting to "discuss the situation" as soon as possible. Benita felt sure this signified another layoff, meaning that her household was about to consist of two unemployed adults with two children to feed and clothe. While a part of her wanted to postpone the inevitable, another part wanted to get it over with. She agreed that Stacey and her brother could come to the house at three that afternoon.

Benita hung up the phone. *Here we go*, she thought. The lawn mower stopped and a moment later Ken came around the corner of the porch, wiping his brow.

"Can you be here when they come?" she asked after telling him about the call. "However this goes, I don't want to repeat everything and I won't have to if you're here."

"I'll be here," Ken said.

He showered and changed clothes while Benita tidied the house before their guests arrived. "God," she muttered, "if you're listening . . . what sort of twist is my life about to take now?"

CHAPTER 19

Benita poured steaming coffee into Stacey's mug while Rod sipped his ice water. She'd invited them to join her and Ken on the back porch, where they admired the antique silver suitcase beside Benita's chair. Both of them had inherited their father's fiery red hair and freckles. When she heard Rod chuckle as he joined his sister on the porch swing, Benita detected Brian's laugh.

Now that the small talk and condolences were behind them, Benita braced herself for getting down to business.

"Naturally Benita and I are curious about your intentions for the store." Ken stirred sugar into his coffee.

Benita gave her husband a glance, unsure whether she was resentful or grateful that he'd broached the subject so quickly.

"Yes. That's why we're here." Rod cleared his throat. "We've had a chance to look at the store's books and ask around about the real estate market. Stacey and I share fond memories of growing up in that place. We hate the idea of selling it, but neither of us is in a position to run it. Yet selling it now doesn't make economic sense, either."

"We think, with a little initiative, the store can still be a viable enterprise," Stacey said, drumming her fingers against the side of her mug. "It would be ideal if we could hire someone with retail experience, who knows the neighborhood—"

"—and who wouldn't mind living right there over the store," Rod continued. "That way the rent could be part of their salary—"

"—someone with a knack for sprucing things up, maybe some interest in interior design . . ."

Benita's eyes grew wider by the second. "Are you asking me to manage the store?"

"No, Benita." Stacey smiled. "We are asking both of you. Believe me, running the place is two full-time jobs." She looked at Benita's husband. "We know you've been without work awhile, Ken, and to us it seems like the timing couldn't be better. Benita already knows the ins and outs of the store, and you have experience with a big chain. Would you two consider it?"

Benita and Ken stared at each other in shock. This was the last thing either of them had expected. Benita looked around. It would mean moving into much smaller quarters. But if they accepted the offer, they could crawl out from under their mortgage, maybe even use their home equity to pay off the debts they'd accrued since Ken's layoff.

"When do you need an answer?" Ken thumbed through his pocket calendar.

"Oh, we know you'll need some time to think about it," Rod said. "But the sooner, the better. In the meantime, we really need to reopen so we don't lose Mom and Dad's loyal customers. If the two of you could see your way to start Monday morning and run the store while you make up your minds, we'll gladly pay you for your time."

"Consider it a trial run." Stacey set her mug on the table. "If you decide not to take the positions, you can step back. No hard feelings."

"That's more than fair," Benita said after exchanging another silent look with her husband. "Wow. I really thought you came here to tell me you were closing the store. I'm pretty overwhelmed!"

"I understand." Tears glistened on the ends of Stacey's eyelashes. "We're overwhelmed ourselves. But we really hope you'll say yes. We believe Mom and Dad would want this. And to us . . . well, it seems like a God thing."

After another thirty minutes or so of talking business and looking over some files from the store's office together, Rod rose from his chair. "We're sticking around for church tomorrow morning so we can connect with a few old friends, especially those who couldn't make it to the funeral. Then Stacey flies out in the afternoon. I'll pop in at the store on Monday morning to see if there's anything you need, and then I have to head down the highway myself. Thanks for considering this. Mom and Dad thought very highly of you, Benita."

Ken and Benita followed the siblings to the front door, where they shook their hands and watched them drive away. Once the car was out of sight, they silently returned to the back porch and sank into their wicker chairs with a sigh. A full minute passed before their eyes met, and they both burst out laughing.

"What . . . just . . . happened?" Ken's hands gripped his knees.

"I have no idea." Benita shook her head. The silver suitcase lay at her feet, shimmering in the afternoon sun. *It just winked at me*, she thought.

"We're store managers!" Ken said, shaking his head.

"Well, for now anyway."

"And furthermore," Ken declared with more authority than Benita had heard from him in a long time, "we're going out for supper tonight to celebrate."

Protest immediately rose up in Benita's heart. "Ken, we can't afford—"

"And another furthermore!" Ken stood to his feet, his pointer finger up. "We are going to church tomorrow."

"We are?" Benita smiled up at her husband. Who was this character with the newfound ambition?

He smiled back. "We are. I have some serious thanking to do!"

CHAPTER 20

December 1939

Cornelia wrapped the blanket more tightly around herself and gazed out over the creek as the late afternoon sun glistened on the water. Winter had been mild so far, and although there was now ice along the edges, the middle of the creek still ran cold and clear. In the morning, she would leave for Winnipeg with Henry's parents, but right now she knew where she needed to be—at the spot that had been so precious to her ever since the day she'd practically kidnapped Henry from his cousins' home. Cornelia lost track of how long she'd been sitting there, hardly noticing the cold, still stunned with shock and disbelief.

God is punishing me, she decided. *I did wrong and now he has taken Henry away forever. And he's left me alone to deal with a bigger mess than I can imagine.* How could she bring Henry's child into a world that would only shame Henry's memory, reject his child, and embarrass Henry's entire family? She stood to her feet and picked up icy-cold stones to hurl into the water.

"Punish me if you must," she yelled. "But what did Henry's parents do? Why on earth are you punishing *them*? Why are you making *them* pay for something *we* did?"

With each fist-size stone that she heaved into the frigid water, she flung out a fresh accusation. "You are the meanest God ever. You don't care about any of us. I wish I'd never been born! I wish you didn't exist. Everything would be so much easier . . . if only . . ."

She dropped the blanket and slumped down upon it with a whimper. "If only I could believe for one minute you didn't exist."

Cornelia sat crying for so long, she lost track of time. She lay on the blanket, curled up as tightly as she could, and sobbed. When at last she could cry no more, she lay still. Overcome with exhaustion, she stared into the distance and spotted the frayed remnants of an old rope swing Jimmy had rigged several summers before. She remembered the story of Judas hanging himself after betraying Jesus. *How exactly does one accomplish that?*

How easy it would be to lie here until she froze to death. She closed her eyes and wished for it. *I deserve death for my stupidity. Why did I let myself love him? I should have known he would only get taken away. That's how it works.*

Her mind was made up. She would climb that tree, tie that old rope around her neck, and jump.

As she reached for the lowest branches, Corrie thought she heard a voice. Had the wind picked up? She stopped to listen. It sounded like someone whispering in her ear: "Corrie."

Was it the motion seen out of the corner of her eye or the sound that caused her to look up again, across the water? She felt her pulse quicken when she saw a man standing there, on the opposite bank of the creek. In spite of her impulse to flee to the truck, she remained riveted to her spot. The man looked at her with such intensity, it was as if he stood a mere three feet away. When he spoke, his words sounded as gentle as a whisper in her ear, despite the distance between them.

"Corrie." Although she tried to look away, Cornelia couldn't take her eyes off the man. He began walking toward her, across the creek, yet without creating ripples. Had the creek frozen after all? Why wasn't he sinking?

I'm dreaming, she thought. But it felt more real than anything she'd experienced before. *Wake up*, she told herself. Had she frozen to death? What was happening to her?

"Henry?"

No. As he drew closer, Cornelia realized that this was the tallest man she had ever seen, and his face looked completely unfamiliar. The war crossed her mind. Had Canada been invaded?

"Corrie, don't be afraid," the man said.

Cornelia couldn't say another word, nor could she move. This stranger knew her name. Who was he? Did he know Henry? Had he come here to tell her the details of Henry's death? Better yet, maybe he'd come to tell her it was all a horrible mistake. That it was he who'd died and Henry remained alive and well. *That's it,* she decided. *He's a ghost.*

The man reached her side of the creek and stood a mere six feet away. He'd just crossed the creek, yet his clothing appeared dry. He crouched. His eyes had not left hers since the moment she first saw him. Had he even blinked? His eyes looked sad. He didn't smile exactly, yet she discerned a kindness in him, a tenderness that minimized her fear and gave her the courage to speak.

"Who . . . who are you?"

The man merely turned, gathered a handful of stones, and began pitching them into the water just as she had. He said nothing until he had tossed precisely seven stones into the water. Cornelia instinctively knew that the number of stones he'd thrown matched hers.

"Am I dreaming?"

The man turned back toward her. "What do you think?"

"I—I don't know. This is too strange to be real."

"But . . . ?"

"But it's too real to be a dream. Are you going to tell me who you are? Do you know Henry? Do you have a message for me?"

The man smiled. "Yes. I know Henry."

Know. Not *knew*.

"Is he alive? When can I see him?"

The man reached out and touched the corner of Cornelia's blanket. "Henry is alive. But you will not see him for a very long time."

"I don't know what that means." She looked at him in confusion. "Why don't you speak plainly?"

"As far as your life here is concerned, Henry is dead."

Cornelia stared at him. "Why don't you tell me who you are?"

"I've been sent to you, Corrie." Cornelia had never before heard such a gentle, compassionate voice. "From someone who loves you more deeply than you'll ever know."

Cornelia did not respond. She looked back at the creek, at the stubble field on the other side. Her eyes roamed from her blanket to the hem of her coat to the truck still parked at the top of the bank behind her. She realized she was not the least bit cold. The man emanated a warmth that completely surrounded her. The air seemed easier to breathe somehow, and the sounds of the water and the birds were crystal clear—richer than any sounds she had ever heard before.

Cornelia felt glued to the spot, though a part of her wanted nothing more than to flee. They sat in silence, for how long she didn't know. Minutes? Years?

Who was it that loved her more deeply than she knew? Moments from her life floated past, beginning with her earliest memories. Her mother, rocking her in the old wooden rocker, the creaky rhythm of the chair keeping time to her mother's singing: "*Jesus loves me, this I know . . .*" Sunday school lessons about Jesus and the children, Jesus walking on water, Jesus healing the sick, Jesus dying on the cross. Her father tucking her into bed and praying aloud for guardian angels to protect her through the night, for God's blessing on Cornelia's life.

Praying in Jesus's name. Her father, faithfully thanking God at every meal, though provisions at times were pitifully small. Her little brother getting baptized in the creek last summer, while she herself never took that step of faith, never desired to take her charade that far. Pastor Johnson reading the Twenty-third Psalm at her mother's graveside. "I will fear no evil, for thou art with me."

Cornelia had every reason to feel afraid, but she did not. Why not? She looked at the man beside her.

"Are you Jesus?"

"No. But I consider it an honor to be sent here by him to you, Corrie."

"Are you an angel?"

"We've been called by that name, yes."

"Do you have a name of your own?"

"They call me Aziel."

"Aziel?"

"It means 'God is my power.'"

Cornelia looked around her. No one else was in sight. Who would ever believe her if she told them? Should she take this Aziel character home with her? When she glanced back at him, he was still gazing at her with warmth, and something more. It felt like recognition, as if he'd known her all her life.

Cornelia lifted her chin and looked Aziel in the eye. "Why are you here now? Why have I never seen you before?"

Aziel glanced up at the rope dangling from the tree. "You have never been this desperate before."

"I've had questions for God as long as I can remember. Why did he let my mother die? Why did he let Henry die?"

Aziel took his eyes off Cornelia and looked out over the creek. "Why? It's always the first question, isn't it? Until he multiplied food for the masses or healed a cripple. Nobody asked 'Why?' then. Then, all they wanted to know was 'How?'"

Cornelia felt her anger rise at this. "All right. You like *how* better? Fine." She had waded in too deep to back down now. "How could he have let both my mother and Henry die? If he's all-powerful, like they taught us—if he cares so much, like they taught us—then it makes no sense. Either he is a loving god or he is a powerful god, but he surely cannot be both."

"One of the reasons I'm here, Corrie, is to help you see that neither the *why* answers nor the *how* answers will satisfy your heart. One day, you will have both. But even if you could grasp them now, they would not heal your wounds. Only love can do that. And God loves you more than you can ever understand or imagine."

When Cornelia looked directly into his eyes she could see that he spoke the truth. No one had ever looked at her like that. Not anyone in her family, not even Henry. Though she couldn't explain it, she sensed that this man had access to every thought she'd ever entertained, every ache in her heart, every tear she'd ever cried. And of those, there were many.

"But I've hated him," she insisted.

"I know."

"And that makes no difference?"

"Oh, it makes a difference all right. It pains him, Corrie. It hurts him more deeply than I can say." He reached out and touched her hand gently. "But as to how much he loves you? It makes no difference at all."

CHAPTER 21

April 2006

Church had changed a great deal since Benita attended as a child. Gone were the wooden pews, the pulpit, the hymnbooks. Women were as likely to be wearing jeans as dresses. Ushers greeted her, Ken, and the children warmly at the door and pointed them in the direction of the children's church area, where volunteers in bright red T-shirts welcomed them. James spotted a friend from his grade two class at school, and gladly joined him. Katie-Lynn opted to stay with her parents.

They sat in a gymnasium on chairs that hooked together in rows, and they were led in singing by an upbeat band, complete with electric guitars and drums. The words they sang were projected on a giant screen behind the band, with moving images appearing in the background. Benita looked around her. These people sang as though they'd written the lyrics themselves, some raising their hands in joy, others closing their eyes and simply soaking the music in. One woman rested her hands over her chest, and Benita saw tears streaming down her cheeks. Staring seemed like an invasion of privacy, but it was hard to turn away. She didn't know whether to be in awe or disturbed by it all.

So this was Gram's church. Although the pastor had officiated at Gram's funeral, it had taken place at a funeral home with all the traditional trappings, such as organ music and stained glass windows. She tried to picture Gram worshipping with this crowd, wondered how many people here knew her, and felt a pang of regret for not having participated in this part of Gram's life.

When the singing ended and everyone had taken their seats, Benita felt relieved to see Pastor Gray's familiar face as he walked to the center of the stage. At least one thing hadn't changed since her childhood, if you didn't count his gray hair and casual clothing. Like many of the men there, he wore a simple button-down shirt with no tie or jacket. She guessed he must be close to seventy now. It surprised her that he had changed with the times and welcomed this new style of music and informality into his church. Perhaps it was a matter of survival. Give the people what they want.

Yet as she looked around, she knew there had to be more to the church's appeal than what she had cynically concluded. For a church to be filled to capacity like this, not just with gray-haired folk but many young families, something significant must transpire within its walls.

Today, Pastor Gray spoke about "discovering the gifts God gave you" and using them to "build his kingdom."

"God has uniquely gifted you and put within you a dream to pursue," he said to the gathered crowd. "A dream so big that if you follow it, it will terrify you, but if you ignore it, it will torment you."

Lofty words, Benita thought. *They sound good, but I'm just trying to figure out how to keep our children fed and clothed without running myself into the ground. Who's got time to build God's kingdom, whatever that means?* Her long-held dream of working in interior design lay dying, only rarely raising a weak hand to wave a faint farewell.

She looked over at Ken, who was taking notes on the sheet provided in the program. Her mind kept going to the new opportunity that had landed in their laps the day before. She wondered if there was a way to keep their home in case the arrangement with the Schneider family didn't pan out. Perhaps they could rent the house out for enough money to make the mortgage payments. Selling the house while they moved in above the store seemed like a bigger leap of faith than she wanted to take right now.

Katie-Lynn squirmed beside her and asked for her help in finding a bathroom. When they returned several minutes later, the congregation was rising to sing a final song, so Benita waited at the back rather than try to find her place beside Ken. Pastor Gray said a brief prayer and the service ended.

By the time she caught up with Ken, he had found someone he knew and was deep in conversation. Benita felt in no mood to be sociable. Wanting to hurry home and continue reading Gram's diary, she gripped Katie-Lynn's wrist and went to find James. When they returned, Ken was still conversing with the couple.

"Benita." He waved her over. "This is Bill and Caroline Grainger. Bill and I used to work together. Do you remember?"

Benita reached out to shake hands. "You do look familiar. Are you still with the company?"

"No, I got laid off the same time as Ken," Bill said. "And I'm still looking for work, too. Caroline teaches at the private Christian school the church runs, right here."

"Bill and Caroline knew your Gram." Ken put one arm around Benita's shoulder.

"We're so sorry for your loss," Caroline said. "Ken explained to us about your employers as well. We read about the accident in the paper. That's a lot for you to deal with all at once. It must be pretty overwhelming."

"Yes." Benita didn't know how else to respond.

"Well, your grandmother certainly was a sweetheart. I once attended a women's study group she led, in her stronger days. She had so much life experience and wisdom, but she never forced it on anyone."

Benita knew this to be true. "Now that she's gone, I sometimes wish she'd pushed a little more," she confessed. "There's a lot I don't know."

Caroline smiled and nodded.

"Mom, I'm hungry," James piped up.

"Me, too." Ken reached out to shake Bill's hand. "We'd better get going. Good to see you again, Bill."

"Hope you enjoyed the service." Bill smiled.

"I think you'll see us here again." Ken nodded and the family headed off to their car—and to another meal of macaroni and cheese at home.

"So . . . ?" Ken asked a little later, once they were seated around the kitchen table.

"What?" Benita knew what he was after.

"What did you think? Is this church idea a good one? Do we want to get up every Sunday and do this? Should we go back, or do you want to try another church?"

"I want to go back," James said, reaching for a second helping of macaroni. "We got snacks and played games and some big kids acted out a story about Jesus walking on the water. And Peter too."

At the mention of snacks, Katie-Lynn looked at her brother with wide eyes. "Next time, can I go with James?"

"Of course, sweetie." Benita smoothed Katie-Lynn's hair. "We can go back." It was Gram's place of worship, and that was good enough for her.

After the lunch dishes had been cleared, Ken took James and Katie-Lynn outside with a kite they had been trying to get into the air. Benita grabbed the opportunity to settle back into her spot on the back porch, where she could keep an eye on the kite-flying attempts and dig deeper into the contents of the silver suitcase. She had finished reading through 1936 the evening before, and now she pulled out the diary marked *1937*. Gram would have been fifteen.

Dear Diary,

The only thing anyone talks about is the depression. I don't understand it, I wish it would go away. We used to buy new clothes, or at least fabric to make new clothes, every year. Not anymore. I've mended my stockings so many times, they're more mend than stocking. I think my feet grew because my shoes sure do pinch. We eat porridge every morning and for supper it's eggs and potatoes, potatoes and eggs. Daddy says we should be thankful and people in the city aren't nearly as fortunate. They must stand in long soup lines waiting for a handout. I'd hate that. So I guess I'm a little grateful. I'm trying.

I miss school. Sometimes I help Jimmy with his grade six homework just because I'm afraid I'll forget everything, maybe even how to read or write. Daddy doesn't subscribe to any newspapers anymore. Too expensive. I did spend an afternoon at Betsy Miller's house this week. We braided each other's hair. Betsy says she's going to marry William, and I believe her. You should see the two of them making googly eyes at each other.

I wonder what it would be like to have someone look at me like that. Sometimes, when my chores are done, I go sit under the oak tree in the middle of the yard. I imagine a young man beside me, telling me I'm beautiful and he can't live without me. He brings me flowers and candy and tells me he's never known anyone as fascinating as me. He's really tall and he has thick dark hair and a really big smile. He's kind to little children and animals and he only has eyes for me. He wants to take me away from this and set me up in a fine house. Nothing too posh, not with servants or anything. Just a nice place with a nice yard and we would have some children and he would love me and I would love him back. And in

> *the evenings we would sit and listen to the radio together—to music, not to the stupid news about depression and more depression.*

Benita remembered having the same longings at fifteen. *I guess some things are timeless*, she mused.

She looked out at Katie-Lynn and James, fighting over who got to hold the kite string. Did they have any idea how much they were loved? Ken had helped them get the kite up in the air, and now he was relaxing in a lawn chair. They seemed like such an ordinary family, enjoying life on a Sunday afternoon. No one driving by would guess they had struggled with unemployment for months, now suffered mounting debts, or were grieving the loss of three people who were significant to them.

Or that their lives would look very different in less than twenty-four hours.

CHAPTER 22

December 1939

Finally out of accusations, Cornelia sat quietly with Aziel, studying his face and wondering whether he was aware of the Sunday school picture behind the attic mirror. Every now and then he would say something, and when he did, it went straight to her heart. Sometimes it pained her to hear, like when he assured her Henry really had died in that train wreck. But most of the time, his words soothed her. It reminded her of childhood, when she had come in crying with a skinned knee. How good it felt when her mother washed it off, pulled her onto her lap, carefully applied ointment to the knee, and gently rocked her to sleep. Although the cleansing stung, it was wonderful to feel so loved and cherished.

"You are going to accomplish great things, Corrie," Aziel said. "But it will not be easy. I know you have already endured sorrow upon sorrow in your young life. There is still more to come. But don't be afraid. Jesus will be there with you, and he knows all about sorrow. It's one of his nicknames."

"How can I go on without Henry?"

"It won't be easy, Corrie. Life rarely is. But God will never leave you, I promise. And he will send people along who will support you and help you."

"But, what about—" Cornelia couldn't look Aziel in the eye.

"I know."

"—what I did. With Henry."

"I know. Confession sets you free. So does forgiveness." They sat quietly for a few more minutes, then Aziel closed his eyes. "Listen. Do you hear those sparrows chirping?"

Cornelia closed her eyes in order to focus in and hear the little birds more clearly. "Yes."

"From now on, whenever you hear that sound, or see a sparrow, I want you to remember that you are forgiven and you are not alone. You are never forgotten, Corrie. Never."

Cornelia gazed at him and knew in her heart she had always believed. Although she had been angry with God so long, the foundation her parents had laid in her young life held firm. She believed in a creator, and she believed in Jesus. She had found it difficult to accept that he loved her. But now, looking into this messenger's face, there was no denying that fact. Though she couldn't explain it, she knew she had never experienced this kind of love before.

"But I've hated him." Her voice was barely a whisper.

"I know. I know about the tack in the picture, too." Aziel tapped his left eye. He grinned as Cornelia cringed, trying to hide her face. "It wasn't a good likeness, anyway. Do you remember the promise you made that day?"

She gently shook her head.

"You said one day you would tell the world the truth about Jesus. And you will, Corrie. You will."

Cornelia said nothing, trying to comprehend how on earth she could even begin to tell the world anything.

Aziel snapped a twig between his fingers. "Do you still hate him?"

I am known. The thought felt incredible to Cornelia, as though she had finally awakened out of an eighteen-year-long dream and everything was at last crystal clear.

"No." She swallowed. "How can I? It would be . . . unthinkable."

Aziel smiled. "He loves you too, Corrie. And he *likes* you. He likes the way you dance in your room when you think about Henry. He likes how you punch down your bread dough in time to the song in your head. He likes how honestly you write in your diary. He loves how you respect your dad and treat Jimmy kindly—most of the time. And he loves your determination. He loves how you don't pretend to like cars just to please the boys. And did you know he shares your taste in books? He's so proud of you for all the things you've learned to do without your mother. He is very proud of his girl."

Aziel reached into a jacket pocket and pulled out a chocolate bar. He took his time unwrapping it, then snapped the bar exactly in half and offered one piece to Cornelia.

"Jersey Milk," she said softly. "Mother used to buy us these."

She couldn't remember the last time she'd tasted chocolate.

"It's her favorite," Aziel said. "Each time she tasted one, she liked to think it might be made from the milk of one of her own cows."

Cornelia looked at him, wide-eyed. "And are they?"

Aziel chuckled. "No."

They sat quietly, savoring the chocolate. Cornelia lay with her head in Aziel's lap, and it felt perfectly natural to do so. She knew she was loved, and for this moment, that was all that mattered.

She closed her eyes and listened to the song of the sparrows, the trickle of the water in the creek, and the sweet humming from Aziel's lips. When the humming stopped, she opened her eyes.

He was gone.

A neatly folded Jersey Milk wrapper lay on the blanket near her feet.

Cornelia bolted back inside the house, hoping that her family hadn't sent out a search party. Her father would be so worried. She knew it must be getting late, although the sun still shone in the sky. She could hear the voices of Henry's parents and her father coming from the living room, and glanced at the kitchen clock. *That can't be right,* she thought. She crossed to the living room doorway, and one look at the mantel clock made her knees almost buckle.

"Was the walk helpful, Corrie?" Daddy asked.

A mere ten minutes had passed since she'd left the house.

CHAPTER 23

April 2006

On Monday morning, Benita rose at five and headed out the door before six. Leaving Ken to get the kids up and off to school, she went to the store and took stock. The place had been closed for nearly a week. Outdated milk and spoiling produce required disposal, shelves needed restocking, and signage needed changing. *First things first,* she told herself, grabbing a large garbage bag and tossing in a loaf of stale bread.

By the time Ken arrived at nine, Benita thought the place looked pretty good. "You can unlock the door and turn the 'Open' sign around," she instructed. "We're in business!"

The morning flew by, with some customers coming in to shop and some to express their condolences and their loyalty. A new shipment of dairy and eggs arrived. Delivery orders needed to be taken by phone and packed into boxes. Between customers, Benita tried to teach Ken how to run the cash register and debit machine.

"I'm not an idiot, you know," he said. "I've used these before. You don't have to be so condescending."

"Fine. I figured you need to learn as much as you can, as fast as you can. I can't be here all the time." Benita shrugged.

"I know that. Have you been upstairs yet?"

"No. I was only up there once, when they were alive."

"Well, Stacey and Rod said they got it all emptied and cleaned out, ready for us to move into. I mean, if things work out that way."

"Yeah. I'm still in no hurry to go up there. Seems a little . . . I don't know . . ."

"Creepy?"

"Well, no. Invasive, I guess."

"You just need some time. There's no need to go up today. Plenty to do down here."

"That's for sure." Benita picked up a box cutter and opened a carton of creamed corn. She started stacking the cans on a shelf.

"I brought some lunch. Are you hungry?" Ken asked when the church bells up the street struck twelve.

"You're kidding."

He looked up from the counter he was wiping. "What?"

"We're surrounded by food and you brought a lunch?"

"Why, what do you usually do? Don't you bring a lunch?"

"Never."

"I didn't know that. What do you do?"

"Most days, there's no time for lunch at all—lunchtime is the crazy hour. Then, and after school when the kids show up." Benita added the last can to the shelf and broke down the box.

"No lunch?" Ken raised his eyebrows.

"Well, I've always been invited to help myself to whatever I wanted from the store—fruit, chips, granola bars. Those ready-made salads."

"Well, no wonder this place isn't exactly making anybody rich. Where do you write down what you eat?"

"Nowhere. What's the big deal? It's just an apple or banana here and there, and I had permission. It's not like I was stealing."

"I didn't say that. I'm saying those are lousy business practices. How on earth do they keep track of inventory? What happens when the auditor wants to look at the books?"

"Ken, why are you getting so crazy about this?" Benita put one hand on her hip.

"Where did you write down all the spoiled food you tossed out this morning?"

"Nowhere, Ken. Good grief! You are so—"

"So what? Eh? Business savvy?"

"Anal-retentive," she muttered, as a customer walked in. Benita waited on the woman: a young mother with two preschoolers in tow. After they left, she saw Ken in the back room finishing a sandwich he'd brought from home. After polishing off his apple, he began carrying the delivery boxes out to the car without another word.

"Are you taking those now?" Both of Benita's hands knuckled her hips.

"No, I thought I'd let them sit in the van where the sun can beat on them for a couple of hours and then deliver them later. Yes, I'm taking them now."

"Ken. It's still the noon hour. If you do the deliveries now, I'll be here alone during the crazy rush."

"Crazy rush?" He looked around the empty store. "Oh, I'm sorry. What was I thinking? Okay, you take those two over there, and I'll look after the lineup at the counter."

Benita couldn't believe what she heard. "It's not usually like this, trust me. The minute you leave, they'll all show up, and let me tell you, there are some sticky fingers among those junior high kids. I can't keep an eye on them all. And why are you so sarcastic all of a sudden?"

"Because you've done nothing but boss me around since I got here, that's why."

"Well, I know the ropes around here and you don't. Once you've learned everything, I won't boss you around anymore."

"In case you hadn't noticed, Stacey and Rod hired both of us. They didn't specify which of us would be the boss. It could just as easily be me. I do know a thing or two about running a business, you know."

"You're being ridiculous." Benita shook her head.

"Am I? If I don't deliver those orders now, when are they going to get delivered? Huh? One of us has to pick up the kids from school at three . . . if we wait till after that, the phone will be ringing off the wall with people demanding their purchases."

Benita thought about that for a moment. "Whatever."

He had a point. Besides, Mrs. McLaughlin from next door was shuffling in for her daily newspaper and Benita knew that, as was always the case when Mrs. McLaughlin came in, she was about to hear a litany of concerns and suggestions. Sure enough, the woman poured out her most heartfelt sympathy and then began to explain to Benita precisely how the Schneiders' car accident could have been avoided.

As she did so, Ken slipped out the back door and began the day's deliveries.

CHAPTER 24

December 1939

The fence posts whizzed by as Cornelia stared out the window from the backseat of the Robertses' car. She had hugged Daddy and Jimmy tightly when they said their good-byes that morning. Only one stop at a filling station interrupted their silent three-hour ride to Winnipeg. Each member of the trio seemed lost in grief. Henry's mother would periodically dab at her eyes with her hanky or blow her nose. Now she rested her head on the car seat and tried to sleep. Cornelia couldn't tell what Mr. Roberts was thinking, but she knew this must be the most painful experience of his life. She had overheard him tell her father, "I'd give my other arm and both legs, too, to have my boy back."

Her own thoughts drifted back and forth between the incredible experience she'd had at the creek the day before, her grief over losing Henry, and the deep secret she still carried. When would be the right time to tell Henry's parents? *I must wait until after the funeral,* she decided. *Because if they get angry and send me back to Daddy, I won't even get to attend.*

And poor Daddy. This will break his heart. She imagined the endless *I-told-you-so's* and lectures they would both receive from Aunt Miriam. If only she had asked the angel about all this while she had the chance. She thought back to yesterday—was it really only yesterday? She had recorded as much as she could in her diary late last night and wished she could fish it out of her suitcase to reread now. *I must write every detail down,* she thought, *before I forget.*

"I can't believe I almost forgot," Henry's mother said from the front seat. She reached into her purse and pulled out a tattered envelope. "This was found on Henry's body, addressed to you. There was one for us as well." She handed the letter back to Cornelia and dabbed at her eyes again.

Cornelia was torn between her need for privacy and her desire to read Henry's last letter. Finally she opened it and read what he had written:

> *My dearest Cornelia,*
> *As I write, I am on a train for Halifax where we'll board ship for somewhere overseas. The guys were ribbing me so much about writing to my girl—offering suggestions for what I should say, and so on. I found a freight car at the tail end of the train and settled myself in it. It's full of crates and not really comfortable, but at least I have some privacy.*
>
> *I don't know how to say this, so I'll just get it out there. I wouldn't feel right leaving the country without asking for your forgiveness, Corrie. I'm sure we both know what we did the night before I left was wrong, but I want you not to blame yourself, sweetheart. I took advantage of you in an emotional time and I am sorry. I hope we can start again, forgiven by God, when I return home and we get married. By now, you might know I spoke with*

your dad before I left. We have his blessing, though I feel I've already abused his trust without his knowing. Unless you told him.

I also wanted to apologize for not talking to you more about the Lord. I left my parents' home for Roseburg last summer in anger and resentment. I guess I was trying to ignore God, too. But now that I'm going into battle, I realize I need Jesus more than ever. I wish I'd shared my faith with you, prayed with you, helped you see how much he loves you. I wish I'd loved you better.

I did reconcile with my father before I left for boot camp, at least as best as we could. He can be a harsh man. But my Heavenly Father is always ready and able to forgive completely and give us a clean slate. He's given me one, and I want that for you, too, my darling.

If you are feeling guilty the way I was, ask him, Corrie. He'll clean your slate.

I know it's hard for you to understand why we have to be apart now. But please believe me when I say I miss you, I love you, and I can't wait for the day we are together again, in peaceful times.

All my love,
Henry

Cornelia clutched the letter to her heart, but managed to keep the tears in check. *Oh, my love,* she thought. *I have a clean slate, too. I hope you know that.*

She carefully refolded the letter and placed it in her own purse. *Thank you, Lord.*

Her eyes widened as she took in the sights of the city. She had only been here once before, when she was too young to remember it. Knowing that Henry had grown up here made seeing it now bittersweet. As they approached their own neighborhood, the Robertses pointed out Henry's school, the corner store where he'd worked the summer he was sixteen, and the home of his best friend, Eugene. Eugene was in the army now, too, waiting to be shipped overseas. Henry's parents didn't know whether he had heard the sad news or not.

Mr. Roberts stopped the car in front of a narrow two-story house made of gray bricks. The houses on either side stood dreadfully close to it, Cornelia thought. She couldn't imagine having neighbors so near all the time. *I suppose one gets used to it,* she mused as she climbed out of the car and stretched her arms and legs. The first thing she noticed was a sparrow sitting on a shrub outside the Robertses' front door. It reminded her of Aziel's promise, and this settled her nerves a bit. Henry's father pulled their bags out of the trunk and led her around to the back door.

The house felt cold, and while Mr. Roberts went down to the cellar to adjust the boiler, Mrs. Roberts lit a fire in the cookstove. She then showed Cornelia to their newly acquired water closet, which Cornelia gratefully used.

"Let me show you around while the water heats for tea." Mrs. Roberts took Cornelia's hand.

Cornelia followed her through the simple kitchen. Its cabinets were painted a cheery yellow, and the window curtains and tablecloth were made from the same yellow gingham. In the small living room, heavy drapes covered the front door to keep in the heat. Four overstuffed armchairs and one rocker stood around a low table. The focal point of the room, however, was the books. Lining all four walls, broken up only by the presence of a window or doorframe, were shelves sagging with books. Even Cornelia's school library hadn't housed this many books.

"My goodness! Henry never mentioned the books."

"Oh, yes, we're all quite the readers. He wouldn't have thought to mention it, I suppose, because to him, this is normal."

Through an open door, Cornelia could see Mr. and Mrs. Roberts' bedroom, but they did not go in there. Instead, Eva led Cornelia up a staircase. At the top was a small landing with one room on each side. Mrs. Roberts indicated the one to the left.

"We've turned this one into a library."

Cornelia's eyes grew even wider. More books?

"The other, of course, is Henry's room."

Cornelia looked at the closed door.

"I haven't been able to bring myself to go inside yet." Eva placed one hand on the doorframe. "But, now that you're here . . . well, this is where you'll sleep. I hope that's all right."

Cornelia looked back at the door again and swallowed hard before finding her voice. "I'd be honored."

By this time, Henry's father had caught up with them and overheard the last bit of their conversation. They all looked at one another, then he reached out with his one hand and turned the knob. They stood still for a moment, then crossed the threshold—first Henry's mother, then Cornelia, then Mr. Roberts. Though the room held no memories for Cornelia, she could already sense the essence of Henry there. His mother sat on the edge of the bed quickly, as though her knees might give out. His father turned on a desk lamp, and Cornelia took her time walking around the room.

"I knew him such a short time," she said with reverence. She realized that the room held twenty years of memories for the two of them. "Thank you so much for including me—for coming to get me."

"Oh, sweetie," Eva said. "You were so special to Henry. He wrote to me—to us—faithfully all summer, you know. And every letter was about you. It does our hearts good to have you here."

Over Henry's desk hung photos of his baseball teams, taken from the time he was ten or so. Henry had told Cornelia stories about how he'd loved the game and had started coaching when he was only fourteen. She'd also attended the games Henry organized back in Roseburg the past summer, though the sport itself held little interest for her.

"He took his glove with him, but there's his bat in the corner." Henry's father pointed to it and Cornelia walked over and picked it up. It comforted her to touch something Henry had held in his hands so many times. Hooks on the wall were draped with all the clothing Henry had left behind, which was most of it. She recognized a tan cardigan and stroked the sleeve. Next to the clothing, a narrow window looked out onto the street. The window had a pull-down blind and simple, dark blue curtains. A four-drawer dresser completed the furnishings. Over it hung yet another bookcase that was nailed to the wall and filled to capacity. Among the volumes of classic literature were sprinkled books on baseball and agriculture, including every *Old Farmer's Almanac* going back to 1925.

"Henry read and reread all those throughout his childhood." Eva ran her hand over the books.

The room grew quiet as each person became lost in thought. Finally Mr. Roberts broke the silence. "Are you hungry, Cornelia?"

"A little, I guess. But please, call me Corrie. Everyone does."

"And you must call us Samuel and Eva." He looked back at her without smiling.

"Yes, indeed," his wife agreed. "Let's all go back downstairs and see what we can rustle up for supper. It'll be much warmer down there by now. I think I hear the kettle whistling. I'm so glad you're here, dear."

CHAPTER 25

June 2006

Benita hadn't had one free minute. Between the demands of the store, housework, and laundry, helping the children with homework, and trying to grab a few hours of sleep each night, she hadn't looked at Gram's diary for weeks. The kids had insisted that they all go to church this morning, so she hadn't dared protest. Not that she minded going to church.

But now, at last, Sunday afternoon had arrived. The store was closed, although Ken stayed in the back office working on the books. The washer and dryer were both humming, Katie-Lynn was reading, and James was at his friend Robbie's house. Benita filled a mug with cinnamon apple tea and retreated to her favorite spot on the back porch. She sure would miss this porch when they moved to the apartment over the store. Oh, well. She knew she needed to keep things in perspective and enjoy it while she could.

She reached into the silver suitcase, pulled out the 1937 diary, and turned to where she had left off.

August 1, 1937. I can hardly believe it, but I am 16 years old today. Just when I thought everyone would forget, Daddy came in for lunch yesterday to announce he'd sold one of Daisy's twins and wanted to take me shopping for a new dress and shoes. And not in Roseburg, either! We drove the whole 16 miles to New Pass and visited Mrs. Kimble's dress shop. It was wonderful! I tried on five dresses and ended up choosing the first one I tried on. It's pink with small brown polka dots. It zips up the back, but there's a double row of little buttons all the way down the front for show. It's slim-fitting nearly all the way down, with a nice amount of flare around the bottom, at mid-calf. The puffy sleeves end with a wide band above the elbow. I love it, love it, love it! Jimmy was bored to death, I could tell, but he was really good and didn't complain. After the dress, we went across the street to try on shoes. Jim got a new pair for school, and I got brown pumps to match my new dress. They're beautiful and they FIT! Now I can hardly wait till the harvest dance. I feel like a princess!

Before we headed back, Daddy bought us all ice cream from the soda counter in the drugstore. Instead of going straight home, we went to Aunty Nonie's, where everyone gathered for a birthday supper for me! We filled up on corn on the cob from her garden.

What a great day! It would have been perfect if it weren't for Aunt Miriam. When I showed everyone my new clothes, she told Daddy he paid way too much and she could have made the same dress for half. And brown shoes? What were we thinking? Black would be much more practical, they would go with everything. But while I helped Aunty Nonie clear the table, she leaned over and told me to never mind Miriam. She said "your outfit is beautiful and your daddy loves you very much."

So Aunt Miriam can go suck on lemons.

Now, will George Rollston invite me to the dance or won't he?

Benita picked up her laptop computer from the wicker table in front of her and googled *1937 Fashion.* Only black-and-white sketches appeared, but she found one that could easily have been depicting Gram's sweet-sixteen dress. What would it be like to have had a daddy who loved her like that? Who provided for her needs and for her heart's desires, even when it probably meant sacrifice? She turned back to the diary.

September 29, 1937. Daddy means well and I love him for it. We all dressed for the harvest dance, and when I came out of my room, Daddy said "those boys sure will be sorry when they see you walk in. But that's okay, because it means I get to take the prettiest lady to the dance." I really don't mind that no one asked me. Well, okay. Honestly, I felt pretty disappointed. But still, I thought it would be fine. I made my pumpkin pie and it turned out great. Jimmy helped me whip cream for it and said he and Walter Sylvester planned a contest to see who could eat the most.

We arrived at the hall and stood around for a long time before the music started. Daddy asked me to dance and the Brewster Brothers did "Dream a Little Dream of Me." We were half way through "I Found a Million Dollar Baby" when I saw George walk in with Agnes. I couldn't believe my eyes. Why didn't she tell me George asked her to the dance? She knows I like him, that's why. I didn't even think she liked him, but apparently I was wrong. I finished the dance with Daddy and went to the ladies' room. I wanted to cry, but I didn't. I hated the rest of the night. I danced once with Alex and twice with Pete. George and Agnes stuck together like glue all evening. I'm so mad I could spit. Boys are dumb anyway.

Also—I finished reading Pride and Prejudice. *Again. Sure wish we could find some new books.*

The afternoon flew by as Benita delved into the ups and downs of a young girl's life. Her grandmother had been a typical teenager in so many ways. Yet to think that she'd run a household instead of attending school—where perhaps she would have been a cheerleader or played sports—both fascinated Benita and made her a little sad. The books Cornelia mentioned reading and the precision with which she wrote told Benita she had probably been a good student before she was deemed too old for school.

After breaking for supper with the family, Benita returned to the diary. *I'll just read one more entry,* she told herself. By now, she was up to 1939. When she picked the diary up, a neatly folded but brittle and yellowing piece of paper fluttered into her lap. Benita unfolded it.

It was a Jersey Milk chocolate bar wrapper.

CHAPTER 26

December 1939

Cornelia felt so grateful when Henry's parents insisted she sit with them at the funeral, as part of the family. Together, they had viewed Henry's body for the first time the previous evening, privately, at the funeral home. Cornelia felt her knees begin to buckle when she first looked into the casket, yet at the same time she knew she must.

Eight weeks had passed since they said their good-byes, and this was certainly not the reunion she dreamed of. He looked like a pale, empty shell, as if the real Henry had merely stepped out of his skin and moved on. Eva began to sob, and as Cornelia focused her attention on supporting Henry's mother, she felt her own strength return.

Now as the funeral music played, she sat at the end of a pew with Henry's parents on her left. To their left sat Eva's mother, Henry's grandmother Bridget. Behind Cornelia sat a row of aunts, uncles, and cousins, and when she felt a tap on her shoulder, she turned to see Elizabeth and Trudy, Henry's cousins from Roseburg, with their parents. Trudy patted her shoulder and Elizabeth leaned in for an awkward hug across the church pew. Behind the cousins sat rows of strangers who had come to say good-bye to Henry and support his family.

Throughout the service, Cornelia's mind kept wandering to her secret. She had dismissed each thought that had arisen about how she might raise a child alone. She could not think that far ahead. The shock of this loss was more than enough to handle, but she knew she needed to tell someone soon. The pastor was telling a story about Henry, which drew her attention back to the service.

"I'll never forget the first time I watched Henry play ball," the pastor said. "I think he was about twelve. He invited me to his games many times and, finally, I made it to one. Henry was pitching and doing a fine job. Then a smaller boy with a clubfoot went up to bat. It was clear that even if the boy managed to hit the ball, running around the bases would prove a problem. But you could read the determination on his face. After one strike, he did hit that ball and what followed was the most brilliant display of baseball choreography I've ever seen.

"You would have thought they practiced it. That ball rolled right past Henry, although he could have easily caught it. The second baseman picked up Henry's cue. By the time he threw it to the first baseman, the boy was on his way to second. The ball went back to Henry and around and around it went, each player always too late to tag the runner, who completed the first home run of his life. And oddly enough, the boys never once appeared to be 'trying' to fumble the ball.

"Henry took some criticism for his act of kindness, but I happily watched the coach pat his shoulder after the inning. The next time I saw Henry, I, too, commended him for putting others ahead of himself. What he said next will stay with me forever:

"'It was Jesus,' he said, with a shrug of his shoulders. I asked him what he meant.

"'Who was Jesus?'

"'The boy with the bad foot.'

"'What do you mean?' I asked him. 'Jesus didn't have a bad foot, as far we know.'"

"Henry explained, as though it was an obvious fact everyone should know, 'Jesus comes in all shapes and sizes. You need to learn to see him in every pair of eyes you ever lock onto.'

"Henry recognized his savior in other people. I'll never forget Henry's lesson, and since that day I've tried to live my life looking for Jesus in every person I lock eyes with."

Cornelia would have been surprised to hear this about Henry, had she not received his last letter. Beyond the gift of his hymnbook, he had shared little about his faith during his rebellious summer. His doing so would have only irritated her, she knew. But now, having looked into the eyes of Aziel, she saw things so much differently. Had Henry seen Jesus in her eyes, too?

"There is not one doubt in my mind that Henry lives with Jesus now," the pastor continued. "And there's no doubt they knew each other instantly, for they already enjoyed a great friendship."

The funeral concluded with a hymn Cornelia didn't know, but the words poured into her soul while she listened intently to the congregation sing:

"Face to face with Christ, my Savior,
Face to face—what will it be
When with rapture I behold Him, Jesus
Christ who died for me?
Only faintly now, I see Him, with
the darkling veil between
But a blessed day is coming, when
his glory shall be seen.
Face to face! O blissful moment! Face
to face—to see and know;
Face to face with my Redeemer, Jesus

Christ who loves me so.
Face to face I shall behold him, far
beyond the starry sky;
Face to face in all his glory, I shall see him by and by!"

As the music continued, Cornelia considered whether Henry's pastor might be the one to whom she could take her secret.

At the graveside, Cornelia stood behind Henry's parents as more prayers were offered, and the casket was lowered into the ground.

For a brief moment, Cornelia was back at her mother's funeral, where she and her brother had stood, one on each side of Daddy, holding his hands. Aziel's words came back to mind: *You have already endured sorrow upon sorrow in your young life, and there is still more to come. But Jesus will be with you. He understands sorrow. It's one of his nicknames.*

At the gathering afterward, Eva introduced Cornelia to so many of Henry's relatives and friends, she knew she would never keep them all straight. She wondered how much it mattered. Although they were sharing a profound experience right now, would they ever see one another again?

A young light-haired man in an oversize suit approached her. "Cornelia?"

"Yes."

"I'm Henry's friend Eugene." He extended his hand, and Cornelia shook it. "I wish I could have met you under happier circumstances."

"Me, too."

Eugene told her that Henry had confided his intent to marry Cornelia.

"He said he fell in love with you instantly," Eugene said. "I teased him, of course, but I was happy for him. I sure will miss that guy." Eugene pressed his lips together.

"He was very fond of you, too."

Cornelia had hoped she might find a moment with the pastor and perhaps set up an appointment with him, but by the time the crowd had thinned out, he was nowhere to be seen. She returned with the Robertses to their home, where they all went straight to bed, utterly drained by the events of the day and by their grief.

The next morning, Cornelia was sick. Grateful for the warmth of an indoor bathroom, she tried desperately to be quiet as her stomach emptied itself. When she emerged from the bathroom, it was clear she'd been unsuccessful. Eva looked at her with concern.

"Are you all right, Corrie?"

"I'll be fine." But she immediately turned around and went back to the bathroom for another round of vomiting. When she came back out, Eva invited her to sit at the kitchen table. They sat quietly, sipping tea for a few moments. Cornelia knew now was as good a time as any to tell her secret, but although she had rehearsed the speech throughout the night, her mouth felt dry, her hands trembled, and her heart pounded. She had imagined every conceivable response that Henry's parents could offer, most of the scenarios ending with her boarding the first possible train home.

"Is there something you need to tell me, honey?" Eva gripped her teacup.

Cornelia looked up into the sorrowful eyes of the woman who had been her mother's best friend.

"I—yes." Tears started streaming down her face. How could she add more pain to this already hurting family? But trying to hide the truth was not going to help, either.

"I think I can guess, Corrie."

Cornelia looked up in surprise.

"This is the fourth morning we've been together and the fourth morning you've been sick. Yet you're always better by noon."

Cornelia thought she had done a better job of being discreet. She cried even harder.

Eva's eyes welled up. "Is it true, then?"

Cornelia nodded, trying desperately to hold back the flood of tears. This was the first time she had heard her secret acknowledged aloud. Until now, it had been much easier to stay in denial, even though her body gave every indication it was, indeed, carrying Henry's child.

"Have you seen a doctor?"

Cornelia shook her head.

"Well, then, that's the first thing. We need to confirm it. I'll take you this afternoon. We find out for sure, and if it's true, the second thing we do is tell Henry's father."

Cornelia could tell what Eva's tone meant. She suddenly seemed so businesslike, taking charge and making decisions on Cornelia's behalf. Surely this meant the end of the friendship that had grown through their shared grief.

"Thank you," she managed to whisper as she stared at her shoes in shame.

CHAPTER 27

July 2006

Three months had passed since Ken and Benita took over the management of Schneider's Corner Store. Although the owners were pleased with the state of sales and with Ken and Benita's work, tension between the couple was heavier than it had ever been before. After the first two weeks, they'd moved into the upstairs apartment and begun to prepare their home for sale. Benita tried to convince her husband they should try renting it instead, but Ken wouldn't hear of it.

"Even if we managed to rent it out for enough to cover our mortgage payments—and we won't—the hassles of being a landlord never end," he had ranted. "Things have needed repair around that place for years, but we haven't had the money. Now we don't have time *or* money. If you think for one minute that tenants will put up with that, think again. I don't have time to keep up with everything both here and there. I want to focus on one thing, and do it right."

Benita had to concede that Ken had "done it right" as far the store was concerned. It had never looked this clean and bright before, nor had it offered so much product variety. More important, the books had never looked this promising. With the go-ahead from the Schneider siblings, he spent every available moment repainting, rewiring, and rearranging the store. Benita suspected that after all those months of unemployment, Ken desperately needed to prove his competency, even if it was only to himself.

The frequency of their fights would have been understandable during Ken's time of unemployment, but oddly enough, all the hostility and resentment seemed to be rising to the surface now instead. Every conversation was peppered with sarcasm or escalated into an argument, and it wore her down.

They'd held a huge garage sale to whittle down their belongings, and each of them had seemed determined to part with things the other wanted to keep. The house sold the next week. Benita struggled to wrap her head around the idea. True, the free apartment above the store would greatly reduce their living expenses and give them a chance to catch up on bills, possibly even get ahead—but at how great an emotional price? She felt like she was camping, or a guest in someone else's hotel room. The space seemed too public and too small.

James and Katie-Lynn, accustomed to spending time with their dad, were now adjusting to a new way of life. Benita knew that if they weren't living right at the store, James and Katie-Lynn wouldn't see Ken at all. He went downstairs long before they rose in the mornings and came to bed long after they were settled for the night. Everything had happened so quickly and with too little discussion or preparation. Benita hadn't had time to grieve the loss of Gram, her employers, or her home.

I know I should be thankful, God, she prayed during the silent prayer time at church. *We prayed for work and you provided. Help me be more grateful.*

Ken stopped coming to church after those first few weeks, declaring he needed Sunday morning to work on things at the store. Initially, Benita would have chosen to stay home herself, but the children loved attending and, frankly, it presented a good opportunity to create a little space between her and Ken for a couple of hours a week.

The precious opportunities she found to read Gram's diary were opening her eyes to a new way of doing things, a way that included her creator in the day-to-day of life, as Gram had. And gradually, Benita was discovering the worship times at church to be more meaningful, too.

Before heading home after the service, Benita remained in her seat for a few minutes of quiet reflection.

Lord, you and I haven't had much to do with each other through the years. Well, maybe it's more accurate to say I haven't had much to do with you. I'd like that to change. Show me how to do life better. Please help Ken relax a bit about the store. He acts as if he owns it, and I know that makes for a good manager, but I'm afraid for what's happening in the family. He has changed so much. Show me how to deal with it.

She drove home with a lighter heart.

When lunch was ready, Benita sent Katie-Lynn downstairs to call her father.

"He says he's not hungry," Katie-Lynn reported back. "And he'd *appreciate a little help*."

By the tone of Katie-Lynn's voice, Benita could tell her daughter was imitating the inflections made by an irritated man. She sighed and sat down to eat with the children. She had really been looking forward to an afternoon of relaxation on the one day a week the store stayed closed. She was clearing lunch dishes when Ken's head appeared at the top of the stairs.

"I need an extra pair of hands down there, didn't Katie-Lynn tell you?"

"She did. But we were about to sit down for lunch. Why didn't you come eat with us?"

"We've got more important things around here to worry about than eating every couple of hours, Benita! We won't be able to open the store tomorrow morning if we don't finish that new shelving and put everything back on it. Now put the kids to work on those dishes and get down here and help me!"

"But I promised Katie-Lynn I'd help her finish those cushions for her room, and James needs help with his science project."

"Katie-Lynn can help James with his project and the stupid cushions can wait. That kid already has too much junk in her room anyway. I can't get this done all by myself." He turned around and stomped down the stairs.

Fuming, Benita passed the instructions on to James and Katie-Lynn and followed Ken downstairs, where they spent the remainder of the afternoon and the evening working in icy silence. Their only break came when the pizza delivery arrived, and the four of them sat around the store's counter eating straight from the box. At nine o'clock, James and Katie-Lynn put themselves to bed, and two hours later, Benita's weary feet carried her up the stairs.

At midnight, Benita climbed out of the bath, wrapped her robe tightly around herself, and sat in her bedroom with Gram's diary again. The last entry she'd read had shaken her, and she had set the precious book aside with a sense of having intruded. Now she promised herself she could read one more entry before bed, knowing it might be a week before there would be another opportunity.

After reading Gram's accounts of the loss of her beloved Henry and of her personal encounter with the angel, Benita found that each time she opened the diary she did so with more reverence and awe.

December 16, 1939. I have never felt so alone in my life. Eva guessed about my pregnancy and went with me to visit her doctor. Dr. Colburg is an older man, gentle and soft-spoken. He said it takes a few days for the final, official result to come back, but from his experience he is certain I am pregnant. I was certain already, so this was not surprising.

What came next I couldn't have predicted. Eva took me home and explained it to Samuel. I find him an impossible man to read, and he sat silently and stone-faced for the longest time. Then he said "You will not bring this disgrace upon Henry's memory," and he went upstairs without another word. I didn't know what to do. Was I supposed to leave right that minute? I didn't even have enough money for train fare to get home, and even if I did, I couldn't bear the thought of going home and telling Daddy. This will break his heart! He'll have to find a way to explain it to Jimmy, and he'll have to listen to Miriam's I-told-you-so's for the rest of his life.

Eva told me to go to bed and she would talk to her husband. But in the morning, he laid out a plan. "You will not return home to Roseburg," he said. "If you do, my brother's family will know. You will stay here in the city until the baby arrives, but not with us. I know of a home where you can go. You will not show up at our church or anywhere any of our friends might see you. Eva will write your father, requesting that you stay here with us for a while longer to comfort us in our grief. You will agree to tell no one and you will give the child up for adoption. In exchange, I will provide for your care until the birth and I will pay for you to finish your high school by correspondence while you wait. After that, you will no longer be part of our lives."

And so it seems my future has been decided for me.

Benita wiped tears from her cheeks. That was the last entry for the year. She put the diary back into the silver suitcase. She knew she should get some sleep, but Gram's story compelled her to keep reading. She picked up the next one marked *1940* and took it to bed with her. With pillows propped behind her back, she opened the diary to its first entry.

> *January 1. I endured the most miserable Christmas ever. My heart breaks with grief for my beloved Henry, and though I long to go home to Daddy and Jim, I remain stuck here in Winnipeg with two other heartbroken people. Henry's parents mean well. Eva remains kind and gentle, but she will not challenge her husband's decision. Samuel has not spoken to me since he learned of the pregnancy, except when necessary to make arrangements for my lodging. Eva wrote to Daddy, convincing him to let me stay with them "to comfort them in their grief," and I am expected to go along with this charade.*
>
> *So there was no Christmas tree, no carols, no gifts. The only thing that made it seem remotely like Christmas was the package for me in the mail, from home. Daddy sent me this new diary and Jim sent a beautiful, heart-shaped stone he found at our favorite spot by the creek. On the back, he'd drawn a tiny angel, which of course made me cry immediately. As if he knew! His note said he hoped it would help me to not feel homesick. If only it could.*
>
> *I have been so tempted to run away, but where would I go? Back to Roseburg, where Daddy would have to bear the humiliation of his errant daughter and the never-ending condescension of Aunt Miriam? How could I do that to him? I have no money. I should be grateful, I suppose, for this opportunity. At least I will finish high school, even if only by correspondence. And it truly will be so much better for my child to be raised by two parents who can provide for him. Or her. So I have resigned myself to the decisions made for me, and keep telling myself it will all work out.*

Then they brought me here, yesterday. Mrs. Marshall met us at the back door of her restaurant, looked me up and down, and told me to carry my bag upstairs and leave it in the room on the right. And to be quick about it. I dropped my bag in the room without really looking inside and hustled back down the stairs, my hands trembling. When I returned to the kitchen, Henry's parents were gone. Mrs. Marshall handed me an apron and told me to go to work on the pile of dirty dishes. For the next four hours I scrubbed dishes, pots, and pans while Mrs. Marshall filled customers' orders. How can so many people afford to eat in a restaurant during wartime, and on New Year's Day? Another girl waited tables, and when we were finally done for the night, I learned her name is Linda and she sleeps in the room across the hall from mine.

My room has one bare window that is in desperate need of cleaning. What little plaster remains on the walls is a dull gray, with no pictures hung on it. There's a washstand in the corner and a tiny bed with one thin blanket. When I lie on the bed, the springs sag nearly to the floor. There is no heat in the room except what comes from below through the grate in the hallway floor, so I leave my door open at all times.

My correspondence courses begin next week, and I will need to do my schoolwork around the restaurant schedule. Henry's father insisted that Mrs. Marshall pay me a small wage in addition to providing my lodging, and for that I am grateful. There is plenty of food to eat, although I have little appetite and can't eat anything at all in the mornings. I'm excited about starting my studies. I hope I can handle them. Those Grade Nine courses were a long time ago.

I must turn in. 5:00 a.m. will arrive much too soon, but apparently it's my job to light the cookstove and heat water for the day's supply.

Benita had never before possessed clues about this delicate part of Gram's story, and she wondered whether her mother knew. She wished she could stay up until dawn reading, and she would have if she didn't have to get up early tomorrow. But she did. So she laid the diary on her bedside table and snuggled down to sleep, leaving a lamp on for Ken, who would surely come upstairs soon.

CHAPTER 28

The next morning after the children left for school, Benita stole another look at the diary from 1940 over a second cup of coffee. She quickly became riveted to the pages.

> *February 24. The other girl here, Linda, expects her baby in a month. She is large and awkward, and Mrs. Marshall has her washing dishes so she can stay hidden in the kitchen while I wait tables. It gives me a little glimpse of my near future, I'm afraid. But enough feeling sorry for myself.*
>
> *I completed three lessons in each of my five correspondence courses, and received an "A" on all but one. I received a B minus on a math assignment, but I'm thankful it wasn't worse. I literally fell asleep on top of that one, slumped over at the little table in my room. When I woke up, I had drooled on the page and it was smeared and wrinkled. How mortifying! My brain was foggy, too, so it's a wonder I didn't get an F.*

March 19. Linda had her baby yesterday. In the middle of the night I heard, "Corrie! Corrie!" When I finally woke up, I realized it was Linda calling out for me. When I went to her, she looked horrible. She was in pain, sweating, and so fearful. I ran to find Mrs. Marshall and the two of them left together. I tried to go back to sleep but couldn't, so I stayed up and tried to study but had a hard time concentrating. I couldn't forget that look on Linda's face. It was frightening.

Mrs. Marshall returned in time to open the restaurant as usual and we never talked about Linda all that day. The next morning I couldn't stand it anymore and asked Mrs. Marshall about it. All she would say was "she had the baby." When I asked her whether it was a boy or a girl, she said, "makes no difference. Linda won't be keeping it anyway. Best if she doesn't even see it."

Then she instructed me to clean out Linda's room after the lunch rush ended. I put Linda's few belongings into a box and carried them downstairs to Mrs. Marshall's room off the kitchen. Then I stripped the sheets and washed them, and hung them out on the clothesline to dry. I scrubbed the furniture, the floor, and the window as best I could.

Now it's ready for another girl, I suppose. I wonder who she'll be and whether I will now be relegated to dishwashing duty while the new girl takes my place waiting tables. I will welcome that, actually, because it has become impossible to hide the truth from the customers. I see their eyes wander from my stomach to my left hand, checking for a wedding ring. It's so humiliating.

I feel so sad for Linda. We didn't have a chance to get close, but I wish I could visit her. I don't even know which hospital she's in, where she'll go from there, or whether she'll return for her things.

"Don't you be worryin' about Linda," Mrs. Marshall told me when I asked. "In her parents' home, the only thing more plentiful than money is pride. With this little catastrophe behind them, she'll be fine."

That got me to thinking about Henry's parents, of course. And Daddy too. I miss him so much! Some days I think I should get on a train and just go home. Daddy's not a prideful man. He would take me in, I know he would. He loves me. He has never been one to demonstrate his affections, but I've never doubted my father would die for me if it came to it. I bet he'd defend me against Aunt Miriam, too.

So, what's stopping me? I've asked myself so many times. Is it my own pride, not wanting my community back home to know what I've done? Or is it Henry's reputation I'm protecting? I'm certainly protecting it for Jimmy, that much is true. Henry was my little brother's hero—how could I crush Jimmy's image of him? And how could I do such a thing to Daddy? Not to mention the burden of another mouth to feed after the baby comes.

No, better to go along with what everyone tells me is best. Once the baby is handed over to its new parents, my life can go on. In time, I'll forget it ever happened. Or so I'm told.

One sentence jumped out at Benita and raised a resounding pang of jealous longing in her heart: "*. . . I've never had a doubt my father would die for me if it came to it.*"

She tried to imagine what the unconditional love of a father would be like. Did it even exist? In her experience, men were people who left you alone to fend for yourself. She turned the diary page over and smiled to see a poorly done drawing on the other side. It featured a teenage girl, obviously pregnant, seated on a blanket along a riverbank.

Standing next to her was a man holding out a chocolate bar to the girl. She had clearly penned the words *Jersey Milk* onto the bar. Below the picture were these words:

> *Oh Lord God, how I need you! You have been there for me before. Even when I hated you, you were the sustainer of my life, my every breath. You are the friend I need, the father I need, forever. You have promised to never leave me or abandon me. Thank you, Lord.*

As Benita stared at the picture and reread the words of the prayer, the hungry ache deep inside her grew stronger.

She laid the diary page aside with a sigh and allowed a lone tear to fall to her lap.

CHAPTER 29

May 1940

Just as she had done every spring for three years, Miriam Simpson caught the Monday train for Winnipeg and made her way to the Correspondence Branch offices of the Department of Education, where she would spend one week marking examination papers for extra cash.

She brought along a letter and package from Corrie's father and found her way to the Robertses' home to deliver it in person. When she arrived, Mr. Roberts informed her that, sadly, Corrie was out of town with Mrs. Roberts for the entire week and would not return until after Miriam went back home. She left the package anyway, and returned to the rooming house where she was staying.

Now she was on a lunch break from her work and heading out for some air. *A brisk walk around the block will do me good,* she told herself. She'd never been one to admit that the city fashions in the store windows intrigued her as much as they did any other woman.

When she reached the bottom of the staircase, two young ladies waited to speak to the registrar. One of them appeared to be pregnant, and Miriam found it surprising that a married woman would be taking her high school classes by correspondence. Then she stopped in her tracks. The pregnant woman caught up in conversation looked exactly like Cornelia!

Miriam stepped behind a pillar to collect her thoughts. As she listened, she overheard the young woman explaining that the department had scheduled her to write two different exams in the same time slot. Miriam felt certain the voice was Cornelia's. She couldn't move. Her feet couldn't have been more firmly planted on the marble floor if they'd been tree roots.

She listened as Cornelia resolved her conflict with the registrar and then watched as she left by the front door. Only then did she step out from behind the pillar. Now Miriam had a clear view through the window of Cornelia walking down the sidewalk, papers in hand.

It was most definitely Cornelia, and she was most definitely pregnant.

CHAPTER 30

June 1940

The fragrance of lilacs in full bloom always filled Cornelia's heart with memories of her mother, and the scent swept over her now. She stepped out into the June sunlight and slowly bent down to pick up a milk bottle from the front step. Her size made this quite a feat, but she was determined to do it. Dr. Colburg said the baby could come any day now, and she should expect to stay in the hospital for a whole week. Already she was experiencing cramping that left her anxious about what was to come.

Returning to the kitchen, she poured milk over the oatmeal that was waiting in a bowl and sat down to eat. When the mailman came up the walk, she waddled over to take the mail straight from his hands and happily spotted the familiar Department of Education envelope in his hand. She tore it open and was rewarded immediately by the sight of her name on an official grade eleven diploma. *I did it.* She smiled. With her grade eleven completed, she could again begin to dream of one day becoming a teacher.

After breakfast, and with little else to do, Cornelia turned to her diary.

Dear Diary,

I haven't written for months because I've spent every waking moment either working on my studies or washing dishes in the restaurant downstairs. All of it helps me to forget my circumstances. I'm as big as a house, and the only shoes I can wear on my swollen feet are slippers. I have two outfits I can wear now: one dark blue dress and one gray skirt with a flowered blouse. Both were given to me by Mrs. Marshall, the woman who runs the home for unwed mothers.

It's not much of a home, really . . . merely two bedrooms over a restaurant. Mrs. Marshall sleeps in a room off the kitchen downstairs. I don't know whether it was compassion or desperation that drove her to open her home to girls like me, but I can be thankful to Henry's parents for finding this place and for footing the bill as they promised.

I try hard to save the little cash I earn. Mrs. Marshall says I can stay on after the baby comes if I'm prepared to work long hours . . . but I can only live with her until another girl needs my room. There is one other girl here right now. She is only fifteen and so frightened. But at least she knows she can go back to her parents afterward.

I reached a decision for my future. With the money I've saved so far, and the money I'll earn if I continue working really hard through the summer, I'll have enough to enroll in Normal School in September. I know it won't be easy and I will need to find a job while I'm in school, but I would rather be a teacher and invest my life in other people's children than go home and forever pine for my own.

As for how it will feel to give up this baby, I can't even let myself think about it.

My Grade Eleven diploma arrived today and I feel like celebrating, but I have no one to celebrate with. Eva has stopped by twice to drop off letters from Daddy and Jim, but she never stays long. Between us, we keep up the charade, making it look as though I'm still staying with them. I've never been deceitful with my father before. No, that's not entirely true. He always believed I was a good little Christian girl even when I hated God.

How that has changed! I maintain my friendship with Jesus by talking to him daily—all day, every day, actually. I read my Bible, too, but it's still my experience of last December, of actually having his messenger beside me, which sustains me. The encounter with Aziel has not faded in the least, but remains the most profound thing that ever happened to me. Jesus is far more real to me than Henry now. Though it is Henry's child I carry inside, I carry Jesus in my heart forever.

Yesterday morning, everyone in the restaurant hushed while Winston Churchill's speech to Parliament was broadcast over Mrs. Marshall's radio. I didn't catch it all, but he spoke of the importance of defeating Mr. Hitler and the dark consequences if the man is not removed from power. I grabbed a pencil and copied down the last few lines that Churchill spoke:

"Let us therefore brace ourselves to our duties, and so bear ourselves that if the British empire and its Commonwealth last for a thousand years, men will still say, 'This was their finest hour.'"

Cornelia stopped writing when she realized a trickle of warm liquid had soaked through her dress onto the chair. Her heart started pounding hard.

Though she felt certain she was soon to enter the battle of her life, it seemed highly unlikely that what was about to transpire would be her finest hour.

CHAPTER 31

June 1940

Mrs. Marshall recruited a neighbor, Mr. Lapinski, to drive Cornelia and herself to St. Joseph Hospital, where she stayed long enough to make sure the admitting office had all the information they required.

"Good luck to you." Mrs. Marshall placed a hand on Cornelia's shoulder as she sat waiting in a wheelchair. It was the closest the woman had ever come to any display of tenderness, and Cornelia wanted to beg her to stay. But lunch hour was nearing at the restaurant, and she knew she dared not ask. She watched as the only familiar face in sight turned away and left the building without a backward glance.

A nurse wheeled Cornelia to a labor room, where she was assisted into a hospital gown. Most of the nurses were dressed in nuns' habits, and a crucifix hung in every room and hallway she'd seen. As the pain intensified, Cornelia focused her gaze on the image of Christ on the cross. She reminded herself that Jesus knew what pain was all about, but under these circumstances, the thought didn't make her feel any better.

She hadn't known it was possible to feel this alone. Though one of the nurses, Sister Marcelene, was kind, another treated her with outright disdain and judgment. Sister Estelle looked like she had been nursing at this hospital since it opened its doors seventy years earlier. "The pain will help cleanse you of your sin," she said. "Don't try to fight it."

Sister Marcelene caught Cornelia's eye and shook her head gently without a word.

A small booklet entitled *Preparing for Motherhood* provided the only formal childbirth education Cornelia had received, but back on the farm she'd helped her father birth a calf and a set of twin lambs. The animal mothers never seemed to be in this much pain, and Cornelia wondered if she was doing something wrong. But from the moaning and even occasional screams coming from other rooms, she knew human birthing must be quite different. Determined to get through it, she found herself begging God for help. Hadn't the angel promised Jesus would never leave her? Where was he now? If only she could feel his presence. If only her mother could be here. If only she had told Daddy. With every excruciating breath, another *if only* rose to Cornelia's mind until she thought she would burst from the pain, the fright, and the longing. No one held her hand or spoke an encouraging word.

At long last, Dr. Colburg came and Cornelia was glad to see someone at least a little familiar. He was all business, however, as he told her it was time to push. Through the blinding pain, Cornelia worked harder than ever before. Her resolve to be brave weakened with each exhausting effort. Just when she thought there was no more use in trying, that she must surely give up and die, she heard Dr. Colburg say, "Here it comes!"

In another moment, Cornelia heard the wail of a newborn baby. *Her* baby! In a blur of activity, the baby was hustled out of the room and Cornelia was poked, prodded, washed, moved, tucked in, and told to rest.

It was over.

Two days later, Cornelia stole down the hallway and peered through the nursery window until she spotted a bassinet with a card labeled *Simpson*. Just below the name, in finer print, she saw the words *For Adoption* in brackets. Though Cornelia had not been given the opportunity to hold the baby, Sister Marcelene had told her it was a little girl, and Cornelia had named her Mary Sarah. She studied her newborn daughter's face and let the tears run down her own.

Never before had she felt so overwhelmed with both love and pain. Intense longing for Henry overshadowed the relief of knowing the birth was now behind her, and the grief of losing her mother felt suddenly fresh in the face of this new loss. These feelings were jumbled together with loneliness and with passionate affection for the precious little bundle she longed to cuddle. Her breasts ached, swollen with the milk that would never nourish her little girl.

At the same time, Cornelia tried to feel hopeful for her future, a hope based on what she'd been told—that she would soon be able to put all this behind her. Now she wondered how such a thing could ever be true. She wanted Jimmy to meet his niece and Daddy to meet his first grandchild. She wondered whether she could ever go home. As far as she knew, no one there knew the truth about why she hadn't returned.

In his letters, her father had told her how he bragged about her when folks asked: "She's going to school and providing companionship for the Robertses in their time of grief. We're proud of you, Corrie." He made her sound like a saint. At least the situation spared her father the shame of knowing the whole story.

Now Cornelia's heart felt like it would rip in half. *How can I do this, Jesus?* she prayed. Was giving up her baby a just consequence for her actions? If only Henry hadn't died, they could have gotten married and kept their baby.

A part of her burned with anger at Henry for his insane insistence on going off to a war he never even saw. She could see his features in Mary Sarah's little face. *So this is motherhood*, she thought. *And it is the deepest pain I can imagine.* Had her mother loved her as much as she loved this little one? If Samuel and Eva loved Henry the way she loved Mary Sarah, how could they go on? How would she?

When Cornelia pressed her forehead against the glass and closed her eyes, she thought back to that day by the creek, and she heard Aziel's words to her once again: "There is more sorrow to come. But don't be afraid. Jesus will be there with you, and he knows all about sorrow. It's one of his nicknames."

Man of Sorrows. Cornelia knew the words from an old hymn, and in this moment it was the scarred hands of Jesus that she saw. From some long-ago Sunday school lesson, a memorized snippet of Scripture surfaced: ". . . by his stripes, we are healed." *Oh God, I don't even know what that means,* her heart cried. *I only know I desperately need healing. Jesus, heal my broken heart.*

A nurse gripped Cornelia's shoulders and guided her away from the window and back to her hospital room. "You'll only make it harder."

"Can I at least write her a letter?" Cornelia asked. "Her parents could give it to her when she's older."

"I'm sorry, no. Even if it were advisable, it's too late. They're here for her now."

Cornelia whirled around, but the nurse held her firmly. From this distance, she could tell Mary Sarah's little bassinet stood empty, and her eyes frantically searched the hallway for a couple leaving with an infant.

"Wait!" she called out. Wriggling free from the nurse's grip, she moved as quickly as her aching body would allow, back to her room. There, she rummaged through her purse and pulled out a page torn from Henry's hymnbook.

"Can I just give them this, please?"

"I'll see they get it." The nurse took the page. "You need to get back into bed."

Five days later, Cornelia rode back to Mrs. Marshall's on the streetcar. Mary Sarah's adoptive parents had taken her home, and Cornelia had not seen her again.

She rode along in silence, the hot sun beating through the windows. Everywhere she looked, she was reminded that the world was at war. Large, colorful posters encouraged men to enlist, and women to contribute to the war effort by gathering scrap metal and growing and preserving their own vegetables. Store windows displayed We Accept Ration Cards signs, and women in coveralls walked to jobs formerly held only by men.

Yet the war in her heart trumped it all, at least for Cornelia. She knew the only way to survive her situation was to focus on working as hard as she could, saving the money for Normal School, where she could train to become a teacher, and then studying like crazy. Her father had not been wild about her plan when she first wrote to him about the waitressing job, but he finally accepted it and even offered to send a little money each month.

"You got half an hour to get yourself settled back in upstairs," Mrs. Marshall barked when she walked in the back door of the restaurant. "Then I need you down here for the lunch rush."

And so it begins, Cornelia thought, as she carried her bag up the narrow stairs with a heavy heart.

CHAPTER 32

February 2007

Sunlight beat through the storefront windows, creating a soft glow in Benita's corner display. On a shelf stood her attempt at preserving a fragment of the original atmosphere of Schneiders' Grocery: a collection of old cracker, syrup, and coffee tins. On the floor below sat Gram's ice-cream maker and an old pickle crock. Beside that, Benita sat at an old-fashioned checkerboard table mounted on a wooden pickle barrel, reading the morning paper and sipping her coffee. The early afternoon lull provided her only chance to sit, to breathe, and to think about something besides business. She stared at the paper without reading, stared into her coffee cup, stared out the window.

Her thoughts turned to her marriage, as they always did when she had a spare moment. Her last major spat with Ken had been at Christmas, when she'd spent more than Ken thought she should on gifts for the children. Even as she spoke the words, she'd known they would cut him like a knife, but she hadn't stopped herself.

"What's wrong with getting them what they want for Christmas? You're working day and night to take care of your family. I would think you'd be pleased, now that you're Mr. Big Provider."

"I am not your father," Ken had said with a sigh.

"What?"

"You heard me."

"What does my father have to do with anything?"

"Your father never provided for you, and you've decided I never will, either. No matter how hard I work or how much I earn, it will never be enough for you, will it?"

Benita had stood speechless, shocked by his accusation. As soon as Ken left the room, her eyes welled up with tears. Was it true? Was she projecting her anger against her father onto Ken? But how could she be angry with someone she'd never even known?

That night, she'd again broached the topic of marriage counseling.

"Go ahead. But keep me out of it," Ken told her.

Benita let out a snort of contempt. "Fat lot of good it will do if you won't even cooperate."

Ken had crawled into bed, turned his back to her, and not said another word until morning.

Now the bell jangled on the door as some customers entered, pulling Benita out of her reverie. A man and a little girl walked in, hand in hand.

"Can I get a treat, Daddy?" The little girl eyed the rows of candy on display.

"Not today, sugar." The man turned to Benita. "I'll take a package of Player's Light."

Benita turned, found the cigarettes, and laid them on the counter. As the man counted out exact change, she studied the obvious disappointment on his sweet daughter's face. The man appeared blind to it, and Benita wanted to slap him as hard as she could. She wanted to take the little girl into her arms and never return her to a man who could be so self-centered. She wanted to offer the child anything her heart desired, just to spite him.

Instead, she placed the money in the cash drawer. As she did, she saw her hands shake.

Why this reaction?

Benita stood in silence and stared while the pair left the store and continued on down the street. As she turned to straighten the rows of cigarettes, a business card fell from a shelf and fluttered to the floor. She bent to retrieve it, and when she read it, she instantly recognized the name Rod Schneider had mentioned at his parents' funeral: *Phillip Danson, Counselor.*

It was time.

Benita picked up the phone. Five minutes later, she had an appointment for the following Thursday at ten o'clock. *I did it,* she told herself. *I did something good for myself and for my family.*

Why then, she wondered, did she feel so weighed down with dread?

That evening after tucking the children into their beds, Benita curled up in her own with a cup of tea and Gram's diary from 1940. She hadn't looked at it in months.

> *December 15*
>
> *Dear Diary,*
>
> *It's hard to believe, but I am almost half way through my year at Normal School. After working harder than I've ever worked in my life at Mrs. Marshall's restaurant and now studying, there has been no time to write.*
>
> *I moved into the dorm in September and I'm thankful for the shortage of teachers because without it, I wouldn't be here*

at all. The government has made school affordable. Between what I saved over the summer and what Daddy sends, I've been able to keep up with tuition. I also work in the cafeteria every morning, which means rising at 4:30, so I'm really exhausted every night. Three classes happen in the forenoon and three in the afternoon. Each runs about forty-five minutes long, with a break of about fifteen minutes in between, for changing classrooms.

Mid-term exams are next week, so I thought I'd better write something now while I can steal a few minutes. It's been going well, I think. I love studying, I love my teachers, with the exception of Miss Banning, and most of the other students are all right. I am learning so much. We even received some basic music instruction, something I never dreamed I'd get to learn. I can play "Mary Had a Little Lamb" on the recorder.

The main building is a long, narrow stone structure enclosing offices, the chapel, classrooms, the library, art room, and science room. Above the library, on the third floor, are the female student quarters. I have three roommates: Rose, Noreen, and Ruby. They're all right, although Rose can be loud at times. I mostly keep to myself, focusing on my studies and the work I do in the cafeteria under Johnny's direction.

Across the street sits a small two-room school for neighborhood children. The Normal School uses it as a model school, and Mr. Clarke took our class there for observation one day. I've been assigned to Pinkham School for two weeks to obtain elementary school experience, beginning right after Christmas.

Last week was the anniversary of Henry's death and I went by streetcar to the cemetery. Samuel and Eva were both standing there, but when I approached Henry's grave, Samuel immediately walked back to the car without acknowledging me. Eva took my hand and we stood together for a long time without speaking. A sparrow landed on the grave marker and then hopped within five feet of me, where it stayed for a full minute before flying off.

Eva and I cried and then she said a short prayer. She asked for strength for all of us and for all who are losing their boys to this awful war. And she asked God to watch over Mary Sarah, whom she simply called "the baby." I felt touched. Although I'm grateful to have my studies to keep my mind occupied, not a moment goes by that she is not in my thoughts. It felt so wonderful to be with somebody who knows, even if Samuel remains hostile.

Of course, last week also marked the anniversary of my special visitation and I still have not shared it with anyone. After all these months, it remains the most real experience of my life—more real than Henry, than Mary Sarah; more real than my teachers or classmates. More real than my hand in front of my face. How I wish Aziel would return and make it an annual event. Perhaps he doesn't come lest I make him more important than Jesus.

Or perhaps he is always around and I just don't see.

I'm going home for Christmas! Daddy sent me money for the train fare, and I'll leave the day after exams and stay for two whole weeks. I can't begin to imagine what it will be like.

CHAPTER 33

December 1940

Cornelia saw her father and Jim waiting on the outdoor platform even before she rose from her seat. It warmed her heart to see Daddy blowing on his hands and Jim hopping from one foot to the other in the freezing cold. When she stepped onto the platform, she felt the urge to fly into her father's arms and never let go. But they had never been demonstrative with one another, particularly in public. Instead, she accepted a quick kiss on the cheek while placing one hand on Daddy's shoulder. With the other, she handed Jim her bag and then ruffled his hair, reaching up to do so. Jim seemed a foot taller than when she'd last laid eyes on him, and he wore the biggest grin Cornelia had ever seen on his face.

On the ride home, Jim talked nonstop about how great it felt not having to go to school anymore, how good a cook he was becoming, and how he and his friends Harold and Walter planned to enlist next summer, even if they had to lie about their age. At this, Cornelia cringed, but said nothing.

When they pulled into the farmyard, she thought her heart would stop. Everything looked the same, yet more run-down somehow. She had been away a full year after having never been away from home more than two nights in her entire life. When had the paint on the house started peeling? Had the fence always been crooked? Why had she never noticed the sag in the barn roof or the rusty hinges on the milk-house door? How long had Shep been walking with a limp? His tail wagging, the dog pressed his nose into Cornelia's mitten, and she focused her attention on him for a while, stroking his back and trying to regain her equilibrium before entering the house.

Inside, things looked the same except for a little more clutter and dust than Cornelia considered acceptable. When she had left a year ago, a Christmas tree had stood in the corner of the living room, but of course it was long gone.

"We waited for you to get home before puttin' up this year's tree," Jim said.

Cornelia went upstairs to her own room. It looked as though nothing had been touched. She sat on her bed and looked around, overcome with a longing for Henry and for Mary Sarah that was so desperate her arms ached. She wadded up a blanket and hugged it to herself before lying down. She drifted off to sleep to the sounds of Daddy and Jim down below, donning their overalls and boots, and heading out to do late-afternoon chores.

She awoke to complete darkness and the smell of pancakes cooking. Shocked, she tossed aside the blanket and hustled downstairs.

"I'm so sorry," she said. "I can't believe I fell asleep. I should be doing that!" She tried to take the pancake flipper from Jim's hand, but he wouldn't let go.

"Silly girl. Think I can't make pancakes, Corny? I can make lots of things."

"Sit down and eat some supper, Corrie." Charles pulled out a chair for her. "There'll be plenty of meals for you to cook in the next couple of weeks. Right now, let us treat you." He poured her a cup of coffee, and she sat.

After they'd eaten their modest meal, Jim and Cornelia did the dishes while their father stoked the fire in the living room. The three spent a relaxing evening together, playing checkers and making plans to chop down a Christmas tree the next day. Together they agreed they wouldn't exchange gifts this year, not even their usual homemade ones.

"Having you home is gift enough for us." Daddy smiled.

"And being here is gift enough for me."

When Jim said good night and went upstairs, she remained behind, wanting desperately to have a meaningful conversation with her father but wondering whether that would ever be possible as long as she harbored such an immense secret.

"Daddy, I'm sorry."

"What on earth for?"

"What I mean is—thank you, I suppose. I had no intention when I left here of staying away so long . . . this has been unfair to you, yet you've been so gracious. Thank you for providing for my education. I just . . . can't help feeling bad."

Her father packed the checkerboard and checkers back into their box. Then he reached across the table between them and took her hands in his.

"Corrie, honey. This is something you wanted for a long time. After the loss you suffered, it seemed like the perfect opportunity for you to move on. Much better than coming back here to your same old life."

Cornelia studied him. His blue eyes glistened with unshed tears.

"I'm so proud of you, Corrie. And I'm thankful for Samuel and Eva, more than I can say."

By now tears were streaming down Cornelia's face. Her father was such a good man. One part of her wanted desperately to tell him her story; the other part knew she could never break his heart. And explaining the truth to Jim was unthinkable. He'd practically worshipped the ground Henry walked on.

In her dreams that night, Cornelia placed a doll in a suitcase. She locked the suitcase securely, threw the key into the creek, and watched the key descend slowly to the weeds and rocks below.

CHAPTER 34

March 2007

"I'm so worried about Ken and me." Benita finally said the words aloud. She had been sitting by Gram's grave for ten minutes without saying a word. Sparrows fluttered and hopped about, gathering food in the late-winter shrubbery.

"I wish you were here, Gram. I bet he'd listen to you. I've had two sessions with the counselor now, but Ken won't come. We don't constantly bicker like before, but that's only because we are so distant from each other. It's crazy. Living under the same roof, but living alone—you know? I hate it."

Benita brushed aside some dead leaves and raked through the brown grass with her fingers while she kept talking, getting dirt on her knitted mittens.

"I've been reading your diary, Gram. I sure hope you don't mind. You had to have known someone would, or you wouldn't have left it behind, right? I have the silver suitcase, the quilt, the hymnbook, the ice-cream maker . . . they're all treasures. But the diary is by far the most precious. I had no idea you carried such deep sorrow in your heart. How did you do it? How did you come through all that and end up such a sweet-spirited woman? Did you ever try to find Mary Sarah? Does Mom know? Does she have a sister out there somewhere? I have so many questions. Why didn't you ever tell us?"

Closing her eyes, Benita tried to remember the sound of Cornelia's voice, as though doing so might bring answers to her many questions. But all she heard were the chirps of a few birds and the hum of traffic in the distance.

"I loved your story about the angel coming to you by the creek, Gram. Wouldn't it be wonderful, to have an experience like that for real? Did you make it all up, just to help yourself cope? You were so hurting, so young."

Benita looked at the gray sky and then glanced around at the other graves. Most displayed two dates with a short dash between, representing the span of a person's life. Not Gram's, though. By special request of Gram herself, her stone said:

Cornelia Faith Simpson Baker

Born August 1, 1921

Born again December 11, 1939

Entered Heaven March 16, 2006

Even in death, Gram's life was a testament to her faith. From reading her diary, Benita knew the "born again" date represented Gram's encounter with the angel by the creek. It had been that real to her.

"I've been going to your church, Gram." Benita felt somehow that Gram could hear, or perhaps that God could hear and would carry the message to Gram for her. Either way, it felt good to keep talking.

"The kids like it, and I wish we had started a long time ago—when you were still here. The people who knew you speak so highly of you. And I've been realizing I need more in my life, too, Gram. I want the faith you had. One of the songs we sing says, 'Earth has no sorrow that Heaven can't heal.' I want to believe God can take all our messes and make them good. That he can meet my needs. I need to believe it."

A tear fell unchecked onto Benita's jacket.

"I desperately need to believe it."

CHAPTER 35

December 1940

Sunday morning, Cornelia kept pausing for deep breaths as she prepared for church. She knew people would be happy to see her, or at least pretend to be. They would be kind and consoling about her loss of Henry. How would his aunt, uncle, and cousins respond to her?

She studied herself in the mirror as she dressed. Her body had changed. Would anyone notice or suspect the reason? Did they find it strange that she had lived with Henry's parents even though there was never an official engagement? She also knew enough about the small-town mentality to fear they would find her too uppity now that she was a city dweller. *I'll work extra hard at being warm and friendly,* she decided, pulling on her gloves. So many things to think about. She chewed her bottom lip all the way to church.

As it turned out, she needn't have worried. Henry's relatives embraced her warmly. Old school chums flocked around to ask about her adventures in the city. The Christmas spirit hovered in the air, and when anyone expressed concern about anything, it was about the war overseas. As it should be.

Pastor Johnson prayed for the fighting in Europe to come to a swift end and for conscription to be avoided, as Prime Minister Mackenzie King had promised. This community relied heavily on its few remaining men.

News abounded. Henry's cousin Elizabeth had married Pastor Johnson's son Paul last summer. Cornelia's friend Agnes had delivered her second baby, a little girl named Susan. The schoolchildren were performing Dickens's *A Christmas Carol* the following evening, and Tommy Staples had fallen from his horse and broken his leg. Old Mr. Kitchen had passed away and Elsie Miller's dog had birthed a litter of twelve puppies. Betsy Miller still received regular letters from William, who was somewhere overseas.

Cornelia's heart swelled with many emotions as she joined in the carol singing, starting with "Joy to the World" and "Hark, the Herald Angels Sing." She remembered her visit from Aziel down by the creek and wondered if he had sung at Jesus's birth. She tried to imagine Jesus as a newborn baby—as tiny and helpless as her Mary Sarah. "Happy birthday, Jesus," she whispered. "Thanks for coming."

When the singing shifted to "Silent Night," Cornelia stopped singing, closed her eyes, and listened to the voices around her. How she longed to be swept away to a place where she could sleep in heavenly peace, where memories and longing for all she had lost did not dominate every waking moment. *Jesus, please watch over my baby,* she prayed.

Noise reigned at Aunt Miriam's as the whole family gathered for their Christmas celebration. Aunt Nonie's little ones ran through the house and wrestled with Jim on the living room floor. Everyone peppered Cornelia with questions about college and the city. What were her roommates like? How many teachers did she have? What did she wear to class? When was graduation? How were Henry's parents coping? Did the war overseas make a more noticeable difference in the city than at home? Did she get to ride the electric trolleys? What were people wearing in the city?

She felt like a celebrity.

By four o'clock, almost everyone had cleared out, and Cornelia sat with Daddy, Jim, and Aunt Miriam, who had been, even if not less bossy, surprisingly kind to her. She had been studying Cornelia quietly but intensely, and this caught Cornelia off guard.

"I'm delighted you're following in my footsteps and becoming a teacher, Corrie dear. Good teachers mean everything in a child's life." Miriam pulled her glasses off and wiped them with an embroidered hanky, then held them up to the light for examination before returning them to her face. "We help shape society, we really do. And you'll be one of the good ones, mark my words. Now I have something you need to give some serious thought to."

Cornelia looked up from her tea.

"I happen to know that this year's teacher at Rocky Creek School plans to leave in June, and the board must hire someone new. The position would suit you perfectly. You could live at home, be part of our community again, even walk to school when the weather's nice."

Cornelia swallowed hard, trying to comprehend this change in attitude on the part of her aunt. Why was she going out of her way to be nice?

Miriam walked over to a rolltop desk in the corner and picked up some papers. "I have the application right here. Now I want you to take this and fill it out as soon as possible, and I'll see it gets in the right hands. Of course I'll provide a reference for you, although the trustees know we're related, so you'll need to put the name of one of your instructors at Normal School as well, and . . . oh, perhaps Pastor Johnson? He thinks highly of you. I'm sure you'll have a good chance of getting the position."

Cornelia took the form from her aunt's hands, and Miriam returned to her seat looking as if Cornelia getting the job was a done deal.

"I intended to start applying for jobs soon. I suppose it would be fun to teach at my old school."

"Fun has nothing to do with it. It just makes good practical sense."

"Well, thank you." Cornelia tried to suppress a grin at the return of her aunt's normal demeanor. "Graduation is June fifteenth. It would be lovely if you all could come, although I will certainly understand if it's not possible."

"We're proud of you, Corrie." Her father smiled. Cornelia knew he was staying deliberately noncommittal about attending her graduation, and she could accept that. It was a long trip and money was scarce.

"I feel so privileged," she said. "I can hardly believe I'm getting to do this at all." Though her words rang true, Cornelia wished she could shed the weight of her horrendous deception once and for all.

CHAPTER 36

April 2007

On Easter Sunday, Benita finally found another chance to pick up Gram's diary. The whole family attended church that morning, and after lunch Ken took Katie-Lynn and James to The Forks, a historic site in downtown Winnipeg where the Assiniboine and Red River meet, to watch the ice breaking up. James had grabbed his skateboard and helmet on the way out the door, hoping to have a chance at some of the half-pipes set up there.

Benita breathed a prayer of thanks that Ken was spending time with his children. Maybe something was finally starting to change. They'd even hired a part-time clerk, Richard, to help out in the store.

She poured a fresh cup of coffee and curled up on the couch with the precious pages. She was now beginning 1941.

January 4

Dear Diary,

I'm on the train on my way back to Winnipeg to finish my year at school. I'm going to be a full-fledged teacher! I can hardly believe it. My two-week Christmas break went quickly. It was great to be home, but I'm glad to go back. I could not bring myself to tell my secret to Daddy and I don't know when I will, if ever. I thought about it a lot. I couldn't do it, I'm not sure why. I had no idea it would be so hard. I suspect that's why I'm glad to be going back. Anyway, by saying nothing, I'm keeping my end of the bargain with Henry's father. And so I shall.

I attended Roseburg School's production of "A Christmas Carol" while I was home, and Aunt Nonie introduced me to the director, a young teacher named Stuart Baker. He did a remarkable job with the children and I told him so. He finished Normal School two years ago and had most of the same instructors I have now. Like me, his favorite was Mr. DeVries and his least favorite Miss Banning.

It took me until my last day at home to work up the courage to walk down to the creek—to "our" spot. There was no sign of Aziel. You would think that would make it feel like his visit never really happened, but nothing could be further from the truth. It's still as real to me as ever. Of course, I still miss Henry, and my memories with him by the creek bring back such a mixture of pain and loveliness. I spent my time there crying and praying. It will be good to go back when summer comes again.

Benita awoke to the clattering of the children's footsteps coming up the stairs. She had fallen asleep reading Gram's diary.

"Mom! Look what I got!" Katie-Lynn bounced over to her mother holding a chocolate egg in each hand. The city had sponsored an Easter egg hunt for the children at The Forks. Ice jams and skateboarding had been forgotten amid the excitement of chocolate and bunnies. James followed closely behind his sister. His hands were empty, but his lips and cheeks were sticky and brown.

"To the washroom!" Benita ordered, sitting up and tucking Gram's diary safely back into the silver suitcase. Ken appeared at the top of the stairs, James's skateboard in one hand, a couple of chocolate eggs in the other, and a grin on his face like Benita had not seen in months.

"Boy, did we hit it lucky." He held out one of the eggs to Benita, who accepted it gladly.

"For me? I thought the Easter Bunny would have forgotten all about me."

"He did, but I wrestled him to the ground for ya. I said, 'Your chocolate or your life, Rabbit!'"

"We had a good time, didn't we, Daddy?" Katie-Lynn gave her father a chocolaty grin.

"We sure did," Ken admitted. "How about you, sport?"

James walked back into the room, drying his hands on his pants. "I wish we could do that every day. No more school, no more store, just play and find eggs and eat chocolate. Every day should be Easter. Or maybe Christmas."

They all agreed that would be awesome, and when Katie-Lynn grabbed the game of Twister out of the closet, Ken lowered himself to the floor to play with her and James.

As she popped corn for their evening snack, Benita got an idea. She crept downstairs to the store and soon returned with cream, fresh strawberries, a bag of ice, some chocolate sauce, and Gram's ice-cream maker. No one had used it in decades, but tonight would be the night.

Benita's guess was right: The children, fascinated by the antique, fought over turning the crank. After what seemed like an eternity spent cranking, there was enough for them all to enjoy the delicious frozen treat.

"I didn't know ice cream ever tasted like this." James licked the bottom of his bowl.

"You're going to be so sugared up, we'll have to peel you off the ceiling," Ken said, which sent both children into waves of giggles. Benita couldn't remember the last time their family had had this much fun together. She hoped with all her heart the experience would convince Ken to close the store occasionally, before the kids grew too old for this. Before it was too late.

After she'd tucked James and Katie-Lynn into their beds that night and was headed off to her own, she breathed a prayer of thanks. *I don't know what you're doing to change things, God, but it must be you, because I sure haven't done anything. The only thing I've done is pray.*

Whatever it is you're doing, please don't stop now.

CHAPTER 37

August 2007

The rain beat against the windshield as Ken, Benita, Katie-Lynn, and James drove home from an evening at her mother's. They had filled up on barbecued chicken, corn on the cob, fresh garden tomatoes, and rhubarb crisp. They'd watched an old Jimmy Stewart movie, *No Time for Comedy*, which even the kids seemed to enjoy. Ever since Easter weekend, Ken had agreed to close the store on Sundays, and their family had been doing more things together. Now the children dozed in the backseat as the wipers kept time with the rain.

"You're quiet," Ken said.

"Mm."

"You asked your mom a question tonight that sure made me curious."

"I did?" Benita was pretty sure what he meant, but had thought he wasn't listening.

"I heard you ask if she'd ever wondered what it would be like to have a sibling, or to discover a long-lost brother or sister somewhere.

That doesn't have anything to do with stuff you've been reading in Gram's diary, does it?"

Benita had indeed asked her mother the question. She learned enough to be convinced her mother had no idea of Gram's story or of Mary Sarah's existence. When her mother asked why, she'd shrugged it off.

"Oh, no reason," she'd lied. "I saw a movie the other night where something like that happened, and it made me wonder what it would be like."

Her mom had jumped to the wrong conclusion. "You weren't adopted, Benita, if that's what you're thinking. And you're my one and only. I would have liked more children, but when your father left us . . . that was the end of that."

Benita had let the matter drop.

But Ken obviously wasn't satisfied. "I don't recall you watching any movies lately, about long-lost siblings or anything else. You sure have been reading that diary a lot, though."

Benita wasn't ready to share what she knew with anybody. She tried to form an answer while they rounded the corner of their block. The first thing they spotted through the rain was a broken window and the front door of the store hanging open, banging back and forth in the wind. Benita gasped and Ken stepped on the gas, racing up to the store and then braking hard. He pulled his cell phone out of his pocket and called nine-one-one before Benita could even comprehend that the store had actually been broken into.

"Oh, no." She was about to climb out of the car when Ken reached out an arm to stop her.

"They might still be inside," he warned.

She craned her neck, trying to see inside the store through the pouring rain while Ken made the report by phone. They were instructed to stay in the car until the police arrived. When they did, two officers went inside while a third invited Ken to sit in his patrol car and answer some questions. The children were awake by this time, and Benita did her best to keep them calm.

After the police determined that there was no one inside, they allowed Ken and Benita to go in. Benita sucked in her breath when she saw the damage. Besides the broken window that had left shattered glass everywhere, an entire rack of canned food had been toppled over, and cans had rolled all over the place. The cash register was smashed, even though Ken had left it empty and the drawer open, as was part of their closing procedure. Cans of pop had been shaken and opened, making a spray that left a sticky residue over everything. A computer was missing from the back office and the thieves had ransacked the desk drawers, no doubt looking for cash. James stood wide-eyed and Katie-Lynn started to cry. Benita looked at Ken and felt sure that they were both wondering the same thing. Had the thieves gone upstairs?

Benita flicked the light switch at the bottom of the stairs, but nothing happened. Her heart sank. She climbed the stairs in the darkness and when she felt for the doorknob to the apartment, she knew the lock had been smashed.

The first sight that met her eyes was that of open cupboards and drawers, but it was not immediately obvious whether anything was missing. In the living room, the thieves had overturned couch cushions and taken the television, stereo, and DVD player. The laptop computer they'd left lying on the coffee table was gone.

The children's rooms appeared untouched, and Benita wondered if the culprits had run out of time. But when she got to her own room, her heart stopped. Although nothing else appeared to have been touched, she saw a clear outline on the carpet where Gram's treasure had been sitting.

The silver suitcase was gone.

CHAPTER 38

September 1941

Cornelia held the bell high over her head and clanged it as loudly as she could, as if the volume could somehow cover her nervousness. Her first day as teacher at Rocky Creek School had begun.

Every day for the past two weeks, Cornelia had worked in this building from sunup until sundown. She had reviewed the guidelines that were taught at Normal School for teaching multiple grades:

Teach to the oldest and let the learning trickle down.

Do projects that can be adapted to include the smallest child and the tallest teen.

Allow older children to learn by teaching.

She had prepared the first week's lessons for eight grades in six subjects: English, mathematics, history, geography, science, and music. She had covered the walls with bright pictures, maps, and letters of the alphabet. On one corner of the chalkboard, she'd drawn a large calendar for the month of September and decorated it with fall leaves in colored chalk. She had pushed the desks into the most suitable, age-appropriate arrangement for 32 students from seven different families. She'd even written a play the children could perform for the all-important Christmas pageant in December. And she had prayed.

Oh, how she'd prayed.

Lord, help me! I'm barely twenty years old. Some of the older students will remember sitting next to me in these very seats. Help me teach them well. Help me gain their respect. Help my stomach to stop churning. Help me, help me, help me.

As the children filed past her into the building, she smiled and said "Good morning" to each one as brightly as she could. Most returned the greeting with "Good morning, Miss Simpson," but some only looked at their shoes. One little girl clung tightly to her sister's hand. Cornelia recognized the older girl as a Murphy, but couldn't recall her first name.

There were seven Murphy children, including the two who had completed grade eight and moved on, one to high school and one to farmwork. They all had the same flaming red hair and freckles. Cornelia's roster listed five Murphys, so this new little girl must be the last of the clan. Their reputation for misbehavior was widespread. Cornelia had spent all eight of her years at Rocky Creek School being terrorized by the oldest, Russell. Briefly she wondered whether she would run into him now that she taught his younger siblings.

Once all the students were seated, Cornelia stood at the back for a moment to compose herself, taking in the sight of the room. The east wall of windows allowed the bright morning sun to shine in from the students' left. Cornelia knew this was the standard design of every school built in the days before electric lighting. Most students were right-handed and this arrangement prevented them from creating shadows across their work. Those who were naturally left-handed had been strongly, and sometimes cruelly, encouraged to use their right hands.

On the west wall of the room hung a massive blackboard. More blackboards covered the front, with the letters of the alphabet displayed above them and a portrait of King George VI in the center above that. Little had changed since Cornelia had studied here herself.

Breathing deeply, she stepped to the front of the class. She knew these next few minutes would be crucial in setting the tone for the year.

"Hello, everyone," she began. "Welcome back to school. Thank you for finding your seats so quickly. I'm your new teacher, Miss Simpson, and I'm looking forward to a good year getting to know all of you and assisting you through your studies.

"We'll begin each morning with Scripture, the Lord's Prayer, and the singing of 'O Canada.' We'll end each day by singing 'God Save the King.' You may have noticed that I hung the flag this morning, but after today, the older boys will share the task of putting it up in the morning and taking it down after school.

"Now, does anyone know how many chapters are in the book of Proverbs?"

A hand shot up, and Cornelia recognized her friend Agnes's little sister, Trudy.

"Yes, Trudy?"

"Thirty-one."

"That's right. This year, we will read through the Book of Proverbs every month, one chapter a day for each corresponding day of the month. Now, today is September fourth. So which chapter will we read today?" She looked at the youngest children for a response, but a loud adolescent voice cracked from the back of the room.

"Thirty-two!" A round of giggles in various voice ranges followed this answer.

Cornelia looked up to see an enormous grin on the freckled face of the oldest Murphy boy, Randy. His red curls had been flattened on top by the cap he'd worn on the way to school, while the sides still stuck out. A perfect image for the class clown.

"Incorrect, Mr. Murphy," Cornelia said. "But since you are eager to be heard, you may come to the front and read Proverbs chapter four aloud."

The other children snickered as Randy shuffled to the front, took the Bible from Cornelia's hands, and turned to face his peers.

"Hear, ye children, the instruction of a father, and attend to know understanding," Randy read without hesitation. This brought another round of giggles from the room. Cornelia let it pass. She listened, impressed with his ability, as the boy read the remaining twenty-six verses.

"You read very well, Mr. Murphy. Thank you." Cornelia smiled at him and watched his face turn the same color as his hair. She led the class through the Lord's Prayer and a badly off-key version of "O Canada." When the last strains of "We stand on guard for Thee" had dwindled, she surprised the students with her next words.

"Since today begins our first year together, we will spend some time getting to know one another. I'll ask each of you to tell me your name, age, and your favorite summertime activity. We may take until recess to do this, but I want everyone to take a turn. Afterwards, I'll answer questions about myself. Who would like to begin?"

The boldest of the grade seven girls, a blonde with long braids, raised her hand. "I'm Connie Webber and I'm twelve. My favorite summer activity is swimming down by Rocky Creek."

Next to Connie sat her younger brother, Ernie. He raised his hand high, but spoke softly when Cornelia acknowledged him. "I'm Billy Webber. I'm twelve and I like fishing."

From bravest to shyest, the students all took their turns. But Cornelia had difficulty concentrating. The mention of the creek had hit her in the face like a blast of hot air, and memories of Henry washed over her. She had thought she would easily avoid memories here, in this building that should hold none of him. Now she could see how wrong she had been. What other things might catch her off guard?

She steeled herself and tried to focus as, one by one, her students stood to introduce themselves. Some enjoyed their chance in the spotlight while others said as little as possible.

"My name is Brenda Murphy. I'm ten and I guess I like going into town for ice cream on Saturdays."

"I'm Bert Rogers. I'm nine years old. I like playing with my puppies."

"I'm Clara Rogers and I'm eleven. I like riding our horse, Champ. He's a great big bay and he's twenty years old. He was my daddy's when he was a boy, and he can run like the wind."

"My name's Teeny Webber. I'm almost eight and I like helping my mom cook food."

When Randy Murphy's turn came, he stood and looked around the room. "Uh . . . yeah, like you already know, I'm *Mister* Murphy. I'm 124 years old and I like catching leprechauns and tying their beards together just to watch 'em wrestle."

This, of course, triggered a burst of laughter throughout the entire room.

"So." Cornelia smiled. "It seems we have a centenarian in our midst." The children laughed again. "Do you know what that word means?" She turned and wrote the word on the chalkboard.

"I'll tell you what, Mr. Murphy. At recess time, you will stay in and look up this word. You'll write the definition on the board, and when you're done you may be excused to go outside with the others."

"Sure, I can do that in a minute." Randy's changing voice cracked on the word *minute,* and the others laughed again.

"Furthermore," Cornelia continued, "if you can bring me one of those leprechauns before the weekend, I'll believe you. If you can't, I will expect a one-page report on the history of St. Patrick's Day on my desk by Monday."

A chorus of *oooooh*s waved across the room as Randy took his seat. On his way down, he punched the elbow of his nearest neighbor, Allan

Black. Allan was the only student with no siblings in the room. He stood.

"My name is Allan Black and I'm thirteen. My favorite thing in the summer is fishing, but my dad won't let me go anymore." He scratched his arm self-consciously and sat. Cornelia wondered what the boy might have done to lose fishing privileges, but thought better of asking.

Only one child hadn't introduced herself—the shy little Murphy girl who had held so tightly to her sister's hand earlier. Cornelia approached her and got down to her eye level.

"And what is your name, Miss Murphy?"

No response. Cornelia saw only the top of her head; a crooked part separating two red braids that looked like an older sister had hastily created them.

"Do you have a name?" Cornelia asked.

The red braids bobbed.

"Can you say it?"

The faintest of whispers came from somewhere below the red tresses, but Cornelia couldn't make out what the voice said. The girl's sister, Brenda, spoke up.

"Her name's Ivy."

"Hello, Ivy," Cornelia said. "Are you six years old?"

The braids bobbed again.

"She don't talk," Randy Murphy stated from the back of the room.

Cornelia looked up. "Doesn't. And I bet she can speak quite nicely, can't you, Ivy? All you need is a little courage, and I happen to have some extra courage in my desk. I'll get it for you at recess."

That's when Cornelia saw the edge of a puddle on Ivy's seat, where it had begun to form beneath her. It was slowly beginning to drip to the floor.

"You are dismissed for recess," Cornelia announced to the class. Then she quietly pulled Brenda Murphy aside.

"It seems Ivy needs some assistance. Can you help me with her?"

While Randy busied himself at the large dictionary on the corner table and the others went out for a round of dodgeball, Brenda and Cornelia cleaned Ivy up as best they could under the circumstances. To her credit, the little girl didn't cry.

She didn't speak, either. Once they'd finished, Cornelia took her by the hand and led her to the big teacher's desk.

"Remember how I told you I keep some extra courage in my desk?" she said.

Ivy nodded.

Cornelia leaned in and spoke in a conspiratorial tone. "I needed some this morning, because I felt nervous about teaching all these children for the first time. Lucky for me, I have a good supply right here in this drawer. Go ahead and pull it open."

The little girl looked up to make sure she'd heard correctly. When Cornelia nodded, Ivy slowly pulled on the handle and opened the drawer a few inches.

"See that little tin?" Cornelia said. "Go ahead and take it out."

Cornelia sat in her own chair at the desk and took the small, colorful tin from Ivy. "Whenever I need a little courage, I sprinkle a little of this on my head, and it makes me very brave. I've been very brave today, don't you think?"

Ivy nodded again.

Cornelia opened the tin and the girl looked inside. Then she looked up at Cornelia, confused.

"Oh, I know what you're thinking," she said. "You think it's empty, don't you?"

More nods.

"That's because I forgot to tell you this special courage dust is invisible. You can't see it, and you can't feel it, either. But it only takes a little, like this."

She put her fingers into the tin and sprinkled the invisible contents over Ivy's head and hands. "See? Just like that. It might not work immediately, but mark my words. You'll feel braver and braver as the day goes by."

A hint of a smile played at the corner of Ivy's lips. Cornelia couldn't help but think of her own tiny daughter, now sixteen months old. Walking, no doubt. Perhaps beginning to speak, too. Was anyone encouraging her to express herself?

"Now, let's close the tin and put it away before anybody else finds out our secret, okay?"

Ivy nodded and obeyed.

Cornelia looked up to see Randy Murphy watching from where he stood at the blackboard, chalk in hand. She took Ivy's tiny hand and led her out to the playground, where she supervised another ten minutes of energetic play before ringing the bell again.

This would be one interesting year.

CHAPTER 39

August 2007

On Monday, Schneiders' Grocery remained closed while Ken and Benita spent their time at the police station and at their insurance agent's office, filling out forms. It had been a sleepless night, even for the children. Though their rooms were untouched, and Benita had tucked them into bed with prayers and stories and tried to keep their routine as close to normal as she could, they naturally felt traumatized by the violation of their home.

The police dusted for fingerprints and collected Benita's initial list of missing items. Ken had stayed up late nailing boards over the broken window and rigging a makeshift lock on the door. The two of them had finally collapsed into bed around three o'clock, but no sleep followed. Every little sound, inside or out, was cause for alarm.

When she finally did doze off, Benita dreamed of strangers carrying away her children, and she awoke with her heart pounding. Whenever she allowed herself to think about the silver suitcase, she was unable to hold back the tears.

Now she was filling out still more forms and trying to assess the value of the electronics taken from their home. Benita was thankful that Ken had faithfully backed up important documents from the missing computers. The external hard drives lay safe in a file cabinet.

When it came time to assign a dollar value to the silver suitcase and its contents, she had no idea what to write. As an antique, it might possibly hold a small value, but for other reasons it was priceless. She decided to put it in the special column titled *Sentimental Items.*

Once they had filed all the necessary forms with the police and the insurance company, they returned to the store to begin the cleanup. Two workers from the glass company pulled up in front of the store at the same time as Ken and Benita. Ken put them to work fixing the window while Benita restacked the fallen canned goods and mopped up soda pop. Katie-Lynn and James helped, and while they worked, Benita said a silent prayer. *God, help me somehow to turn this awful experience into a valuable life lesson for the kids. Make something good out of this.*

"The guys who did this should have to clean it up," Katie-Lynn grumbled, dipping her rag into the bucket of hot soapy water she was using to scrub shelves.

"You're right, sweetie, they should," Benita said. "That would be a lot more fair, wouldn't it?

"Yes!"

"Do you suppose they will?" Benita's test question hung in the air for a moment.

"Well, if the police catch them, won't they make the bad guys come back here and clean up?" James said.

Benita stopped to look at her son. "I don't know. I suppose they might. But they may not catch them. Or it could take a long time . . . months, or even years. Meanwhile, the store would have to stay closed, our customers couldn't buy what they need, and we'd have no income and no way to pay our bills. Do you think it would be wise for us to just sit here and wait for them to come back and clean up?"

"I guess not," Katie-Lynn admitted. "It would end up costing a whole lot more."

"That's right. And fair or not, life is like that. People do things that hurt us. Sometimes they come back and make things right. But more often, they don't. The choice is ours. We can sit there and say 'I didn't make this mess and I'm not going to clean it up' and continue to live in the mess. Or we can do what we need to do to clean it up."

"Like if someone hurts your feelings?" Katie-Lynn said.

"Yes, that's what I mean."

Benita wished she could practice what she preached. In counseling, Phillip had helped her understand how much her father had hurt her by his abandonment, even though she had no relationship with him. She'd projected her pain onto her husband, which only pushed *his* pain buttons and kept the conflict spiraling.

James looked at the boarded windows. "But what if you don't know how to clean it up?"

"Sometimes that means hiring professional help, like those window guys and the locksmith. They can see the problem and they have the right tools and skills to fix it."

"Is that why you visit Phillip?" Katie-Lynn asked. Benita had explained to the kids that she was getting help with sorting through some struggles.

"Yes. He has tools to help me," Benita said. "After this little adventure, I suspect it would be a good thing for us all to talk to someone like Phillip."

"I hope you're not including me," Ken said from the next aisle.

Benita hadn't been aware that Ken was listening. "Don't you think it would be a good idea?"

"And who will mind the store if we all go traipsing off to see the shrink? Has it not occurred to you this wouldn't have happened if we'd been here?"

Benita looked at him with raised eyebrows. "Ken, we can't be here twenty-four-seven!"

"Listen, I took your advice and started closing the store and spending more time with the family. Look where it got us." Ken tossed a screwdriver into his toolbox and closed the lid. "I won't let this happen again."

"How do you know the thieves wouldn't have come anyway, while we were here, and hurt one of us?" Benita studied her husband's face. "Here I've been thanking God we were gone when they came, that we're all safe—and you're blaming yourself for not being here!"

"I'm not blaming myself. I'm blaming you."

Benita couldn't believe what she'd heard.

"You and the kids can go talk to your precious Phillip if you must, but somebody has to stay grounded in real life." Ken picked up his toolbox and walked out the back door, leaving Benita and the children standing as mute as statues.

By the end of the week, they had reopened the store. Customers were quick to commiserate with them and some even bought a little extra as an expression of support and empathy.

Benita acquired a replacement computer and created posters for the lost suitcase. She found a photo online of an identical one, and even offered a reward. On the bottom of the poster, in fine print, appeared these words: *This suitcase contains the handwritten diaries of Cornelia Faith Simpson, dating back to 1934.*

Benita and the children went around the neighborhood posting the signs wherever they could. They dropped them off at police stations, pawnshops, recycling depots, and schools. Who knew where it might turn up?

Phillip allowed them to hang one in the waiting room at his counseling office. She and the children spent an hour telling him how the break-in had made them feel violated, disillusioned, and unsafe. Phillip asked about the silver suitcase, and Benita told him that she'd inherited it from the grandmother she loved and missed so much.

"What's really hard is I never finished reading the diaries. I learned so much about her life, so many things I never knew. I guess it felt like sort of a lifeline for me."

"Can you talk about that? How was it a lifeline?" Phillip prompted.

"Gram's faith inspired me to start going back to church and discover God for myself. She lost her mother early, but she had a sweet relationship with her father, which was something I never had with mine."

Benita nervously tapped the arm of her chair. "Gram went through some really hard things, yet I never saw any sign of bitterness in her, only faith and joy. I want to know her secret. I don't want to end up a bitter old woman, but sometimes I'm afraid I will—even without facing the kinds of loss my grandmother did."

With the children there, she didn't talk about her contempt for Ken or the accusations he had dumped on her. She sat quietly while Phillip asked the children questions and they answered in their childlike fashion.

"Sometimes," Phillip told them, "when bad things happen to us, we might think it's our fault somehow. If you ever feel like that, you need to know it's not true. In no way is the break-in your fault. You could not have prevented it. Do you understand what I'm saying?"

James and Katie-Lynn nodded their heads solemnly, but tears trickled down Benita's cheeks. She suspected Phillip's words were directed toward her. She hadn't told him how guilty Ken's words had made her feel. How did he know?

"And if anyone tries to make you feel like it is your fault, it might be because that person feels guilty for not being able to prevent it, and wants to put the blame on somebody else."

"I know it's not our fault." Katie-Lynn twirled a brown braid around her finger. "Mom says we should just be thankful we're all okay."

Phillip nodded. "That's right. That's the main thing, isn't it?"

Two weeks later, summer break officially ended. Ken had focused fully on the store since the break-in. Although no physical evidence of the event remained—other than the absence of the silver suitcase—emotional tension charged the air more than ever. Ken's workaholic tendencies had kicked back in, and he'd taken his behavior to a completely new level. He rose by five every morning and was downstairs by six, poring over spreadsheets or prices online, rearranging stock, or talking on the phone with suppliers. He rarely returned to the apartment before midnight, except to eat, and often skipped that as well.

"If that's the way he wants to live, it's his loss," Benita told Phillip on her next visit, when she had the chance to talk to him alone. "But what really bothers me is that he expects me—and even the kids, to some degree—to live the same way. He tries to make me feel guilty for not working as long and hard as he does."

"Do you?"

"Do I feel guilty?"

Phillip nodded.

"Well, yes . . . sometimes. I feel guilty for coming here, actually. I feel guilty for taking time to go for a haircut or even to church."

"What else do you feel?"

"Mostly I'm ticked off," Benita admitted. "James joined a soccer team, which I'm thrilled about. He plays his first game next week and I know Ken won't go."

"How can you be so sure?"

"It's during store hours. I'm not sure he's left the premises since the break-in, except to file reports with the police and insurance company."

"Would he go watch James play soccer if you offered to stay at the store?"

Benita thought about that.

"Possibly. But I don't want to miss James's game."

"Would you be willing to make that sacrifice?"

Benita scowled. "That's so unfair." Even as she said it, she heard Katie-Lynn using the exact words . . . and recalled her own answer. "But . . . yes. I suppose I could. Right now it's more important for James to know his dad cares . . . and maybe if Ken went to watch, he'd realize what he's missing." Benita fiddled with the edge of her skirt as she watched Phillip write on his notepad.

"And if all is well at the store when he returns, maybe he could lose some of his anxiety about leaving it," Phillip suggested, tucking his notepad into a file folder that displayed Benita's name across the top.

"Maybe."

"Think about it. You can at least make the offer and see where it lands."

CHAPTER 40

December 1941

As Christmas approached, Cornelia threw herself into preparations for the annual pageant the school board insisted be held, regardless of the chaos reported in world news.

On December eighth, the United States had joined the war, the day after Japan bombed Pearl Harbor, Hawaii, an attack that killed more than twenty-four hundred Americans. Three days later, Cornelia quietly remembered the anniversary of Henry's death by going to their special spot at Rocky Creek. This year was much colder, however, and she stayed only minutes before returning to her father's truck and driving home. So much had happened in two years.

Glad to have a distraction from her own memories and from all the fears surrounding them, Cornelia had put together a simple play for the children to perform. Much to her relief, one of the mothers, Mrs. Rippley, volunteered to come to the school three times a week and help the students form a choir. They prepared three Christmas carols for the children to perform and three more that would include audience participation. Mrs. Rippley's daughter, Rose, accompanied the children on the accordion. This gifted girl was in grade eight, and on the second day of school, she had volunteered to lead the singing of "O Canada" every morning and "God Save the King" at the end of the day. Cornelia had gladly surrendered the duty.

A makeshift stage was erected at the front of the classroom with curtains pulled across it, from wall to wall. As the school filled with families, Cornelia tried to organize the nervous children behind the curtain. She had never felt so much in demand.

"Miss Simpson, I can't find the lamp I'm supposed to carry in."

"Miss Simpson, she's wearing my costume!"

"Can you tie my apron, Miss Simpson?"

As the children took their places before the play, Mr. Rogers, the board chairman, stood in front of the curtains to welcome everyone. Cornelia could vaguely make out what he said and thought she heard her name mentioned in the context of the board's appreciation. Just then she spotted little Ivy Murphy inching dangerously close to the edge of the stage. Cornelia dashed toward Ivy, hoping to move her to safety before the applause died down and the curtains opened.

Instead, Cornelia herself slipped too close to the edge and down she went, landing on her rump in front of the crowd.

Mr. Rogers stopped mid-speech.

"Uh . . . It appears Miss Simpson has fallen off the stage," he said in a voice as dry as dust.

The audience roared. Cornelia couldn't remember having ever been so embarrassed in her life, but she merely smiled to the crowd and returned to her place as gracefully as possible. She consoled herself with the knowledge that if there had been any tension in the room before her fall, it was gone now. The curtains opened and the play began.

More than ever, the theme of peace dominated this Christmas. The students presented their little story about two families who feuded and then realized in the end that no one could recall what had started the fight. A little child, played by none other than the timid Ivy Murphy, became the first to initiate peace and friendship, and the two families became a community. The audience applauded with gusto and joined in on "Joy to the World," "Silent Night," and "Dona Nobis Pacem."

Once the concert had ended and the children were running about with bags of peanuts while their parents visited, Cornelia felt a tap on her shoulder. When she turned, she recognized Stuart Baker, the young teacher from Roseburg School whom she'd met last year and saw occasionally at church.

"Great concert," Stuart said.

"Hello, Stuart. I didn't know you were here." Cornelia reached out to pull a young Murphy boy away from his third trip to the cookie table.

"I especially loved the opening act. Excellent stunt work."

Cornelia grinned even though she could feel her face flush. "Well, I was about to thank you for coming, but now I'm not so sure."

"I try to take in as many of these Christmas concerts as I can. You know how hard it is to find good material. Yours was excellent. Do you mind sharing your scripts for the play, or telling me where I can order it?"

Cornelia laughed. "Well, you can't order it. But you're more than welcome to use it. I wrote it."

"You didn't." Stuart looked at her with appreciation.

"It's a lot easier to provide parts for everyone if you create them yourself, don't you think? What did your school do this year?"

"Teaching at a bigger school has perks," Stuart smiled. "It was one of the other teachers' turn to take the lead on the Christmas program, and she picked a musical about bears and rabbits. I only had to set up a stage and play stage manager. And manage, I did. Barely."

One of the parents, Cecil Black, waited behind Stuart for his chance to talk to Cornelia. She turned to acknowledge him.

The man stood with his arms crossed on his barrel-shaped chest. "I must say, I'm a little disappointed in this year's concert, Miss Simpson.

I assumed you knew Rocky Creek School always does a nativity scene. It was missed."

Cornelia fought the instinct to apologize. She looked the big man in the eye. "Actually, I attended school here myself, Mr. Black. So yes, I am aware." She gestured toward her students. "Actually, it was the children who requested something different."

"Well, we can't allow the children to decide everything for us, now can we?" Before Cornelia had a chance to respond, he walked away to collect his son, Allan. Stuart looked at Cornelia with one raised eyebrow.

Just then Cornelia's father approached them and patted her shoulder with enthusiasm. "Great job, Corrie!" He turned to shake Stuart's hand. "Merry Christmas, Stuart. I suppose you'll head home to spend Christmas with family?"

Stuart hesitated. "Uh . . . no, actually. I'll be sticking around here. I'll probably spend the holidays trying to fix my radio. It's kaput and I can't afford to replace it. Sure would like to get it going again, though."

"Well, bring it on out to our place. I don't know much about them, but Jimmy likes tinkering with those things. He got ours working again a time or two. And if he doesn't succeed, well, you can stay and listen to ours."

"Really?" Stuart spoke to Charles, but his eyes rested on Cornelia. "When should I come?"

"Nobody should be alone at Christmas, and tomorrow's Christmas Eve. Why don't you come on out for supper and stay for the evening? Corrie here can cook as well as she can pull off a concert."

"Well then, I'll look forward to a fine meal. Thank you."

Cornelia could feel her face getting hot. If she didn't know better, she'd think her father was setting her up.

Cornelia, Charles, Aunt Miriam, and Jimmy all pitched in to prepare and serve roast chicken with mashed potatoes, gravy, stuffing, creamed corn, and Aunt Miriam's dill pickles. Cornelia had made an apple pie for dessert. Before the meal, Charles asked Stuart if he would do the honor of saying grace, and Cornelia figured it was one of the finest prayers she had ever heard.

"Lord, in a world where so many go hungry, may we be truly grateful for all we have to eat. On a planet where war rages, may we bring peace wherever we can. And to the most precious gift you sent at Christmas, your son . . . may we devote our very lives. Amen."

The five of them managed to refrain from talk of war during the meal, but later they took their coffee to the living room, and while Jimmy messed with wires in the back of Stuart's radio, they tuned in the news on the Simpson family radio in time to hear a live broadcast from Washington, DC.

England's prime minister, Sir Winston Churchill, was staying at the White House with President Franklin Delano Roosevelt. Only seventeen days had passed since the bombing of Pearl Harbor and the entrance of American troops into the fray. The president spoke first.

"We have joined with many other nations and peoples in a very, very great war. One of their great leaders stands beside me. He and his people have paved the way, encouraged, and sacrificed for the sake of little children everywhere. So I'm asking my associate, my old and good friend, to say a word to the people of America, old and young. Winston Churchill, prime minister of Great Britain."

The cheering of the crowd could be heard through the crackling static. Then the prime minister spoke.

"Fellow workers in the cause of freedom . . ." he began. "This is a strange Christmas Eve. Almost the whole world is locked in deadly struggle. We are in the midst of war, raging and roaring over all the lands and seas, creeping nearer to our hearts and homes. Here, amid all this, we have tonight the peace of the spirit in each home. We may cast aside for this night at least, the cares and dangers which beset us. Each home throughout the English-speaking world should be a brightly lighted island of happiness and peace before we turn again to the stern task and formidable year that lies before us. Resolve that by our sacrifice and daring, these same children shall not be robbed of their inheritance or be denied their right to live in a free and decent world. And so, in God's mercy, a happy Christmas to you all."

For the remainder of the evening, the group enjoyed listening to Christmas carols, playing Parcheesi, and drinking coffee. Miriam took her leave at nine. At ten thirty, Stuart stood to leave.

"You can't go yet," Jimmy said. "Your radio's not fixed. I think I know what it needs, though."

"Well, maybe he'll have to come again." Charles smiled. "You're not busy tomorrow, are you, Stuart?"

And that's how schoolteacher Stuart Baker came to spend almost the entire 1941 Christmas school vacation at the Charles Simpson farm.

CHAPTER 41

September 2007

When Benita returned to the store, a curious message waited for her on the office desk, written in fine-point felt-tip by Ken's deliberate hand. *Call Ramona Stanford re: the suitcase* was all it said, followed by a phone number.

"Who's Ramona Stanford? What does she know about the suitcase?"

"No idea." Ken shrugged and went out front to wait on some customers.

Benita scowled at his back. A quick search for the area code on her computer told her the number originated in the Toronto area, over two thousand kilometers away.

"How on earth could the suitcase have turned up in Toronto?" she muttered, dialing the number.

A voice-mail message informed her the cell-phone customer was out of the area. While she waited to try again, Benita tried to focus on household tasks. *Could it be this easy to get the suitcase back?* She'd received only one other call since the posters went up, but the caller had turned out to be someone with a similar antique suitcase, looking for a buyer.

About an hour later, Benita was watching the store while Ken worked on books in the back office. When she heard the overhead bell clang, she looked up from her rows of produce and did a double take. A woman walked in looking so much like Gram, Benita's heart began to race.

Calm down, she told herself. She'd heard of the phenomenon that causes people to think they see their deceased loved one, still alive, but she hadn't experienced it before. She watched while the woman scanned the store, spotted her, and started toward her. She even *walked* like Gram!

"Excuse me, are you Benita?" the woman asked.

Benita swallowed. "Yes."

The woman resembled a younger version of Gram, the Gram she'd known as a child, but in contemporary clothing. The same soft curls framed a similar round face. The same gray-blue eyes met Benita's, and when the woman smiled, it was Gram's smile.

The woman held out her hand. "I'm Ramona Stanford. I called earlier?"

"Oh!" Benita returned the handshake. "I thought it was a Toronto number. I tried to call, but—"

"It is. I flew to Winnipeg yesterday, after my son called me. He saw one of your posters about the silver suitcase and the missing diaries."

"Do you know where they are?" Benita could feel her heart beating faster.

"No, dear, I'm afraid not. He called me because of the name at the bottom. The poster said they were the diaries of Cornelia Faith Simpson. Is she a relative of yours?"

"Yes, she was my grandmother."

"So . . . she's passed away then?" Ramona's smile faded.

"Yes, last year. I inherited her diaries, but they were stolen from our home about six weeks ago. Were you a friend of Gram's?"

"No, dear. The fact is . . . well, I was born in Winnipeg in June of 1940 and given up for adoption."

Benita sucked in her breath.

"The only information I've been able to obtain is my birth mother's maiden name—Cornelia Simpson. I've been trying for years to find her. Is there any chance this could have been your grandmother?"

Benita thought her heart would stop beating. She hadn't told a soul—not Ken, not even her mother—about Gram's secret. She had given only a few brief thoughts to the idea of trying to find her long-lost aunt. Never in a million years would she have foreseen this happening now, as a result of her posters. She steadied herself against the cooler.

"I'm sorry, dear. I should have realized this might be a shock. I should have waited for you to return my call. I was just so excited, I wanted to come to the store myself and see if maybe—"

Benita felt as if she might pass out. She directed Ramona to the two chairs set up in the corner, then sat down beside her and took a deep breath.

"Yes, I'm just a little . . . um . . . yes . . . there is a good chance this is the same Cornelia. Although, if you'd come a year ago, I'd have told you it was impossible."

Benita explained about the suitcase and told Ramona that she hadn't finished reading the diaries before they went missing.

"Oh, this is exciting! I have a million questions. Are your parents alive? Do I have brothers and sisters? Who was my father?"

"Please. Can you give me some time? I'll need to talk to my mother, for one thing. Can I call you tomorrow, Ramona? I need some time to process this."

"Yes. I'm sorry. I should have realized. I've been searching for so long, I forget this might be brand-new to you. Can I ask one question before I go?" She paused only briefly. "You still have your mother, but you didn't say whether Cornelia was your maternal or paternal grandmother. Is your mother my . . ." Her voice faltered. "My sister?"

"If it's true, then yes. My mother would be your half-sister. She was an only child. But we don't know for sure, do we?" Benita stood to her feet, glancing toward the back office. Had Ken overheard? "Please, I really need you to go now."

"Of course, dear, I apologize. I'll look forward to hearing from you tomorrow, then." Ramona walked to the door, where she turned to give Benita one last smile. "Good-bye."

Benita said good-bye, locked the door behind Ramona, and turned the Closed sign around just as Ken wandered back into the store.

"Who was that? Why are you locking up early?"

For the next half hour, it was as though angels stood at the door, preventing customers from trying to come in. Benita poured out the whole story to Ken: about the child Gram had given up, the diaries, and now the visit from Ramona. She left out the part about Ramona's resemblance to Gram, just in case that had been her imagination. *Let him see it for himself, if it was real.*

"And your mother doesn't know anything about this?" Ken was incredulous. "I would think the first step would be to talk to her. She'll need some preparation if Ramona is really Mary Sarah. And it sure sounds like she is."

"You're right. Oh, man. Now it's more important than ever to find that suitcase! Why would they take it, Ken? Where is it?" Benita felt hot tears on her cheeks. "What on earth would petty thieves want with an old suitcase anyway?"

"I've wondered that, too," Ken said. "But those silver suitcases sometimes hold large amounts of cash—at least they do in the movies. From what the police said, it was most likely a bunch of kids on a dare, or an initiation. Maybe they decided to grab the suitcase and run, and check out the contents later."

"This is so unfair." Benita paced around the office. "We've got to find it!"

CHAPTER 42

January 1942

"Are we playing train today, Miss Simpson?" Ivy Murphy asked, looking at the flash cards lined up along the ledge of the blackboard.

"We might." Cornelia smiled. The little girl's confidence had improved greatly since September, boosting Cornelia's own confidence as a teacher. The formerly shy student would surely be one of her success stories.

The train game had proved to be a favorite with the youngest students. They would line up to form a "train" along the row of flash cards. When they could correctly read the word on the card at each "station" as they chugged along, they picked up that card and carried it as "freight" until the ledge sat empty. Then the children would begin again. This presented a challenge for the older students who weren't playing, as they had to keep copying their own homework questions from the board into their notebooks and try not to get distracted by the entertaining little ones.

Cornelia had distractions of her own that day. It was the fifteenth of January, and Stuart Baker had offered to pick her up from school so they could go out for supper together before attending the district teachers' meeting at the Roseburg School. A speaker from the university would be explaining the government's initiatives for the war efforts as they related to education.

That morning she had carefully chosen the green wool dress her aunts had given her as a congratulatory gift when she began teaching. She determined to delegate all chalk-brush duties to the students today, lest her date arrive to find her green dress covered in yellow dust.

Stuart's attentions were not unwelcome. Cornelia found him intelligent, kind, and genuinely interested in his students. She sometimes wondered why he had not volunteered for military duty along with most fellows his age, but she hadn't worked up the courage to ask him about it. Perhaps tonight would provide an opportunity.

Things went reasonably smoothly for most of the day. By now, Cornelia felt quite accomplished as a one-room schoolteacher and believed she was competent at the juggling her work required. While Brenda Murphy dictated spelling words to the youngest children, the students in grades four and five each paired off with a "buddy" from grades seven or eight for practice with reading aloud. Since Clara Rogers was the only student in grade six, she assisted Cornelia in copying worksheets on the hectograph for the next day.

This serene, organized scene abruptly ended during afternoon recess.

With the abundance of snow, the boys had decided to bring shovels from home so they could build an enormous snowslide in the schoolyard. They had begun working on it during morning recess, enlarged it further at noon, and were excited by the prospect of making it even bigger during their last break of the day. Cornelia was bundling into her coat and boots when Teeny Webber dashed into the school. She was crying so hard and talking so fast, Cornelia could hardly make out what the girl said.

"Miss Simpson, Miss Simpson, come quick! Bert Rogers cut off my brother's ear!"

Cornelia prayed that the child was exaggerating as she ran behind the wailing girl. The impressive snowslide on the playground stood well over her head, and the first thing she noticed were red stains running the length of it. She found the entire student body clustered around someone at the foot of the hill. As she approached, they cleared a path and Cornelia saw twelve-year-old Billy Webber lying on the snow, clutching a hand to his right ear. His mittens, hair, and the snow under his head were drenched in blood.

"Oh God, help me," Cornelia managed to mutter. Normal School had not prepared her for this. If the training manual contained anything relevant to this situation, it likely would have instructed her to "call for the school nurse" or "telephone for help." Rocky Creek School possessed neither a nurse nor a telephone.

The nearest town, Roseburg, had no hospital or clinic, and the nearest medical facility was at least an hour's drive away. Allan Black lived closer to the school than any of the other students, but Allan was absent today.

Taking a deep breath, Cornelia pushed down the rising panic. *Wounds to the head always bleed the most* came to her from somewhere deep in her memory. She unwound her scarf while several students shouted at once.

"Quiet, everyone!" she commanded. "Now calm down. Randy, tell me what happened here."

"We were shoveling snow onto our pile," the boy said, his voice shaky. "Bert's shovel got too close to Billy's ear. It was an accident. He didn't mean nuthin.' We'll still be able to sled on our hill, right?"

Closer examination revealed that Billy's ear was still attached, but the gash looked severe, and he was losing a lot of blood. Removing her own mittens, she pressed them tightly against the ear and wrapped her scarf around Billy's head to hold them in place. While she worked, she instructed the children.

"Randy, I want you to run as fast as you can to the Blacks' house. Ask them to call Billy's parents and then come back quickly. If no one is home, I want you to go into their house and use the telephone yourself. If you get no answer at Billy's house, keep calling other parents until you reach someone. Then hurry back here as fast as you can. Do you understand?"

"Yes, ma'am." Randy was on his way.

Cornelia helped Billy to his feet. "Let's get back inside," she instructed. "Bert, please add two big pieces of wood to the stove. Brenda and Marlene, I want you girls to fill a basin with clean water and put it on top of the stove. Everyone else, please put away your coats and boots and sit at your desks. Pray for help to come quickly."

The students had never been so quiet or cooperative. The sight of Billy's blood put the fear of death into them, and Cornelia thought immediately of all the young men, not much older than these children, who were fighting real and bloody battles even at this moment.

Twenty minutes later—though it seemed as if it had taken hours—Randy returned with Cecil Black at the wheel of his farm truck. Cornelia had slowed the bleeding and cleaned most of the blood off Billy's face. The boy was trying to put on a brave face, but he continued to shake as Cornelia bundled him in her own dry coat and kept him close to the stove.

Mr. Black burst through the doors.

"What's happened here?" his voice boomed, startling the children. Before Cornelia could answer, he had assessed the situation and herded Billy to the door. "Billy's mother is on her way. The other Webber children are to come with me, and we'll meet her on the road. Hurry, now."

While he waited for Connie and Teeny Webber to grab their coats and schoolbags, Cecil Black turned to Cornelia with a cold stare. "I don't know who was supervising these children when this happened," he said. "But you can be sure the board will hear about this."

Cornelia swallowed hard and watched them leave. The students looked at her in expectation, and she could tell that Bert Rogers was fighting to hold back his tears.

"Class," Cornelia said. "Please bow your heads while we pray for Billy." They did so, and sniffles registered around the room.

"Lord, thank you that Billy's ear is still attached. Please help him see a doctor quickly. And help him heal completely. Now calm our hearts and bring peace to this room, I pray. Amen."

By this time, parents were beginning to show up to collect their children. Most students normally walked to school and home again year-round, but thanks to the efficiency of the party line, word had spread. Cornelia was comforting Bert when she glanced out the window and saw Mr. Rogers and Mr. Murphy shoveling fresh snow over the blood spots. Other parents gathered their children and reclaimed shovels. Rides were offered to students whose parents had not come.

When Mr. Rogers came in to collect Bert, the boy remained at his desk, alone in the classroom.

"You responsible for all the commotion?" Mr. Rogers said.

Bert looked at his lap. "Yes, sir."

"It was an accident, Mr. Rogers," Cornelia interrupted. "The boys were just—"

"Oh, I know it was an accident, Miss Simpson. But I teach my children to take responsibility for their accidents. Come on, Bert. You'll make amends to the Webber boy once we know how much damage was done." The two headed toward the door, Bert's eyes remaining downcast. "Looks like you might be buying Miss Simpson a new dress, too."

Cornelia looked down at her blood-spattered dress and closed her eyes with a heavy sigh.

Just as the Rogers family left, Stuart Baker arrived.

"Looks like I missed the party," he said, surveying the room.

Cornelia resisted the temptation to cry and told him the story as calmly as she could. "How could I let it happen, Stuart? I wasn't watching them! This is all my fault."

"Corrie, you cannot possibly keep your eye on thirty-two children at the same time, all day long."

"But I was inside when it happened. I should have been—"

"And you can't be in all places at once, either." Stuart put his hands on her shoulders. "Come on, I'll help you clean things up."

Together, Cornelia and Stuart restored order in the room. He carried the basin of bloodied water to the outhouse rather than pouring it out where it would stain more snow. She straightened desks and swept the floor. Tomorrow was another school day, and the janitor, Mr. Cox, came only on weekends.

"I need to go home and change clothes before we go anywhere, Stuart," Cornelia said when he came back inside. "I'm so sorry."

"I have an idea." He grinned at her. "I'll take you home first. But let's go out for supper and skip the teachers' meeting. They won't miss us. And if they do, they'll understand once they hear about your day. Besides, *No Time for Comedy* is playing at the Roxy in New Pass."

Cornelia smiled up at him. "That does sound good."

That's when she realized her coat, scarf, and mittens had gone out the door with Billy Webber.

That night, Cornelia took time to write in her long-neglected diary.

January 15, 1941

Dear Diary,

I must be the worst teacher in the history of Rocky Creek School. Maybe even the world. I don't know what the School

Board will do when they hear how Billy Webber almost lost an ear today. I only pray he heals completely, and quickly.

Stuart is proving as valiant as he is kind. He wrapped his own coat around me after school today and drove me home. While I bathed and changed into a clean outfit, leaving my green wool dress to soak in cold water, Stuart explained to my father what happened. I don't think I could have recounted the story one more time.

Then we drove all the way to New Pass and ate the loveliest supper in the Garden Restaurant. We dined on roast beef with all the trimmings, and it was easy to pretend all was peace and prosperity. Stuart regaled me with stories from his own classroom and embarrassing mistakes made his first year. We lingered over coffee and shared a slice of chocolate cake, which made us late for Jimmy Stewart's movie. All we missed, though, were the newsreels and we really weren't in the mood for more scenes from the war anyway.

We're hearing rumors that Prime Minister King may go back on his word and introduce conscription for overseas service. On the drive home, I worked up the nerve to ask Stuart if he worried about being drafted.

"No. Health issues would prevent it for me," he said, and left it at that.

CHAPTER 43

September 2007

Benita approached the front porch of her mother's house with a pounding heart. She had called to ask if she could come for the evening, saying only "I have something pretty serious to discuss."

Grace opened the door before Benita reached the bottom step, a worried frown on her face. "Benita, honey, come in." She led the way to the kitchen, where a pot of coffee was nearly done brewing. Her mother seemed to be studying Benita's face, looking for clues, a worried crease across her forehead. "Let's sit on the back deck. It's a nice night and it's quiet out there."

Benita accepted a coffee mug from her mother and followed her to the deck. She settled herself in a wicker chair across from the one her mother had taken, and decided to jump right in.

"Mom, like I said . . . I have something serious to talk about. I don't know how to begin."

"Is this about you and Ken, sweetie? I've been sensing a little tension there."

"Oh! No, Mom. It's not that. Well, I mean—you're right, there's tension there. More than a little. But it's something else. Remember the night I asked if you ever wondered what it would be like to meet a long-lost sibling, given up for adoption?"

Grace shook her head. "Honey, I told you, you weren't adopted, I promise. I remember every contraction." She chuckled and rubbed a hand around on her tummy.

Benita sighed. "It's not that, Mom. It's . . . well . . . you know I had been reading through Gram's diaries, right?"

"Before those awful hoodlums stole them, yes." Grace placed her mug on the table between them and smacked her right fist into her left palm "I'd like to get my hands on those rascals. I looked forward to reading Mother's diaries myself when you finished, and now I may never get to."

"Mom, Gram revealed a pretty big secret about something that happened to her when she was a young girl. Before she met your father. Did you ever hear of her having a boyfriend named Henry who died in the war?"

Her mother thought for a few seconds. "Yes, I did. His relatives lived in our community, but he was a city boy. I asked her once—when I was in my teens—if she had any boyfriends before Dad. 'Just one,' she said. It was a short summer's romance, though, nothing serious. He went off to join the army and died in a train wreck. What a tragedy. So young."

"Turns out it was a little more involved than that, Mom. Did you know Gram stayed with Henry's parents here in Winnipeg for a while after he died?"

Grace thought a minute. "I think she may have mentioned it, although I wouldn't have remembered if you hadn't told me."

"Did you know she didn't return home for over a year?"

"Really? Well, she wouldn't have, would she? She went to Normal School in Winnipeg."

"But before Normal School, Mom. Something happened. In June of 1940. Gram gave birth to a baby girl."

Her mother went silent and her face started to turn pale. Benita let this revelation sink in for a minute before continuing.

"The baby was Henry's. Gram gave her up for adoption, then went to Normal School for a year. She graduated in 1941."

Grace seemed to regain her composure, but then she shook her head and her rate of speech picked up to double time.

"You've got your facts mixed up, Benita. Mom started teaching back in Roseburg as soon as she finished Normal School. That's when she met Dad, and they got married in '42. Dad was a teacher, too, as you know. The army would have drafted him, but he couldn't serve because of a bad knee. Mom used to tease him and say that was the reason she married him, because she knew he wouldn't go off to fight. They moved into Grandpa's farmhouse when I was born, although I don't remember living there. They built the new house in '46 when I was two. After the war ended."

Grace paused for a quick breath. "Grandpa passed away when I was ten. I remember it, because I was so heartbroken. He was such an old sweetheart. Had the bluest eyes you ever saw. I used to tag along with him when he did the farm chores. 'My right-hand girl,' he called me. They let me go to the funeral, though, and I was the only kid in my whole school who ever attended a funeral, so I felt pretty important. I can still remember what I wore. This little navy suit with a white—"

Benita jumped in. "Mom!"

Her mother stopped talking, but her eyes continued to dart about the room like she was tracking a fly.

Benita tried to proceed gently. "I'm sure your grandpa was a wonderful man, Mom. The diaries indicate she never told him her secret. It's possible she didn't even tell your father. Do you think he knew?"

Grace stared at a spot on the floor, then slowly shook her head. "There was no secret, Benita. No baby. You're mistaken. It's not possible."

Grace gathered up the coffee mugs and headed for the kitchen.

CHAPTER 44

January 1942

Cornelia sat on her hands to keep from biting her fingernails. The school board had called a special meeting and asked her to attend. Now she sat in Cecil Black's living room waiting for the rest of the board members to arrive. Mrs. Black had placed cookies and teacups on the coffee table, but they sat untouched. Cornelia's Aunt Miriam sat perched on the edge of a hard-backed chair. Mr. Rogers, the chairman, had chosen an overstuffed armchair. When Mr. Johnson and Mrs. McKinnley arrived, they completed the quorum, and Mr. Rogers wasted no time before calling things to order. While he read the minutes of their last meeting, Aunt Miriam leaned over and whispered in Cornelia's ear.

"I won't be defending you, Corrie. Not because I agree with Cecil Black, but because you need to stand up for yourself."

Cornelia's thoughts turned to the conversation she'd had with her father the previous evening.

"Daddy, what if they fire me?"

"Sweetheart, they're not going to fire you. Where would they find another teacher in January?"

"Oh, thanks. That helps a lot."

Charles chuckled. "Honey, Cecil Black has been nothing but a bully since he and his family moved to this district five years ago. I don't know what's eating him, but you remember these words and you'll do fine: 'The Lord shall fight for you, and ye shall hold your peace.'"

"Is that one of your Sunday school Bible verses, Daddy?"

"You know it."

"Where's it found?"

"Beats me. Chapter and verse were your mother's specialty. Somewhere in Exodus, maybe." He kissed her cheek and headed up the stairs to bed. "You have yourself a good sleep. It will turn out all right. You're smarter than that whole school board put together."

Mr. Rogers's abrupt "Carried!" brought Cornelia back to the moment. The minutes of the board's last meeting were approved.

"Miss Simpson," Mr. Rogers said, "I'm sure it's no surprise to you that we've called this meeting to discuss the events of ten days ago at your school. I'm turning the floor over to Mr. Cecil Black. Cecil?"

Mr. Black cleared his throat, adjusted his glasses, and studied his notes. "On January 15, 1942, I was shovelin' manure in my barn when I heard a young man runnin' toward my farm yellin' at the top of his lungs. It was Randy Murphy, all out of breath. The boy told me there was an accident at the school with one of the Webber children. I immediately ran into the house and telephoned Mrs. Webber. We agreed I would pick up her children and meet her on the road. The Murphy boy got into my truck and we hurried back to the school.

"When I saw all the blood on the playground, I was sure the Webber child would be a goner. I carried him and his sisters in my truck quickly down the road, where I met their parents at the corner of the old river road and the Kelm road. They was some upset. Mrs. Webber was cryin' and carryin' on. The lad required stitches and stayed in the hospital overnight."

The man paused, and Cornelia hoped he was done. But he flipped his paper over, scratched his ear, and continued.

"I believe if the children had been properly supervised, this event could have been avoided. Why did Miss Simpson here let 'em bring shovels to school in the first place? I understand Miss Simpson was not outdoors watching the students but inside the schoolhouse at the time. I'm only thankful my own boy stayed home with a cold that day, or it might have been his ear what almost got cut off. This type of serious neglect is completely unacceptable to me as a parent, and as a member of this here board, I move that Miss Simpson's position be exterminated immediately."

Cornelia's head snapped up. *Just like that?*

"You mean *terminated*," Aunt Miriam muttered, rolling her eyes.

"Is that a second?" Cecil Black asked.

"Now just a minute, Cece," said Rupert Johnson. "I don't think you or anybody else should make any motions until we've heard Miss Simpson's side of this story."

Mr. Rogers spoke up. "Rupert's right. It is indeed regrettable that this happened, and we're all aware it could have been far worse. But according to the reports of my own children, Miss Simpson handled the situation admirably."

"Of course you'd say so, it was your boy what done it!" Cecil Black bellowed.

"Hold it, gentlemen." Ruth McKinnley pressed her palms together, then laced her fingers. "It's no secret we have our share of conflict of interest on this board. It's unavoidable in such a small community." She gestured toward each person in the circle as she referred to them. "A child was the victim of an accident at the hands of Mr. Rogers' son. The teacher is Miss Simpson's niece. It seems everyone's related to someone! If we can't work within these boundaries, there won't be anyone qualified to serve on the board."

Rupert Johnson spoke again. "I think we should give Miss Simpson the floor. The younger Miss Simpson, that is."

Cornelia took a deep breath and swallowed. She stood and moved to the side of the room where Mr. Black sat, then faced the board. "Thank you, Mr. Johnson. Everything Mr. Black said is true. I was inside the school when the accident occurred. I had dismissed the students and stayed behind a few minutes to organize their papers for the last class of the day. I was putting on my coat when Teeny Webber ran inside to tell me what happened.

"I agree it is most unfortunate, and I will do everything in my power to learn from this situation and not let anything like it happen again."

"Well, I should hope not!" Mr. Black shouted.

"I do believe I learned from it," Cornelia continued. She addressed her next thoughts directly to Cecil Black. "Mr. Black, you are a caring and devoted parent. You would not serve on this board if that weren't true. I appreciate your concern for your son and for the other students. May I ask you something?"

Cecil Black grunted, and Cornelia took that as a go-ahead.

"When your son Allan first learned to walk, did you and his mother praise and encourage him?"

"Well, of course."

"And in his inexperience with walking, did he fall sometimes?"

"Well, of course he did. What kind of question is that? Every child falls down. What are you getting at?"

"Mr. Black," Cornelia continued, "because you are a wise and kind parent, I assume when little Allan fell, you did not kick him or hit him or forbid him to walk again. Did you?"

Cecil Black frowned at her, then looked around at the others, and finally back at Cornelia. "Well, what kind of fool would do that to a little child? Of course not!"

"Mr. Black, I have been teaching for five months. I am responsible for the safety and the education of thirty-two children for seven hours a day, five days a week. By myself. I am still learning. Sometimes I fall. I humbly ask you to extend to me the same grace you would extend to your own child, even if that child were to stumble or make a mistake."

The room grew unexpectedly quiet. Aunt Miriam cleared her throat. Mr. Rogers shuffled papers. Finally, Cecil Black rose and went into the kitchen. The board members looked at one another. Mr. Johnson raised his eyebrows and Mrs. McKinnley responded with a shrug.

Rather than return to her seat, Cornelia turned to study the family photos displayed on the mantel. She recognized several of little Allan Black, but another boy appeared in some of the pictures beside Allan. She turned her head when she heard the sound of the outside door slamming. A moment later, Mrs. Black stood in the doorway to the kitchen, holding a pot of tea.

"Cecil said to tell you he went out to finish his evening chores," she said, placing the pot on the coffee table. The board members looked around the room. No one seemed to know what to do next. Mrs. Black stood straight and finished delivering her message. "He also said he would like to retract the motion he laid on the table. I hope you know what that means, because I don't see anything on the table but the cookies and tea."

That broke the ice, and some board members sighed while others chuckled softly. Mrs. Black moved over to where Cornelia stood at the mantel. She picked up a photo of her son Allan with the other boy and held it tenderly.

"This is our oldest son, Freddy," she said. "We lost him six years ago, just before we moved here. Drowning accident. Please forgive Cecil. He still blames hisself. He isn't truly mean-spirited." She replaced the picture and walked back to the kitchen without another word.

Cornelia returned to her chair, and Aunt Miriam reached over to pat her knee.

"Does anyone have anything else to offer?" Mr. Rogers asked. The board members shook their heads. "Then I move we adjourn this meeting. Good night, folks."

"You did fine, Corrie," Aunt Miriam said as she dropped Cornelia off at home twenty minutes later. "You missed a golden opportunity, though. I've been pushing to have a telephone installed at that school ever since they elected me to the board. Maybe next time."

Cornelia raised her eyebrows as high as they would go and glared at her aunt through the darkness. "Next time?"

But Miriam just laughed, shooed Cornelia out of the car, and drove away.

CHAPTER 45

September 2007

Benita couldn't believe what she'd just heard. She followed her mother into the kitchen.

"Mom. Didn't you hear what I said? It was all in Gram's diary. She even named her little girl—"

"No. She would have told me. You're mistaken."

"Believe it or not, I *can* read, Mother. It was in the diary."

Grace placed the cups in the sink and turned around to face Benita. "It was probably just the romantic notions of a young drama queen with a boring life."

Benita raised her face to the ceiling, as if looking for answers elsewhere. "Why would Gram make that all up?"

"Why would *you*?" her mother accused. "I don't know what your plan is, honey, but now you've gone and lost the diaries—probably forever—and all I have is what you're saying." She put a sugar bowl back in the cupboard. "For all I know, you dreamed it. Did Ken read them? Did anyone?"

"No." Benita shook her head slowly and sank into the nearest chair. "Just me. Gram wrote it, Mom. I'm not making this up, and neither did she." Benita tried to stay calm, though her mother's words stung.

Grace joined her at the kitchen table. "Well, why didn't you tell me this when you first read about it, then? Why didn't you show me the diaries right away?"

"I intended to, Mom. I wanted to get all the way through them first. I don't know why . . . maybe I wanted to have something special, some connection to Gram all to myself for a little while. I don't know."

"Well . . . you and Gram were pretty close. But that doesn't explain why you're telling me this now."

Benita sighed. "I got a visitor today."

She explained to her mother about Ramona's visit and quest to meet her blood relatives.

"She's anxious to meet you, Mom. I guess everybody wants to understand about their roots."

Grace sat silently for a long time. Perhaps her mother just needed time for it all to sink in, Benita thought. She would probably come around in a few days. Benita finally decided to call it a night.

But as she picked up her purse to head out the door, her mother surprised her.

"She looked for us once before."

"What, Mom?" Benita took a step back toward Grace's chair. She had spoken very softly. Benita knelt beside her and looked up into her mother's face.

"I said she looked for us before. Years ago." Grace sighed. "I still lived at home at the time—it was a summer between college semesters, so I must have been around twenty. The phone rang one day when I was home alone, and the caller was a young woman looking for a Cornelia Simpson. She said that was the name of her biological mother, and I told her she had the wrong person. I believed it, too. Until now."

"Did you tell Gram about the call?" Benita asked.

"No. I never breathed a word. I guess, deep down . . . I don't know. I was afraid it might be true and I didn't want it to be, so I made myself forget. I never told anyone."

Benita rose from her knees and sat in the chair again. "Would it have been so horrible if it were true?"

Grace considered this. "I suppose not, looking back on it now. It's just . . . I don't know, when you're that age, and you think you know who your parents are and that they'd never do anything deceitful . . . somehow the idea felt like a threat. Like I would lose something important. Maybe it's silly, but it would have been painful to think my mother kept such a big secret from me."

"Do you think Gram ever tried to find Mary Sarah . . . er, Ramona?"

"I don't know. Is that what she named her? Mary Sarah?"

"Yes."

"After her own mother, then."

Benita waited quietly, allowing Grace to process the information.

"Mother always told me my name had special significance, too." Grace turned to gaze out the window where the leaves were beginning to turn yellow. "She said I was God's special gift of grace to her. She was a good mother. She should have had lots of children. I had her all to myself."

She stood up and walked over to the window, turning her back to her daughter. "I miss her, Benita. I really, really miss her."

Grace's shoulders began to shake as the tears came in earnest. Benita crossed the distance between them and wrapped her arms around her mother. She gently rubbed Grace's back until the sobs subsided and Grace had a chance to blow her nose and regain her composure.

"Mom, Ramona's come all the way from Toronto. I'd like to tell her she can meet all of us. But I won't if you don't want her to. But please don't decide tonight. Get some sleep, and let's talk some more tomorrow."

Grace nodded, and they said good night.

On the drive home, Benita wondered whether she would ever sleep again. But exhaustion took over and she fell asleep with a minimum of tossing. That night she dreamed of Gram. In her dream, Gram wore a fuzzy blue bathrobe and sang while she rocked Katie-Lynn on her lap.

Something woke Benita suddenly and when she looked at the clock on the dresser it read 3:16. She felt a desperate need to remember the song Gram had been singing in her dream. But no matter how hard she tried, she couldn't.

When she finally fell back to sleep, she slept soundly until the alarm clock rang.

CHAPTER 46

July 1942

Dear Diary,

Life has been such a whirlwind, I haven't had time to catch my breath, let alone record the events of the last many months. But summer is finally upon us and the wedding behind us. Yes, the wedding!

On February 14, Roseburg held its annual Valentines dance. Although so many boys from the community are away, the Committee felt it an important display of optimism to hold the event as usual. Stuart and I were seeing each other two or three times a week by then. He came to our home for supper and stayed for the evening. Some nights we sat together at the kitchen table, marking students' papers. Other times, the four of us held checkers tournaments. Some evenings we listened to the radio. Stuart and I regularly stayed up talking after Daddy and Jimmy went to bed. Daddy always left his bedroom door part-way open. Stuart usually managed to collect a good-night kiss at the door, though.

Of course, I fully expected Stuart to ask me to the dance. But Valentine's Day approached and he hadn't mentioned it. I wondered if it would be another evening at home. Surely he hadn't asked someone else.

I even prayed about it. "Lord," I said. "I don't know what your plans are for Stuart and me. It seems he cares about me a lot, and I like him too. But if this is going nowhere, it would be just as well if we ended it now. I can't go through any more loss. Not yet. Not for a long time, I hope. Please show me what to do."

School dragged that week. The brutally cold weather made my students tired of being cooped up. I would send them out for extremely brief breaks, and then only after checking each child for mittens, hats, and scarves. I couldn't wait for the end of each school day.

When Stuart came for supper Tuesday evening, I thought for sure he'd mention the dance. On Wednesday, he didn't come. On Thursday, the weather warmed and the atmosphere at school brightened. In art class, the children made valentines out of items brought from home. I worked on some as well—one for Stuart, one for Daddy, and one for Jim.

That evening, Stuart came for supper. By seven or eight o'clock, I felt my throat getting scratchy and my eyes were watery. Stuart left early without a word about the dance and I went to bed with a hot water bottle.

By Friday, my symptoms had worked themselves into a full-blown cold. Daddy, bless his heart, drove to the Blacks' and arranged for Mrs. Black to take school for the day. He and Jimmy even rustled up some homemade chicken soup for me. I haven't felt that miserable for a long time.

Saturday proved no better. Not only was I sick, I felt completely blue. Valentine's Day. No date, no dance, no Stuart, no friends. I tried desperately to think of something to be thankful for, and finally came up with one thing. I no longer lived at Mrs. Marshall's boarding house/restaurant. What a dark time. So alone, waiting on tables, still trying to keep my secret from customers, studying in my freezing room, and crying myself to sleep at night over what lay ahead.

Now, thankfully, that is all behind me. I may have felt rotten that Saturday, but at least I had a warm home and loving family around me.

By mid-afternoon, Stuart arrived. I didn't particularly want him seeing me with my awful red nose and all. But it beat being alone. It annoyed me, though, when he spent more time with Jimmy than he did with me. The two of them stayed outside for the longest time. When they came in, they banged around in the kitchen for another couple of hours and every time I tried to see what they were up to, they'd shoo me back to the living room, where I had set up camp on the sofa.

Then I got the surprise of my life.

Daddy and Jimmy left for the evening. They claimed they had promised to help at the dance. Finally, Stuart allowed me into the kitchen, where I discovered an impressively set table for two and a dinner of fried perch. If it hadn't been for my cold, I definitely would have smelled that fish stinking up the house.

Stuart and I enjoyed a lovely meal, in spite of my cold, and then he excused himself to go out. I assumed he needed the outhouse, and began clearing the dishes. When he came back inside, he said, "Leave the dishes for now, Corrie. I want to show you something."

Taking my hand, he led me to the dark living room and then to the picture window. Earlier in the week, that window had been so covered in frost, you couldn't see a thing out of it. Now, though, the frost congregated around the edges like a beautiful, lacy picture frame. When I looked out, I discovered Stuart and Jimmy's secret. There, upright in the snow, stood dozens of candles placed in the shape of a heart and burning brightly.

I don't remember exactly what I said, something like "Oh, Stuart! It's beautiful!" I couldn't believe he'd got them all burning at once, or that he'd done this for me.

I definitely remember what he said, though.

"Happy Valentine's Day, Corrie." He turned me toward him. "I love you. And I want you to marry me. Will you?"

My face started scrunching up and I'm sure Stuart thought I would cry. But instead I let out a massive sneeze! The moment every girl dreams of, and I sneezed! Stuart valiantly offered me a hanky and together we watched the candles flickering outside, the snow sparkling all around. It really did feel magical.

"I suppose Daddy and Jimmy were both in on this?" I asked.

"I spoke with your father a couple of weeks ago, Corrie. He said he'd be happy to see me join the family and that I could help with the farming around my school schedule."

I laughed. That sounded like Daddy, all right. The two of them had even discussed a spot on the property to build a house for us. Once again, I had the vague feeling my life was being planned on my behalf. But was that really so awful? Stuart was a good man. I had not told him everything about my past, but then, neither had he shared his. I hadn't met any of his family. I knew he had a brother overseas, but it seemed Stuart's family was disconnected in a way I couldn't comprehend.

Gradually, the candles went out and I hadn't yet given Stuart an answer to his question. My heart pounded. One thing I did know: No matter how long this war lasted, Stuart would not be going off to fight. In that moment it seemed like the most foolish thing in the world to refuse his proposal.

"Corrie?" he said when the last flame died. "Are you going to make me ask twice?"

"I'm sorry," I teased. "I was so distracted by the blaze outside my window I didn't catch what you said. Could you repeat the question?"

"With pleasure," Stuart said without hesitation. "I love you, Corrie Simpson. Will you be my wife?"

"Yes," I said.

We set the date for Saturday, July 11. The remainder of the school year, it took every ounce of concentration to stay focused on my classes. The distraction of school and the busyness of wedding planning made the time go by very quickly. In March, I signed a contract for my second year at Rocky Creek School. And on June 24, we celebrated the last day of school with a field day and picnic.

July 11 started out rainy, but just as we left for the wedding, the sun came out and turned it into a gorgeous day. Pastor Johnson married us at the Roseburg Community Church, with all our students, friends, and my family there to celebrate with us. Jim served as Stuart's best man and Agnes was my matron of honor. I wore a light blue summer suit Aunt Nonie helped me select on a trip to Winnipeg in early

May and carried a bouquet of white daisies from Mother's garden.

Stuart looked very handsome in his double-breasted, gray suit. The girls in my school filled the church with flowers. Everything looked and smelled heavenly. When we stepped out onto the church steps after the ceremony, a sparrow landed on the railing and stayed there as long as we did.

Now July is almost over. Stuart and I settled into the little teacher's cottage beside my school. It sat vacant all last year, but the School Board pitched in to spruce it up with new paint and a few repairs. Aunt Miriam helped me sew curtains for the windows and gave me several of the rag rugs she braided over the years. We have four small rooms, if you count the screened-in porch that will be useless come winter but makes a lovely dining room now. The kitchen has a small pump at the sink, an oil-burning furnace fills half the living room, and the bedroom barely has room for our double bed. It's tiny, but it's home.

Stuart's been working with Daddy and Jimmy. We put in the garden at Daddy's as usual and I'll soon be busy with vegetables, preparations for a new school year, and finding my place in the community as a married lady.

God is good.

CHAPTER 47

September 2007

Benita waited until the children left for school before she tried to call her mother. Just as she went to pick up the phone, it rang.

"Honey, I didn't sleep a wink," her mother said, a new energy in her voice. "But I've given it a lot of thought. I'm sorry I accused you of making it up."

"It's okay, Mom, really. I know it was a shock." Benita took a seat on the couch.

"You told Ramona you'd call her back today, right?" Grace said. "I think we should meet. If we don't, we'll both wonder forever."

"Oh, I'm glad to hear it, Mom. I think you're right. I figured out Ramona is sixty-seven years old. If she's the one who tried to contact the family when you were in college . . . she's been looking for an awfully long time."

"I know." Benita could hardly believe the difference in her mother's voice compared to the evening before. "I already thought about that, and I feel terrible. She would have been about twenty-five then. She could have known us all these years. She could have known Gram.

Now it's too late. And it's all because I refused to tell anybody about the phone call!"

Grace's speech picked up pace and rose in pitch. "What if she realizes she contacted the right family all along, Benita? What if she remembers? What if she can't forgive me?"

"One step at a time, Mom." Benita rose from the couch and wandered to the window. No customers approached the store. Ken should be fine down there by himself for now. "For all we know, yours was just one of many such phone calls. But even if she does remember—better late than never. She can meet her sister, her niece, Uncle Jim—"

"Oh, I don't know about that. Uncle Jim would be so confused."

"Well, we wouldn't have to tell him who Ramona is, Mom. It would just be for her sake. Anyway . . . let's cross that bridge when we come to it. And just think—her son lives right here in Winnipeg. So we have relatives we didn't know we had, too!"

"Assuming she is indeed the right person. How do we go about confirming it?"

"I have no idea, Mom. But we'll find out. Ramona will have researched it by now." She turned and wandered into her kitchen. "So . . . should I tell her to come over? Do you want to call her yourself?"

"No. You call her. I might panic and hang up."

Her mother giggled like a teenager, and Benita was struck by a feeling of longing on her mother's behalf. What would it have been like for her to have a sister when she was younger? What would it be like for her now, if it was true?

They said good-bye quickly, and Benita immediately dialed Ramona's number. She pictured the woman waiting impatiently by the phone, eager to begin unraveling the mystery of her life. In fact, Ramona did answer on the first ring.

"Hello?"

"Hello, Ramona. It's Benita."

"Oh, yes, dear. I know. Thank you so much for calling me. Did you speak with your mother?"

"I did. She wants to meet. Of course, we want to take steps to confirm this one way or the other. I'm sure you do as well."

"Certainly. I have a good feeling about this, though, Benita. You sound like family."

"I . . . what?"

"Maybe I shouldn't even say this, you'll think I'm crazy," Ramona said with a laugh. "But I have two daughters—Nancy and Vicky—likely around your age, dear. I can never tell them apart over the phone; they sound so much the same. And you . . . well, maybe it's because I want so badly for this to be true, but . . . you sound a little like them too."

This news left Benita speechless. The only cousins she'd known about were on her father's side, all boys. When her father disappeared from her life, the cousins soon did as well. The idea that she might have more cousins—women her own age—had not crossed her mind.

"Is tomorrow too early? I'm staying with my son, David, and haven't booked my flight home yet, so I can give you as much time as you need if tomorrow's too soon."

Since she and the children had appointments scheduled with Phillip the next day, Benita wanted to wait. She arranged for Ramona to come to the apartment on Monday, and then she hung up the phone. She spent the rest of the day in a fog. All she could think about was Ramona's pending visit. How wonderful it would be if she could find Gram's diaries before then! Her posters hadn't generated any other calls, however, and Benita knew that with each passing day, the precious records were less likely to be found.

Benita decided to prepare the children for their special visitor. At first, she felt inclined to say Ramona was her aunt, but since they hadn't established whether or not that was true, she settled on "old friend of the family." In the meantime, she began jotting down whatever details she could remember from the diaries: Henry's parents were Samuel and

Eva Roberts, and Samuel had only one arm. Henry was an only child and graduated from a Winnipeg high school around 1938. He loved baseball. They had relatives with the same last name in Roseburg, or at least they did back then. If any family members remained, she figured it might be easier to unearth them in a small community.

Benita's next session with Phillip revolved around her processing despair over the lost diaries, guilt over not having told her mother sooner, excitement about the meeting with Ramona, frustration with Ken's ongoing detachment, and worry for her children. Since the break-in, Katie-Lynn had been having bad dreams and James had gotten in trouble for sassing his teacher at school. When his turn came to talk to Phillip, he bit his lip and said he wanted his old house back.

"What do you miss about your old house?" Phillip asked.

"I don't know," James said with a shrug. "We did stuff together. I liked it when Dad didn't work."

"But when your dad didn't work, wasn't that hard on the family?"

"No. We used to do fun stuff."

Benita cringed to think that Ken's period of unemployment was a fond memory for her son. She remembered it as endless days of worry and running up debt, trying to make ends meet. But the children knew only that their dad had been more available. *Perspective really is everything*, she thought.

"What's wrong with this picture?" Benita asked Ken when she summed up the counseling session for him that evening. It was one of those rare nights when he'd actually come up to the apartment before she fell asleep.

Ken sighed. "What do you want from me, Benita? The entire time I was out of work, you worried and fussed and cried and complained.

Now that I'm working, you won't quit going on about how I'm not spending enough time with the kids. Well, you can't have it both ways! You blame me for all our problems, no matter what I do."

"Ken, I'm not blaming you for all our problems—"

"Oh no? What do you call it? Look, I can't be in two places at once. You decided the kids needed counseling . . . how did you think we'd pay for that if I worked less?"

"Well, I've been working too . . . !"

"Have you?" Ken looked her in the eye. "You've been so wrapped up in this visit from your long-lost aunt lately, you haven't been much help around here. Honestly, sometimes I wish you'd never seen those stupid diaries."

"Stupid diaries?" Benita could not believe her ears. "How dare you? Those diaries are a rare treasure! How many people can say they possess such a thing?"

"I don't know. But you can't exactly say you do, either, now can you? And yet *they* still somehow possess *you*."

Benita thought she might explode if she stayed in the room. She grabbed her jacket, purse, and car keys and headed out the door.

"I can't talk to you! If you're looking for me, I'll be at my mother's. I'll come back in the morning to get the kids ready for church. Heaven forbid you should have to do it!"

She flew down the stairs and ran out the door.

CHAPTER 48

January 1944

Dear Diary,

I'm going to have a baby! I started to suspect last month, and Dr. Thompson confirmed it this week. Aunt Nonie went with me, but I'm so glad she stayed in the waiting room. When asked whether this was my first pregnancy, I had to tell the doctor the truth. He didn't press for details, but when I asked, he assured me Stuart need not see the form in my file. The baby should arrive in late June or early July.

Stuart is delighted, as are Daddy and Jimmy. Jimmy insists it's going to be a boy and he'll teach his little nephew how to fish.

As for me, I can't even begin to describe my emotions. Fear, yes. I feel some sadness as so much of my last experience comes back to me. Mostly, I am overwhelmed by the grace of God. My heart is full.

Oh tiny baby, whatever and whoever you are, rest assured I love you with all my heart. I can't begin to tell you how much happiness you have already brought into my life, you precious little person. Sometimes I can't wait to hold you in my arms and look at you. Other times, I want to hang on to you and carry you around inside me forever so you won't have to face the difficulties of life.

Your father and I will do our best, but we're only human and we'll fail you at times. I pray you'll forgive us our shortcomings and grow into a good, healthy man or woman in spite of us. I worry about what kind of mother I'll make. But, others have done it. I guess I can, too. Mostly I'm just SO happy. Thank you, God. Thank you, thank you, thank you!

Daddy prays for the war to end before the baby comes. We all do.

Cornelia sat behind her big teacher's desk and looked around the room. It was the thirtieth of April and, as ordered by the school board, it was her last day at the school.

"It's not proper for an expectant mother to be instructing our children," Mr. Black had told Cornelia. He'd pushed for a March resignation. Cornelia had assured him she could teach through June. In the end, the board compromised and hired Aunt Miriam to finish out the months of May and June. They offered next year's contract to a newly graduated teacher.

Now the time to say good-bye had arrived. Three school years had taught Cornelia more than they had taught her students, she was certain. She'd learned to maintain discipline, even with eight grades in one room. She had learned how to organize a parade for the district field day. She knew how to keep the students busy while giving individual attention to those who struggled most. She'd seen shy children blossom and coldhearted ones warm to her. Most of all, she had learned to love these young people, even the ones she didn't particularly like. She prayed for them regularly, and felt confident she had seen God's hand at work in their lives. As much as she looked forward to her baby's arrival, she knew she would miss this classroom.

Connie Webber raised her hand. "Mrs. Baker?" She stood when Cornelia acknowledged her.

"Since this is your last day, may we take a few minutes to present you with something we've been working on?"

Cornelia smiled. "Of course."

Five students came to the front of the room: Brenda Murphy, Randy Murphy, Bert Rogers, Teeny Webber, and Ivy Murphy. They stood in a diagonal line, facing Cornelia's desk and their classmates.

"We wrote a limerick for you," Bert said from the center of the lineup, then he looked at the others. Cornelia laughed. The students had been learning about limericks and found them quite a challenge. What had they come up with?

Brenda delivered the first line and Randy the second, and so on down the line:

"There was a nice teacher at our school;"

"Who never once looked like an old fool."

"She taught us all well;"

"And then rang the bell;"

"Then put up her feet on a stool."

Cornelia laughed and clapped. "Terrific work! You don't know how relieved I am to know I never looked like an old fool."

"We have a gift for you, too," Brenda said. "It's from the whole class."

At that, the two smallest boys came forward carrying a big box wrapped in tissue paper. A large homemade envelope was stuck to the top and when Cornelia opened it, she saw the words *We'll miss you, Mrs. Baker* on the front in a beautiful script that could only be the work of Clara Rogers, the school's most talented artist. When she opened the envelope and looked inside, she realized that every student had signed the card. She peeled back the tissue paper and opened the box, pulling out a pink and blue baby quilt. Embroidered on the center square were the words *Rocky Creek School, 1941–1944* and a line drawing of the schoolhouse in tiny neat stitches.

"How wonderful," Cornelia said. "What a treasure! Thank you all so much. I will miss you all, too."

"You'll come back to visit us, right, Mrs. Baker?" Randy Murphy asked.

Cornelia looked at her class clown and grinned. "I sure will. But I don't expect to find you here, Mr. Murphy. You'll have moved on to high school—I hope."

"Oh, yeah," Randy said, as though it only now dawned on him that his years at the one-room school were ending. This brought another round of laughter from the class. Then two of the oldest girls brought out a plate of oatmeal cookies to share.

Half an hour later, the room stood empty and Cornelia sat alone. She placed her personal belongings into a box and headed for the door, turning to look around one last time.

"I'll be back," she whispered.

July 1944

Cornelia laid the laundry basket at her feet and sat on the doorstep to wait out another contraction. The familiar pains had been coming on and off all day, and she knew it was time to tell Stuart. He'd been staying close to home in anticipation of the baby's birth, keeping the car filled with gas and ready to go at a moment's notice.

Determined to put away the last of the laundry, Cornelia wrestled the basket into the kitchen and began folding items until the next contraction forced her to stop and lean over, one hand on her stomach and the other on the table for support. This was how Stuart found her when he walked in from the living room.

"Corrie! What's wrong? Is the baby coming?"

"It's all right, this will pass." Cornelia puffed air out, waiting. Then she calmly picked up a towel and folded it.

"How long has this been going on?" Stuart asked.

"For a while, but I just want to finish this—ooh!" Another contraction. Corrie clutched her abdomen again.

"It's time to go! I'll grab your bag. Do you need help to the car? Go to the car. Can you make it to the car, Corrie?"

"Yes, I can get to the car. Give me a minute," Corrie said. When the contraction passed, she went directly to the car and climbed in, just as another contraction hit her. Stuart was already behind her with the suitcase she had prepared. He tossed it into the backseat and they took off down the road.

"Wait a minute, shouldn't we tell Daddy and Jimmy we're going?" Cornelia said.

"They'll figure it out!"

Cornelia had never seen Stuart this anxious, but he drove skillfully, and within an hour they arrived at the hospital. It seemed to Cornelia that things progressed much faster than they had the first time she went through this.

She kept the thought to herself.

"She's perfect." Stuart held his new baby daughter and admired her soft skin and wispy hair. "I can't take my eyes off her. Wait until your father and brother see her! They're not going to believe how perfect she is."

Cornelia smiled, enjoying this new side of her husband. He was great with his students, but always maintained his position as teacher and authority. With this little girl, he seemed completely smitten.

"You're nothing but a big ball of mush," Cornelia teased.

"I won't deny it." Finally he looked up long enough to say, "Thank you, Corrie. Thank you for this beautiful little girl."

"I'm not the one who deserves thanks," she whispered.

What a contrast from four years earlier when she had felt so lost and alone as her child was carried away by others. No one to share the joy or the sorrow. No one to share the love. No one but Jesus. *Thank you, God*, she prayed. *Thank you for being so gracious to me. For giving me a new child to cherish.*

"Jimmy had us so convinced we were having a boy, we never got around to discussing girl names," Stuart said. "What should we call her?"

CHAPTER 49

October 2007

"A wiser woman would insist you go back to your family," Grace said as they shared hot chocolate at her kitchen table. "But I'm selfish enough to want the company of my only daughter. Please don't see this as taking sides, because I'm not."

"Maybe you should tell Ken. He might not see it that way." Benita played with her spoon.

"Surely this will blow over."

"Yeah, by tomorrow. I just need some space and time to cool off."

"This is the first time you've walked out like that," her mother said. "Isn't it?"

"Yes. Although it's not the worst fight we've had. But somehow . . . I don't know . . . his calling Gram's diaries stupid felt like a slap in the face, you know?"

Grace sipped her hot chocolate. "I always thought Ken had a special bond with Gram."

"We all did, Mom. That's the kind of person she was."

"Do you suppose there's any chance Ken feels a little left out concerning the diaries, as if you were keeping secrets from him?"

Benita looked up, considering this suggestion. "I suppose it's possible. But they were there for him to read any time he wanted."

"Did you ever tell him so?"

"No, I guess not. And he didn't ask. I guess he didn't know the extent of the mystery they contained until they went missing—or rather, until Ramona showed up."

"I guess it's true. You don't know what you've got till it's gone." Grace sighed. "I know I'm certainly not the only one missing my mother. I went to see Uncle Jim the other day. He's more confused than ever."

Jim had lived with Gram until her stroke, and then his son Andy had arranged for him to live in a nursing home. The transition had not gone smoothly, but Grace tried her best to make things easier for him. He often called her "Judith" and she simply let him believe she was his late wife.

"Ken never knew his own grandparents, did he?" Grace asked. "Do you think he ever really grieved for Gram?"

"That's easy—no! Ken has never really grieved over anything. He faced the loss of his parents with hardly more than a shrug. When he lost his job—which he loved—he always wore a brave face and said things like 'That's life' when people asked how he was doing. They commended him for handling it so well."

"In the meantime it ate him up inside, I bet," Grace said. "Not that I'm a psychologist or anything."

"And that's another thing. I've been seeing a counselor for months. Ken refuses to go. He figured the kids and I were the ones who needed fixing. I suppose we do need fixing, but I think he does, too."

Grace took another sip of her hot chocolate. "We all need fixing, honey. I'll tell you what my mother always said. 'When it comes to marriage, if both don't win, nobody wins.' The longer I lived with your dad, the more I saw the truth in that. In the end, nobody won."

"Well, at our house, it certainly seems like nobody wins." A single tear ran down Benita's cheek, running out of steam at her jawline. She wiped it away with the back of her hand. "I'm just so tired of it, Mom. So tired."

Grace said nothing at first, allowing her daughter to sit with her thoughts. After a while, she gently reminded Benita about Ken's reading of the eulogy at Gram's funeral. "He did such a beautiful job. Remember?"

Benita sighed. "I guess I was in too much of a fog that day to remember anything he said. Or what anybody else said, for that matter."

"That's why we keep stuff." Grace leaned her chair back and pulled a decorative box off the counter behind her. She opened it and began pulling out mementos of the day—the funeral program, a dried rose, a bundle of sympathy cards, and Ken's eulogy. She handed the typed, neatly folded sheet of paper to Benita, who paused a moment before taking it. She took another sip of her drink before reading it to herself.

> *Cornelia Faith Simpson Baker was born August 1, 1921, in Roseburg, Manitoba, the first child of Charles and Mary Simpson. She attended Rocky Creek School and Roseburg Community Church. Cornelia attended Normal School in Winnipeg, graduating in 1941, and then returned to Roseburg to teach at Rocky Creek School until the school's closing in 1968, taking a break during her daughter's early childhood. In 1942 she married Stuart Baker, also a teacher in Roseburg. In 1972 Cornelia moved to Winnipeg to be closer to her daughter and granddaughter. Predeceased by her mother in 1932, her father in 1954, and her husband Stuart in 1960, she leaves to mourn her passing one brother, James; her daughter, Grace;*

her granddaughter, Benita, with husband, Ken, and grandchildren James and Katherine, all of Winnipeg.

Benita stopped reading to look up at her mother. "Wow, Mom. I guess I never really clued in to how young you were when you lost your dad."

"I was seventeen."

"What happened to him?"

"Cancer. He fought a long battle. Most of my teenage memories include Dad being sick and Mom taking care of him."

"All this while she taught school?"

"Yep. Seems incredible to me now, looking back. At the time, I mostly worried about how it all affected me, of course. But my mother was a remarkable woman. Dad died in late June, so Mom had the summer off and went right back to work in September."

"Did you know she only completed grade nine before . . . well, before she lived with Henry's parents?" Benita asked.

"No. That can't be right. How on earth did she get into Normal School?"

"She finished high school by correspondence, while she waited for the baby to come. She worked hard in a restaurant to save money, both before and after the birth. According to her diary, in order to attend high school in Roseburg, she would have had to board in town and her father couldn't afford that."

Her mother looked incredulous. "I can't believe you know all this when I didn't."

"It was all in the diaries." Benita turned back to the eulogy Ken had written.

That brief paragraph, containing the barest of facts, cannot begin to sum up the person Corrie Baker was. We called her Gram, and from the moment I met her when I began dating her granddaughter, she was one of my best friends. That may sound like a strange thing to say, but it's true. She had a quality about her I can't describe. Easy to talk to, she invited me to share my heart and my life. She demonstrated her faith in ways I haven't seen in anyone else. She knew Jesus so well, you'd think she'd seen him face to face. Or knew someone who had.

And from the time our children came along, they were the delight of her life. She took them to the zoo, to the park, out for french fries and ice cream. We loved having her in our home because she could light up a room with her laughter. When you spoke with her, she had a way of making every conversation about you . . . maybe that's why we don't know more about her life.

One day when Katie-Lynn was about three years old, she fell asleep on Gram's lap in the rocking chair. Gram didn't hear me come in or she likely would have stopped singing; she was pretty self-conscious about her singing, which, I'll admit, was not one of her better talents. I'll never forget the song she sang because it made me laugh and it was all I could do to cover my mouth to stifle the laughter so I could keep listening. How can I describe the picture of this 78-year old woman singing a hit song from the 1960s to a tiny girl cuddled in her arms, damp curls stuck to her forehead and hands clutching a ratty blanket? But there she was, in the most lullaby-like manner, crooning "Groovy Kind of Love." If Gram had not already won my heart before, she certainly would have in that moment.

Benita recalled the chuckles that had risen from the crowd when Ken had told the story, and she realized this was the song Gram had sung to Katie-Lynn in her dream the other night. Although Benita didn't witness the actual event, she had heard Ken tell the heartwarming story about it many times. Somehow she had missed what a special moment that represented for Ken. She continued reading.

> *As some of you know, our family has been going through a bit of a rough patch recently. My job came to an unexpected end several months ago and I haven't found work yet. Gram, even throughout her failing health, has been my greatest source of encouragement. "Don't worry, Ken," she would say every time I saw her. "God's got something for you, and it will come along at the right time. He's never too early or too late."*
>
> *Then she'd mysteriously produce a twenty-dollar bill from out of nowhere and press it into my hand. Or, on her better days, she would bake cookies, muffins, brownies, bread, you name it . . . and share it, not only with us but with everyone she had opportunity to give to. Neighborhood children all knew her as "Gramma Corrie, the Cookie Lady."*
>
> *What I will miss most, though, are her prayers. I know she prayed for us every day because she told us so every chance she got. We'd tell her our troubles and she'd say "I'm taking that one to Jesus."*
>
> *And I, for one, know beyond a doubt that she had his ear.*

Benita sat stunned. She could not remember Ken delivering, let alone writing, this personal and deeply insightful tribute to Gram. How could she have missed it? Was she really so wrapped up in her own grief that she hadn't seen or heard anything about his experience?

"Mom . . . I don't know what to say. This explains so much. I had no idea."

"I kind of thought as much," her mother said. "I confess I didn't hear much of what Ken said that day either, and I only reread this a few days ago. It's beautiful, don't you think?"

"I need to go home, Mom" was all Benita could say. She gathered her purse and keys and fled.

CHAPTER 50

April 1946

Feeling glad for the warmth of the spring day, Cornelia tightened the strings on Gracie's new bonnet. At nineteen months old, the chubby-cheeked girl had no idea what all the excitement was about. She was just happy to be on an outing, held securely on her father's shoulders.

The parade was impressive for one organized by such a small community. Nearly a year had passed since VE Day, Victory in Europe Day, and Cornelia remembered sitting with her family around the radio in her father's living room as the glorious news was made official. Three months later, Japan surrendered.

The soldiers started trickling home, married men first, in the fall of 1945. Most made it home by Christmas, with two more groups arriving in February and March. At last, Roseburg was ready to celebrate, and the little town went all out. Each one-room school in the district put together its own version of a marching band. Most had few instruments but were made glorious by their marchers' voices and feet. Cornelia waved to some of her former students, marveling at how much some of them had grown.

At the end of the parade came the soldiers. Most of them were in uniform for the first time in months, and their solemn faces told the crowd that their hearts were with those who did not march alongside them. Roseburg had lost three men besides Henry. Of those, only two bodies had been recovered and positively identified. They lay buried in Europe. Leif Valdurson had lost a leg and was now pushed along in his wheelchair by his brother, Valdi. Everyone knew Bill Wilson had stayed home and refused to participate. Shell shock, they called it.

The parade led to a celebration at the town hall, where speeches were given and awards presented. Each soldier received a leather wallet, and a plaque was reverently unveiled, inscribed with the names of the fallen. Cornelia felt pleased that the committee had included Henry, even though he had not died in battle and had been part of the community for only a short time. When his name was called, Stuart reached over and took his wife's hand. She looked up at him, at Grace, and sighed. This day would look entirely different had Henry not died.

Afterward, Cornelia helped the other women serve sandwiches and coffee. She felt thankful to be part of this little world, a married mother surrounded with people who loved and needed her. Still, a dull ache lingered deep inside, one that she suspected time would never erase.

CHAPTER 51

October 2007

On Sunday morning, all four members of the Watson household were in church for the first time in more than a year. Benita sat feeling humbled by the response Ken had given her when she returned home the night before, well past midnight. She had found him in bed but awake. With tears in her eyes, she had apologized.

"I read the eulogy you wrote for Gram," she said. "Ken, it was so special, so beautiful. I didn't understand. I didn't hear it that day, and I really didn't know how much she meant to you. I was too wrapped up in myself."

Ken looked at her with sad eyes. "You've never apologized to me before."

His words landed like a knife to her heart because she knew they rang true. But she knew that right now, she needed to make this about Ken, not about herself. Phillip had taught her that much.

"You lost a dear friend, and you need to grieve your loss." Benita stroked Ken's arm.

Ken looked away. "I don't think I know how to do that."

They talked late into the night about Gram, their marriage, their failings, and their hopes for the future. In the morning, when Ken announced that he would attend church with the family, Benita could tell his heart was softening.

Now the worship band led them in an old hymn set to an upbeat tune:

Be still, my soul
The Lord doth undertake
To guide the future as he has the past
Thy hope, thy confidence let nothing shake;
All now mysterious shall be bright at last
Be still, my soul
The waves and winds still know His voice
who ruled them while he dwelt below.

Benita stopped singing and let the words wash over her heart as thoughts swirled in her head. She thought of the lost diaries and of Ramona's pending visit, only one day away. Benita didn't know whether to hope Ramona really was Mary Sarah or to hope it was all a mistake. What if she turned out to be an awful person? What if the diaries were never found? She felt responsible for them and for their loss. Her concerns for her marriage, for Ken, and for the children made her soul anything but still. She desperately needed her soul to be still, if only for a little while. The band was repeating the first verse:

Be still my soul, the Lord is on thy side
Bear patiently the cross of grief or pain
Leave to thy God to order and provide
In every change he faithful will remain
Be still, my soul
Thy best, thy heavenly friend
Through thorny ways leads to a joyful end.

Benita found the words beautiful and longed for them to be true. *God, are you really on my side? Help me trust you, with all of it.* She wanted a friendship with God like the one Gram had. It had seemed nothing could shake Gram.

That's when a brand-new thought crossed her mind. Maybe that's why the diaries were lost. Maybe it was time she quit reading about Gram's faith and started growing her own. Maybe she should be reading God's book and looking to it for answers instead. Was that what God was trying to say?

That afternoon Ken and Benita were napping when James ran up the stairs to their apartment.

"I found it, I found it! Mom, I found it!" he shrieked. Ken reached him first.

"Son, what's going on? What did you find?" Ken placed a firm hand on both of James's shoulders and tried to settle him.

"Gram's silver suitcase!" he yelled, wiggling free from Ken's grip and heading back down the stairs. "Come on!"

Benita was behind him in a flash. At last! Had it really been nearby all this time? Had someone returned it? She asked James a question with every step, but he wasn't answering, merely leading the way. He headed out the back door of the store office onto the tiny patch of yard, and scrambled over the wooden fence to the vacant lot behind them. The children had been warned about playing in there, as the tall grass no doubt concealed broken glass and other dangers. Apparently James and his buddy Robbie had been playing there anyway.

Benita and Ken went around to the piece of fence that served as a crude gate, and opened it. James reached the spot he sought, and at his feet lay what remained of Gram's suitcase. Wide open, one hinge completely broken off, rust growing on every side, it had no doubt lain here for the entire two months since the robbery. They had obviously missed it in their initial search, but now the fall grass was dying off, exposing an assortment of litter.

Ken took in the scene. “The thieves must have taken off over the fence, stopped here long enough to break it open, and then abandoned it once they determined it held nothing valuable.”

“I didn’t touch it, Dad,” James said. “I remembered what you said. Do you think the police could take fingerprints off it?”

“I don’t know, son. I doubt it, with all the dust and dirt on it now. And I’m not sure it will be an important enough case for them to bother with anyway. But let’s leave it here for now, and see if they’ll take a look.”

Benita had stopped in her tracks when she saw the suitcase lying there. Now she ventured closer to it. Would they find anything left inside? All the feelings of violation that she’d experienced the night of the robbery now returned in a flood. When she got close enough to peer inside, the first thing she spotted was Henry’s old hymnbook, still intact. She lifted it carefully and tucked it inside her sweater. Two or three diary pages stuck to the bottom of the suitcase, held in place by something gummy enough to make them stick and wet enough to make the ink run. Benita peeled off what she could and examined the pages. Bits were still readable, but it was mostly a lost cause.

“Let’s look for more diary pages,” she said. By this time, Katie-Lynn had joined them and the four of them spent the next hour covering every square inch of the empty lot. They recovered four pages, then continued through the afternoon searching streets and back alleys in the neighborhood. They carried garbage bags with them and gathered every speck of litter they could find, stuffing four large bags to near bursting. In all that garbage, James found one sheet from the diaries in a gutter, and Benita found two more mixed in with old garage-sale signs between a fence and an electric pole.

A phone call confirmed Ken’s guess about the police not wanting to check the suitcase for evidence. With a heavy heart, Benita carried it inside, where she spent another half hour sponging off the dirt and debris from its surface and repairing the broken hinge.

"I'm so sorry, Gram," she whispered through her tears. "This wasn't supposed to happen."

This time, she determined to include her mother and Ken in the experience of reading the diary, regardless of how little remained. She called Grace, who arrived within the hour carrying a tuna casserole.

The adults waited until after the children went to bed to sit at the kitchen table with the retrieved pages. Benita set up an extra lamp to ensure the best possible lighting, while Ken made a pot of tea. Together the three of them sat and looked at the sorry little stack of pages. They each picked one or two sheets and took turns attempting to read them aloud.

Ken started. "This one looks like it starts in the middle of an entry, so there's no date. How far did you say the diaries went?"

"The most recent was from 1965, five years before I was born. I checked that out when I first got the suitcase," Benita admitted with a sheepish grin. "If there had been anything written after I arrived on the scene, I'd have read those first to see if she wrote anything about me."

"Then she must be writing about you here, Grace," Ken said. "It's quite easy to read, actually:

> *". . . and today she said the cutest thing. I wanted to write this down before I forget. I was bringing in the clothes from the line and she said 'Mommy, can you hang me on the clothesline after my bath too? I want to swing back and forth in the breeze like the sheets. Whee!'"*

"Oh, yes, I remember hearing that story well into my teens," Grace said. "Mom thought it was the funniest thing and told it every chance she got."

Ken continued reading.

> *"Words can't describe how blessed I feel to be a mother. My little girl is the light of my life and I thank Jesus for her every day. How I hope and pray she grows up to know him too."*

"Then there's about two inches of stains running across the page . . . I can't make it out." Ken slid the paper toward Benita, but she couldn't read it either. Below the smudges, she saw more, and picked it up from there.

> *". . . it's the same dress I wore to Jim's wedding and I was glad for the chance to wear it again. Speaking of Jim's wedding, now that he's moved off the farm, I worry about Daddy. Stuart and I help with the farmwork as much as we can, but he is really starting to look old. I wish he'd consider selling some of the cattle and pasture—it's too much. A smaller milk quota would be a lot more manageable, but he won't listen to reason. I even chatted with Aunt Miriam about it, and she agrees with me. But I fear if she tries to persuade him, he'll only dig his heels in more.*
>
> *"My students and I are walking across Canada! We've calculated the miles from Halifax to Vancouver and made a giant chart on the wall. We keep track of how many miles we walk—around the borders of the schoolyard, mostly—and each of us fills in our number for each day. Then the students take turns calculating the week's total and moving the marker on the map to show our progress. I have assigned each student a city to write a short report on, and they give their report when we reach their city. We're somewhere around Port Arthur now, and I think we can make it to the Pacific by the end of June at this rate. They are learning their geography and*

improving their physical fitness and health at the same time. As am I."

"She was a great teacher." Grace wiped her eyes. "I had her for history and geography three years in a row, and even I loved her."

"Former students attended the funeral," Ken said. "One of them pulled out of her purse a note written by Gram, encouraging her in her writing talent. She'd carried that thing with her for thirty years or more."

"I think that's all we're going to get out of this page." Benita smoothed the sheet out as best she could. "Some kind of dirt or ashes covers the rest. At least I hope it's nothing worse than that. What have you got there, Mom?"

Grace put her glasses on and picked up the sheet in front of her.

"This one begins in the middle of a sentence, too. Ken, why don't you pencil in the approximate date on that one we just read? Sounds like I was a preschooler . . . it was after Uncle Jim got married but before Grandpa died, so . . . somewhere about 1947 or '48, I'd say."

She turned to the page before her.

". . . and I worry I won't be much of a mother because I only had a mother of my own for such a short time and for much of that time, she was sick. Most of all, I have this nagging fear something will happen to me when Gracie turns 12 and she'll be left motherless, like I was. I know it's not a reasonable fear, but I can't seem to shake it. It's so real. And her twelfth birthday falls on Monday—"

"Okay, so this would have been . . . um . . . 1956." Grace grabbed the pencil and jotted the year on the corner of the sheet before continuing.

"—so naturally, I've been unusually distracted by the significance of it. I haven't said a word to Stuart about my anxiety. I know he'd think I was silly. And of course I wouldn't tell Gracie. There's no point in giving her cause for alarm, although I suspect the poor girl wonders why I'm so clingy these days. I even went to my spot by the creek to pray. I know, deep down, I hoped for Aziel to come to me there . . . and he did, in a way. Although I couldn't see or touch him, I could feel a supernatural presence and I think God wants me to relax and enjoy my daughter.

"Of course, not a day goes by that I don't also think of her sister—"

At this, Grace's voice began to quiver and she paused. But when Benita offered to finish reading for her, Grace shook her head and continued.

"—and God, I pray she is all right. In my imagination, the two girls play together and squabble over clothes and boys as I've seen sisters do. She must be sixteen now. Oh Lord, please watch over my Mary Sarah. Give her parents all the wisdom and love you can spare, God. May they shower her with love and goodness. And give me strength to be the mother Gracie needs. I love her so much, it hurts. If she should lose me now, well . . . I just don't want her to go through what I did."

Grace had reached the end of the entry and the end of the page. She sat silently for so long, Benita finally spoke. "Are you okay, Mom?"

Grace blew her nose and took a sip of her tea. "Yes. It's just . . . becoming real, I guess. Seeing this in my mother's own handwriting . . . that I really do have a sister somewhere. Takes a while to sink in, you know?"

"Does it make you more eager to meet Ramona?" Ken asked.

"A little. But if it turns out she's not Mary Sarah . . . it will be harder still. On all of us."

"Well, we don't have much longer to wait." Ken glanced at his watch. "It's almost Monday."

"Mom, do you want to stay overnight?" Benita gathered the diary pages into a stack. "We can finish reading these in the morning. It's a lot to take in at once."

Grace agreed, and they placed the few tattered sheets into the broken suitcase and slowly closed the lid.

CHAPTER 52

July 1950

Cornelia was hoeing a row of thigh-high corn during the hottest part of the day when the sight of an old red car going down the gravel road almost made her heart stop. She watched as the car made dust fly across the field to the north. In an instant, the previous ten years disappeared and Henry Roberts once again drove his father's 1932 Pontiac Coupe, bringing his mother to visit.

Who on earth could own a car just like that? And why were they slowing down, coming down Cornelia's driveway? She felt her stomach do a flip and her palms tingle. She looked over at six-year-old Gracie, playing under the shade trees next to the house. Seated on a blanket, Gracie was busy putting doll clothes on a patient mother cat. Cornelia's instinct was to snatch up Grace, carry her inside the house, and bolt the door. Instead, she wiped her brow, dusted off her hands, and walked slowly toward the car.

A woman sat behind the wheel. As she climbed out of the car, a light switched on for Cornelia. Eva Roberts stood before her, ten years older and alone.

"Hello, Corrie."

Cornelia tried, but couldn't speak. Gracie ran up beside her and shyly hid behind her mother's apron. The tabby cat wriggled from Gracie's grip and trotted off, shaking herself free of a pink bonnet. Cornelia put a hand on the little girl's head and stroked her hair.

"I'm sorry I didn't call. I hope I haven't come at a bad time. I—" Eva's voice trailed off.

Finally, Cornelia took a deep breath and found her voice. "Eva. What a surprise."

"I hoped—well, I stopped in at your father's and he pointed me this way. He said he'd phone you to let you know I was coming."

"I've been in the garden all day."

"Yes, I see. I hoped we could talk."

Cornelia glanced down the road toward her childhood home, where she could make out Stuart and Daddy hammering new shingles on the old house. They would be at it until dark, she was certain. "Come in," she said softly.

While Eva used the bathroom, Cornelia washed her hands at the kitchen sink and made a fresh pot of coffee. She poured a glass of milk for Gracie and placed a plate of gingersnaps on the table.

"This is my daughter, Grace," Cornelia said when Eva entered the kitchen.

"Well, hello, Grace. It's lovely to meet you, sweetie." Eva smiled at the little girl, who gave no response.

"What do you say, Gracie?" her mother prompted.

"How do you do?" It was barely a whisper, but she said it.

"Fine, thank you," Eva replied. "What a lovely little girl. Congratulations, Corrie."

"Thank you. Have a seat. I'll get the coffee."

Eva had questions. "Your father tells me you're teaching at the very school you attended as a student. That must be nostalgic."

"Yes." Cornelia had taken two years off when Grace arrived, but she'd been back for four years now. Aunt Miriam babysat for her during the day, and took great pleasure in preparing Grace for school. "Gracie will start this fall. Her father teaches also, at the town school."

"Tell me about him."

"Well . . . his name is Stuart Baker. We met after I moved back home, and . . ." Cornelia couldn't continue. "Why are you here, Eva?"

The woman paused, then took a deep breath. "Does Stuart know?"

Cornelia swallowed hard. "Gracie, sweetheart, why don't you take a cookie and go look at your books in your room for a while? It's time for some afternoon quiet."

Both women watched Grace leave. Once her daughter was out of earshot, Cornelia repeated her earlier question. "Why did you come?"

"Samuel passed away, Corrie. Last winter. He had a stroke."

"I'm sorry. You must be very lonely."

"I am. I wanted to see you again. I wanted—" Eva put her head down. "I've wanted to see you for ten long years. I always wanted to stay in touch."

"He wouldn't allow it?"

"No."

Cornelia sighed and took a sip of her coffee.

"I was hoping . . . now that he's gone . . . you could forgive us for the way we treated you. Perhaps we could be friends. Gracie doesn't have a grandmother, and I don't have—"

"I do forgive you, Mrs. Roberts. Eva. But I don't think that's wise."

"Because . . . ?"

"Well . . . you and I really have—had—only one thing in common. Henry. And he's gone." Cornelia looked around her sunny kitchen. "I have a new life. I'm sorry for your loneliness, but I'm not sure I can do this."

"We have more in common than Henry, Corrie. We have the baby."

"She's ten years old already, Eva. She doesn't even know who we are."

"All the more reason why we need each other." Eva searched Cornelia's face. "You've never told Stuart, have you?"

Cornelia could feel the tears immediately. She ignored them and let them drop, one by one, down her cheeks and onto her lap. She stared at her apron, blackened with garden dirt.

"What about your father? Does he know?"

Cornelia moved her head only slightly. The two women sat without a word for what felt like a full five minutes. Finally, Cornelia broke the silence.

"It was part of the deal."

"Deal?"

Cornelia nodded. "Don't you remember? Samuel promised to support me through the completion of my high school and the baby's birth, provided I never said a word. He kept his end of the bargain and I've kept—"

"Oh, Corrie. Sweetheart. You are not bound by anything. Not then, not now. Samuel is gone. You cannot hurt his precious pride."

"What possible good could it do to tell anyone now?"

"This is too great a burden for you to carry alone. If you cannot bring yourself to tell anyone else, then all the more reason for us to be friends. I can help you carry your secret."

"My husband does know about Henry. Wouldn't he find it odd if you and I suddenly began corresponding, or—" Another thought hit Cornelia. "You're not moving back to Roseburg, are you?"

"No. My home is in the city. My friends. Church. It's where my son and my husband are buried, and it's where I want to be. But knowing I have a grandchild out there, somewhere—"

"I know. Don't think for a moment I don't feel that ache."

"Maybe one day we can find her, Corrie. Together."

Cornelia slowly shook her head. "And how would I explain that to Stuart? To Gracie?"

"You'd find a way."

"What about Daddy? He'd only be that much more hurt that I kept such an enormous secret from him all these years."

"We cross that bridge when we come to it, Corrie. We don't have to think about that yet. For now, I'm asking to be your friend."

"Friend?"

"We'll write, we'll get together a couple of times a year. You could bring Grace and visit me for a few days each summer. We could take her to see the zoo, go shopping. Oh, did you know the spring floods wiped out the band stage at Kildonan Park? They're going to put up a brand-new one, with an arch of lights over the top to look like a rainbow!" Eva demonstrated the shape with her hands. "It will be wonderful! We can go see all sorts of concerts and—"

"Eva," Cornelia said firmly, holding both palms toward the woman.

Eva stopped talking and turned her eyes toward the floor with a sigh. "I'm sorry. I've dropped in here completely unexpected after all these years. Of course, you need some time."

"No, Eva. I don't. I do appreciate your apology, but I really don't need more time. I have a new life. I don't need reminders of things that are no more, things that can never be. I'm sorry."

Eva swallowed hard. "I see." She picked up her purse.

Cornelia stared at her own knees once again as Eva walked to the door and opened it. She didn't turn around when Eva said, "If you change your mind . . ." After a long pause, Cornelia heard the door close. She looked into her coffee cup as she heard the Pontiac start and drive away.

"Oh God. Have I done the right thing?" she whispered, wiping tears from her cheeks and looking toward the ceiling. "If only I could know."

CHAPTER 53

October 2007

Happy shrieks from Katie-Lynn woke Benita long after her alarm should have rung. Surprised to see their grandmother still there, both children were determined to make her breakfast—cornflakes, toast, and orange juice. Benita grabbed a bathrobe and hustled to the kitchen, where she put on the coffee. Ken was already downstairs at work, and the children were due at school in thirty minutes. As soon as they'd prepared Grace's breakfast and eaten their own, Benita shooed them to their rooms to get dressed.

"I can't imagine how I forgot to set the alarm." Benita poured two cups of coffee and sat across the table from her mother. "Did you manage to sleep okay on that old hide-a-bed, Mom?"

"Oh, I've had better nights." Grace accepted the mug with both hands. "But I'm not sure I'd have slept better at home anyway. The countdown is on till Ramona arrives, and that's all I can think about. Listen, since I'm already dressed, why don't you let me drop the kids at school on my way home?"

"Don't you want to stick around here for a while?"

Grace's eyes sparkled. "The idea came to me in the night to round up old family photo albums and the like. Ramona will want to see pictures."

"Sure, Mom, but don't you want to finish reading what we salvaged of the diary?"

"You know I do. But what would you think about saving them for a bit? If Ramona does indeed turn out to be our girl, we could really make an event out of it."

"Yeah. Okay. You're right." Benita swallowed a pang of disappointment.

"Isn't it funny?" Grace gathered up her purse and casserole dish. "When you first told me about this, I wanted nothing to do with it. But now I keep imagining what it would be like to have a sister—a real, live sister of my own. I always wanted one when I was little. I even used to bug Mom about it. How that must have crushed her heart! If only I'd known."

"Well, Gram chose not to tell. How could you have had any idea?"

"I know. But things like that weren't talked about back then. It just wasn't done. Poor Mom. It must have been so lonely, keeping such an important secret."

Benita gave her mother and both children a hug before they walked out the door. After they left, she showered, dressed, and cleaned the apartment from top to bottom. In one corner of the living room, she gathered the things they would want to show Ramona: the silver suitcase, Gram's quilt from Katie-Lynn's bed, photo albums from her wedding and the kids' baby years, and the old ice-cream maker. The store was quiet and Ken didn't complain about Benita abandoning him. He must know her mind and heart were focused elsewhere today.

Grace arrived in the middle of the afternoon, out of breath, her arms laden with photo albums.

"My goodness, we're going to overwhelm her." Benita smiled. "Come on in, Mom, I want to peek at those."

"Oh, no, you don't." Grace held the albums tightly. "Not until we can show them to Ramona together."

"But I haven't seen some of those for years!" Benita protested.

"Maybe not, but Ramona hasn't seen them at all. Trust me, it will be more fun this way." She added the albums to the growing pile in the corner.

"Oh, fine. Have it your way. I should get downstairs and help Ken anyway. He's being incredibly patient with me."

Grace was full of nervous energy and more animated than Benita had seen her in years. To keep busy, she prepared supper for the family after picking up Katie-Lynn and James from school. Benita worked in the store alongside Ken through the late afternoon and they closed at six o'clock sharp. As soon as the store was locked up, all five of them sat around the table and enjoyed Grace's lasagna. Benita alternated between taking trips to the washroom, checking her watch against the clock on the kitchen wall, looking out the window, and glancing at the items in the corner of the living room. James and Katie-Lynn tried everyone's patience with their dish-towel snapping and bickering over whose turn it was to wash or dry.

When the phone rang, the three adults looked at each other, and Benita picked up the phone.

"Hello? Yes, hello, Ramona." She smiled at Grace and Ken. The children, not fully understanding the drama unfolding in their midst, could sense something more important than the arrival of an old family friend was happening, and they paused in their dishwashing.

Benita pointed toward the window and mouthed "They're here."

Grace looked out the window and gasped.

"It's her," she said. Benita looked over in time to see Grace's knees buckle beneath her, landing her on the arm of the sofa. She ran to the window to see for herself what had so startled her mother, but by this time their visitors were at the storefront door and out of sight from where she stood. Ken was on his way down to let them in.

"Katie-Lynn, stay here with Grandma." Benita followed Ken down the stairs. By the time she reached the bottom, Ken had opened the door and was shaking the hand of a dark-haired man in his mid-forties. This would be David, Ramona's son. He didn't look familiar to Benita, but when he stepped aside to make way for his mother, Benita saw Ken's face freeze in shock.

"Oh. Oh my—" was all he said.

The woman before them stood still, smiling Gram's smile. "You must be Ken." The voice sounded different, but otherwise it was as if the Gram of Benita's childhood had walked through the door and back into her life.

The woman reached out a hand to Ken. "I'm Ramona."

CHAPTER 54

July 1950

Eva Roberts had been gone a full twenty minutes and Cornelia still sat at her kitchen table, her coffee now cold. "It's time," she murmured.

She stopped to check on Gracie, who was sleeping in her bed with a picture book across her chest and her beloved stuffed bunny squashed under one arm. Cornelia thought her heart might burst at the sight of her beautiful little girl, so unaware of her mother's past.

She climbed to the attic and dragged her mother's old silver suitcase into the middle of the room, where sunbeams cast enough light into the space that she could see what she was doing. She clenched her teeth and began piling diaries onto the floor, speeding up as she worked. She resisted the urge to stop and read them.

"It's time. It's time," she repeated as she gathered the notebooks into her apron and started back down the stairs and outside with the load. Quickly, she headed for the burning barrel at the corner of the vegetable garden.

"Shoot. Forgot the matches," Cornelia muttered. She dropped the diaries on the grass beside the barrel and headed back into the house.

After checking once more on Gracie, she carried the matches back outside. She'd get a good fire going and toss each notebook in separately, watching to make sure they all burned completely.

Last week's *Winnipeg Free Press* already lay in the barrel, and Cornelia struck a match and lit the newspaper just as a horn sounded behind her.

Stuart. Why was he home so early? Should she toss all the diaries in at once and risk snuffing out the fire?

"Whatcha doin'?" Stuart called to her as he climbed out of their car.

With one foot, Cornelia shoved aside a notebook that had fallen from the stack and headed toward the car, hoping Stuart would go straight into the house. "Just thought I'd burn some garbage."

"I wouldn't start any fires today, Corrie," Stuart warned. "It's too dry. If it rains tonight, I'll burn it for you tomorrow."

"Okay." Cornelia tried to appear nonchalant. "Why are you back so early? You and Daddy can't be done already."

"We're not. Turns out we were short one bundle of shingles. Your dad's gone to town for more, and I thought I'd run home for a snack. And a kiss."

Cornelia kissed her husband squarely on the mouth and ushered him inside. Glancing back, she could tell by the lack of smoke rising from the rusty old trash barrel that her fire had fizzled.

An hour later, Stuart was back at the shingling job with Charles, Grace was up from her nap, and Cornelia knew her resolve had fizzled just like the fire. Back at the burning barrel, now with Grace at her side, she looked at the stack of diaries and sighed.

"I just can't do it," she said.

"I can help you, Mommy," the little girl said. "What are we doing?"

Together they gathered the notebooks. Carrying three of them in her pudgy arms, Gracie followed her mother back into the house and up to the attic. They laid the diaries back in the silver suitcase.

"What are these books?" Grace asked.

"Just some stories, sweetheart."

"Will you read them to me?"

"No. They're grown-up stories."

"I'm going to grow up. Can I read them then?"

Cornelia sighed. "Maybe one day, my girl." She closed the lid and pushed the suitcase back to its dusty corner.

CHAPTER 55

October 2007

Benita drew a deep breath and took Ramona's hand. "Hello, again" was all she could manage. She tried desperately not to stare.

"Hello, Benita." Ramona gestured toward the younger man. "This is my son, David."

Benita shook his hand in silence and finally glanced over at Ken. He continued to stare at Ramona.

"Forgive us, Ramona," he said at last. "You, uh . . . it's just a little overwhelming. You look familiar to us."

"I do?" Ramona looked pleased. "Well, that's good news, don't you think? You . . . said your mother would be here?" Ramona asked, looking around.

"Yes," Benita said. "Uh . . . I mean, yes, she's upstairs with James and Katie-Lynn, our children. Please, come on up."

Benita let Ken lead the way. As she followed at the back of the group, she could see Gram's walk, Gram's gestures, even Gram's fashion sense, in Ramona. She hoped her mother would still be sitting down when they reached the top of the stairs.

"Everyone," Ken said as they entered the room. "I'd like you to meet Ramona and her son, David." He pointed to the kids. "Ramona, this is James, this is Katie-Lynn. And this"—he walked over to Grace and put a hand on her shoulder—"is Benita's mother, Grace."

"How do you do, Grace?" Ramona smiled, but Grace only stared and said nothing.

Katie-Lynn broke the awkward silence. "You look like my Gram. Were you her friend?"

"Oh, sweetie. I, uh—" Ramona looked around at the other adults, eyebrows raised. Finally Grace spoke.

"Katie-Lynn, Ramona is part of our family. That's why she looks so much like Gram."

"But she doesn't look like you," James observed.

"Well, I was always told I looked more like my father," Grace said. "And your mommy looks like me. But Ramona here—oh my." She looked at the visitors. "You must have a seat. David, make yourself at home. Wait till you see pictures. I really don't think we're going to need any official confirmation. It's obvious. At least it sure is to me. Look at that—my hands are shaking!"

Ramona looked down at her own. "Mine, too!"

The two women stared at each other in awe until neither could stand it any longer. Grace stood up from the couch, Ramona crossed the room, and they embraced so enthusiastically it was as if they had known each other all their lives and been separated for only a few weeks.

"I want to hear everything," Grace said at last. She sat and patted the couch beside her. "Tell us how you found us."

Ramona and David stayed long after the children had gone to bed. They pored over the photo albums, exclaiming over and over about the strong family resemblance between Ramona and Gram. Pictures of Cornelia from the 1980s were the most striking, since that's when Gram would have been the age Ramona was now. Ramona explained that she'd been raised near Toronto by parents who'd informed her early in her life that she was adopted.

"They always told me I was extra-special because they couldn't have children of their own. They called me their gift. They were nearly forty when I was born, so they've both passed on, of course." Ramona pulled a black-and-white photo from her bag and passed it around. It showed a young couple, all smiles. The woman was holding a tightly wrapped infant.

"When I turned twenty-one, I contacted the Manitoba Post-Adoption Registry to learn what I could. They told me my birth mother's name—Cornelia Simpson—and her last known address in Winnipeg. At the time of my birth, she indicated on her release papers that she was open to meeting me one day, but she hadn't sent any updates."

As she spoke, Ramona looked around the room and made eye contact with each person. "I came to Winnipeg and found my way to the address. The house had been torn down and the whole area was a big playground. I called every Simpson in the Winnipeg phone directory, but no one had any idea what I was talking about. It seemed like a dead end."

All eyes focused on Ramona as she shared her story.

"After I married and started my own family, I let the issue rest awhile. I did spend one crazy weekend with a fat Manitoba phone book, going through every little town in the province and calling every Simpson I could find. Only once did I get any kind of meaningful response, from a Simpson in Roseburg. The person gave me another number to try, but gave firm orders that if it led nowhere, I was *not* to call the number back. When I called the second number, a teenager answered. It was another dead end."

Benita and Grace gave each other a meaningful glance and then looked away as quickly as they could.

"After that, I gave up," Ramona said. "I couldn't handle the heartbreak and disappointment. But my husband and children knew about my search, and they knew the name Cornelia Simpson. So when David saw one of your posters, Benita, he called me immediately. And here we are." Ramona smiled at Katie-Lynn, who smiled back.

"Wow. I wonder why Gram never updated the adoption registry with her name and address change?" Benita directed this question at Grace.

"Honey, I don't think my father ever knew. I certainly didn't. And Ramona—it breaks my heart to tell you this now, but I remember that phone call. That teenager was me. I'm so sorry. I never told my parents about your call . . . I'm not sure why."

Ramona looked at Grace with sad eyes. "Oh, honey. You were young. Who knows how things might have turned out if we had connected then? Everything happens for a reason, that's what I believe."

"But who do you suppose gave you our family's phone number?" Grace asked.

"According to the diaries, Gram never told a soul," Benita said. "Maybe she did eventually tell her father."

"No, that can't be right." Grace shook her head. "Grandpa would have been gone by the time Ramona made that phone call. He died when I was ten. Her call came when I was . . . nineteen, twenty maybe. What about Uncle Jim?"

"I don't know if Uncle Jim knew either, Mom," Benita said. "I read Gram's diaries up to the point where she met your father and she still hadn't told Jim then. Maybe she told him later. Or maybe he snooped in the diaries."

Ramona smiled. "No. It was a woman on the phone, and she sounded old. I remember. It was listed 'M. Simpson' in the phone book."

"Oh my gosh." Grace's hand rose to her cheek. "Aunt Miriam!"

"What? That can't be right. Gram wouldn't have told Aunt Miriam in a million years," Benita said. "I can't believe it was her. Oh, if only we had those diaries—you'd see what I mean."

"Still no diaries, eh?" David said. He had been quietly listening in on the conversation all evening. The three women, who'd been entirely engrossed in their chatter, looked around them now and noticed for the first time that Ken had slipped out unannounced.

"He went downstairs about ten minutes ago," David informed them when Benita wondered aloud where he'd gone.

"We should probably call it a night." Ramona yawned. "It's been a terribly long day. Can we pick this up again tomorrow? I want to know what you can tell me about my father, too."

Grace and Ramona made plans to meet for breakfast and enjoy some sister-bonding time. After that they would pick up Benita and the three of them would make the drive to Roseburg and see what they could of the place where Gram grew up.

After they'd said their good-byes and the guests had left, Benita found Ken in the tiny backyard, leaning on the fence and looking out into the vacant lot. When she got closer, she heard muffled sobs and saw his face buried in the crook of his elbow. As he became aware of her presence, he took a deep breath and forced his breathing to become more regular. Benita put a hand on his shoulder but said nothing. They stood there for several minutes, looking at what few stars could be seen above the lights of the city. Benita gently rubbed Ken's back.

Ken spoke first. "I miss her so much."

"I know. I miss her, too."

Ken wiped his face on the sleeve of his flannel shirt. "Did you know she told me I had a good head for business?"

"No. But she was right. You do."

"No one else ever saw that in me."

Benita rubbed his arm. "Gram would be very proud of you."

Finally Ken turned and let Benita embrace him in a long hug.

"It's getting chilly out here," Benita said. "Let's go to bed."

Half an hour later, they lay awake staring at their bedroom ceiling in the darkness.

"Ken, I can't tell you how much I regret not sharing the diaries with you. I should have realized how much they might mean to you. I'm so sorry, and I would give anything to get them back so you could read them, too. Will you forgive me?"

"Yes," he said simply. "I already have."

Benita drew a deep breath. "For that, yes. But there's more. I know I've been bitter and resentful toward you for a long time, for things that have little or nothing to do with you." Benita could feel tears collecting in her ears and she rolled over onto her side, facing Ken. "I want you to know I'm sorry, and I'm working on it. I really want to change."

"Is that Mr. Counselor talking?"

As much as Benita wished she'd come to this realization on her own, she knew she couldn't take all the credit. "What if it is?"

"If it is, I might consider seeing the guy once or twice myself. You know, just to say thanks."

Benita said nothing, but found her husband's hand and held it tightly.

"I'm sorry, too." Ken said into the darkness. "I know I've been hard on you. I've been thinking. I'd like to leave Richard in charge of the store tomorrow and go with you to Roseburg."

Benita was delighted. "Are you serious?"

Ken flipped from his back onto his side and kissed her. "Let's take the kids and make a day of it. It will be good for all of us."

Benita fell asleep with a smile on her face that night. Ramona's grand entrance into their lives was bringing good things.

The diaries may have been lost, but Mary Sarah had been found.

CHAPTER 56

It was a glorious Indian summer day when six adults and two children piled into the Watson family's van. David had asked to join them for the excursion, and Grace had invited Uncle Jim along as well.

"He's having one of his better days," Grace said as they loaded her picnic basket into the back of the van. "But I'm not sure how helpful he'll be in talking with folks in Roseburg. He's been calling Ramona 'Corny' ever since we picked him up."

"I suppose that further negates the need for official confirmation." Ken hopped into the driver's seat.

"Well, I do have an appointment with the post-adoption registry tomorrow," Ramona said. "I may as well keep it. You never know what information they might be able to provide."

"Should I call you Grandma or Aunty?" Katie-Lynn asked Ramona abruptly.

Ramona smiled at the little girl. "I think you can call me 'Mona' if you like. All my favorite people do." She looked to Benita for affirmation.

In all the excitement of the previous evening, further explanation to the children had been overlooked. Now, on the two-hour drive to

Roseburg, Benita tactfully explained to them that Ramona was her aunt and David was her cousin.

"Ramona was born when Gram was very young and couldn't take care of her. So because she loved her so much, she gave her to another family so they could adopt her. They moved far away, but now she's found us all. Isn't that wonderful?"

"And just think," Ramona said. "If the diaries hadn't gone missing, I might never have found you." That brought a silence over the van as each passenger thought about the truth of Ramona's words.

"I'm the one who found the silver suitcase," James piped up.

"Yes, you are. You deserve a prize. How about a new hairdo?" Benita reached across the seat and ruffled James's hair as he flailed his arms trying to fight her off.

Uncle Jim hadn't said a word since they left the city, but he joined in now. He looked at Ramona and, with an old familiar glint in his eye, said, "You gonna make your strawberry ice cream, Corny? I'll help turn the crank."

When Ramona raised an eyebrow in Grace's direction, Benita told her the story of the antique ice-cream maker with as much detail as she could remember. Just as she finished explaining, they passed a sign that read Welcome to Roseburg. Population: 453.

Uncle Jim's long-term memory was sharper than they'd predicted. He knew exactly where things ought to be in Roseburg, and the changes in the community annoyed and confused him.

"That's where the Morgan twins live." He pointed as they drove by an old, well-kept house. But the general store he remembered had been replaced by a modern video rental outlet. Their old church was still standing, but it was now a seniors' drop-in center. A new, modern building had replaced the school Grace once attended. Students played outside.

"There's Jean Little and Becky Tarr," Jim said, watching the children. "They sure do like the swings. No one else can ever get a turn on those swings."

James and Katie-Lynn looked at each other, then at their mother. Benita shrugged and smiled.

"Take a left up here." Grace pointed. "This is the way to the farm. I haven't been back since my mother moved to the city. I'm so sorry I never brought you here, Benita. Life has a way of getting so busy. Important things get left undone."

Ken turned left onto the gravel road as Benita quietly observed her surroundings. She imagined Gram as a young girl, riding beside Henry in his red Pontiac coupe down this same road the night they met. She wondered where Gram's special place by the creek might be, or whether a creek ran anywhere nearby. Would Uncle Jim remember? She decided to ask, but when she turned to look at him, she saw that Jim had dozed off with his chin turned awkwardly into his chest.

"Where did you live, Grandma?" Katie-Lynn asked.

"It's up ahead a little ways." Grace nodded toward the road. "My goodness, I feel kind of nervous."

"You think *you* do?" Ramona giggled. "I'm feeling nervous and a whole lot of other things I can't even identify."

"See that white house up ahead on the left?" Grace sat taller in her seat. "That's ours. Someone tore down the old house Gram and Uncle Jim grew up in. Looks like there might be a garage or something in that spot now."

Ken pulled into the yard and stopped in front of a blue Dodge truck parked there. A black and white dog gave a couple of halfhearted woofs and greeted the guests, his tail wagging as if he was greeting old friends. Slowly the group climbed out of the van, leaving Uncle Jim asleep in the back. The dog allowed Ken to pet him while the others stretched and looked around, staying close to the van. Finally a man in rubber boots appeared from around the back of the house and approached them.

"Come, Rascal." He patted his thigh with one hand but stayed focused on the strangers as the dog ran back toward him. "Hello there. Can I help you?"

"Hi! So sorry to intrude." Benita watched her mother step forward and shake the man's hand, wondering what might be going on in her mother's heart. "My name is Grace Gladstone and I grew up on this farm. My parents, Stuart and Cornelia Baker, built this house and my grandfather had a house right over—" But suddenly Grace was overcome with emotion and couldn't speak anymore.

Benita stepped over and placed an arm around her mother's shoulder. "I'm her daughter," she said. "This is my, uh, aunt, Ramona, and her son, David. Uncle Jim is asleep in the car. He would have grown up in the old house. This is my husband, Ken, and our children, Katie-Lynn and James."

"Would you mind if we took a little look around?" Ken said. "We understand if you'd rather we didn't, of course."

"It would mean the world to us if we could." Grace had found her voice again.

The man shook Ken's hand. "Andrew Beckman. I bought the place from a guy named Sanderson in 1995. The old house was gone by then."

"Sanderson, yes. That's who bought it from Mother." Grace had regained her composure. "Oh, I hope this isn't an intrusion. I would so dearly love to just walk around the property."

"Not at all. Take all the time you like, and when you're ready, come on in and see the house too. We've made quite a few changes inside, but you're welcome to see it."

"Oh, thank you. That's very kind." Grace took Ramona by the arm and Benita watched as the pair of them stopped to admire a colorful flower garden in the middle of the yard.

Just then Uncle Jim stepped out of the van. He stood quietly for a moment, looking around. His eyes, which usually held a vacant look, brightened as he began to recognize his surroundings. "My tree." He walked over to an interesting oak tree—four trees, really, that were growing so closely together, their trunks nearly touched and their branches all intertwined as though they came from the same source. The others watched as Jim put his hand on the rough bark and looked up into the branches. "It's big."

"When I was a little girl, I could curl up right in the center of those four trunks," Grace said. "Now, I think they're too close together even for you to try that, James. Want to try?"

James managed to squeeze his body in between the trunks but he certainly wouldn't have been able to curl up there. He hopped out again and chased the dog, Rascal.

"What do you suppose is going on in Uncle Jim's mind?" Benita asked no one in particular. The others followed as he wandered over to an old, dilapidated outbuilding.

"This was Grandpa's milk house," Grace said. Benita could picture Gram there as a young girl, separating the milk and carrying it to the house, just as she'd read. "The old barn is gone, though." Jim seemed to be looking in that direction, too, and he wore a bewildered expression on his face as though he was wondering how the barn had disappeared.

"Gram's diary mentioned a garden many times—and a clothesline," Benita said.

Grace tried to find what had always been their garden spot. "It's hard to even orient myself. The landscape is different, the trees bigger. Yet it all seems smaller somehow. I used to swing on a tire swing right around here somewhere."

For the next thirty minutes they roamed the grounds, Grace keeping up a stream of stories and explanations, Benita offering what details she could remember from Gram's diaries. Ramona ate it all up. Rascal kept the children entertained and seemed delighted to have visitors.

When they were ready to go inside, Andrew Beckman showed them around the house and Grace oohed and aahed over the attractive renovations. The things that remained the same, however, interested her even more, and these triggered memories that she happily shared with Ramona.

"This was my bedroom. I suppose you and I would have shared it if—well, you know."

Ramona squeezed Grace's hand but made no reply.

"Thanks again, Mr. Beckman," Benita said after the tour, as he walked them back to the van. "And when your wife gets home from work, please tell her how much we appreciate you letting us tramp through your house." She paused for a second. "I hate to ask anything more of you, but would you happen to know if anyone by the name of Simpson or Roberts lives in the area?"

Mr. Beckman removed his cap and scratched the back of his head before putting the cap back in place. "Sorry, can't say I do. But that doesn't mean they don't."

"Roberts?" Grace asked when they all sat in the van again. "Who do we know by that name?"

Benita took a deep breath. "Ramona, you haven't asked anything about your father."

Ramona looked at her. "No. I hoped we'd get to that, but was too chicken to bring it up. Sometimes you have to be careful what you wish for, as they say."

Grace looked from Ramona to Benita with raised eyebrows.

"Mom," Benita said, turning to Grace. "Remember when I told you the story of Gram's boyfriend, Henry? He was a Roberts. He lived with his parents in Winnipeg, but he had Roberts relatives here and he came to work for them the summer before he died. That's how he met Gram. He worked on his uncle's farm."

Grace nodded. "Oh . . . yes. You did mention that, I think. Such a shame that he died." Then a realization hit her. "But I suppose if he'd lived, my mother would have married him and there would have been no me . . . and no you, Benita!" She turned to the children and tickled them. "And what about these peanuts?"

James looked at his mother. "Grandma's being weird, Mom."

Ramona watched with amusement. "My father's name was Henry Roberts?"

"Yes. And he loved Gram very much." Benita told the story of how Henry had joined the army but died in a train wreck before being shipped overseas. "He never knew of your existence, Ramona. But he had already asked for permission to propose to Gram when he returned."

Ramona took this in with a sigh. "I wonder what they would have named me?"

"That's easy," Benita said. "To Gram, you were always Mary Sarah, named after her mother."

"Mary Sarah Roberts." Ramona pronounced the name cautiously as though trying on a glass slipper. Then she laughed and shrugged. "That's much too plain and ordinary for me. Believe it or not, I grew up Ramona Olivia Victoria Bartmanovitch. I had to marry Bob Stanford just to tone things down a bit."

The others laughed.

"Mona?" Katie-Lynn piped up.

"Yes, dear?"

"I like your fancy name. Are you a princess?"

"Am I a princess? Well, now." She looked at Grace with a mischievous grin and wiggled one eyebrow. "I might just be the ugly stepsister."

They were coming to love Ramona in the most natural way, and not only for her astonishing resemblance to Gram.

CHAPTER 57

"Uncle Jim, we've packed a lunch," Benita said. "Do you know a nice place by the creek where we can have a picnic?" She knew she was probably grasping at straws, but it was worth a shot. She had already asked her mother, who knew the location of a nearby creek, but knew nothing about any special spot.

Surprisingly, Jim pointed a gnarled finger. "Right up there. Turn right on that road right there. That's where we go fishing, right, Corny? Did you bring my fishing pole?"

Ramona smiled and patted his knee. "Sorry, Jim, I guess I forgot it this time. But if you can help us find our spot, we'll have a nice picnic there, okay?"

Ken followed Uncle Jim's directions down the gravel road a couple of miles, taking a left and then another right down a dirt trail. Though nobody said it out loud, Benita wondered if they were all thinking the same thing: Would they end up stuck in the mud somewhere, or lost? But the farther they drove, the more Jim seemed like his old self.

"Here it is. You can stop the car right here and we'll walk. The creek is over that bank. I'll race ya, Corny."

The "race" consisted of Ramona taking Jim's arm and allowing him to lead her over the bank and down a well-beaten path to the water's edge. Clearly, this special spot was still in use, but no one was around today.

Benita watched from the top of the bank while the rest of the family went ahead, following Jim. If this was his and Gram's fishing spot, it was likely Gram and Henry's special spot, too. This would be where Gram came to cry and where she received the angelic visit. It would be the spot where Gram's faith took a giant leap, the turning point from which she never looked back. Benita felt as though she were about to step onto holy ground. She reverently took in the scene before her: the sparkle of sunlight on the water, the brilliant orange and yellow leaves dancing in the gentle breeze, the scent of fall in the air.

"Gram," she whispered. "Can you see us here? Do you see us together? We've found Mary Sarah."

When Benita caught up to the group, Grace and Ramona were laying out the picnic lunch and the kids were trying in vain to skip stones in the skinny trickle of water. As they filled up on turkey sandwiches, carrot sticks, potato chips, oatmeal cookies, and McIntosh apples, Uncle Jim told stories about the perch they'd caught here, frogs and tadpoles collected, and the rope swing he and Cornelia had rigged. For a moment, he seemed completely healthy. Then the clarity was gone. "You tell one, Corny."

Ramona merely smiled.

"Why don't we take a little walk, gentlemen?" Ken helped Uncle Jim to his feet and David and James joined them. "You want to come, too, Katie-Lynn?"

Benita felt grateful for the chance to sit on the blanket with her mother and Ramona as the men and children explored farther up the creek. The women packed up the leftovers, then sat soaking up the warm sun. Part of her wanted desperately to tell the story of Gram's encounter with the angel here. The other part knew she could never do it justice without having Gram's actual words to read to the others.

"It's so beautiful here." Ramona lay back on the blanket and rested a forearm across her eyes. "What stories can you tell me about this place? Did Cornelia come here often?"

"I never knew this place existed," Grace admitted. "If it was Mother's special spot, it was one she left behind in her youth. What can you tell us, Benita?"

Benita needed no further encouragement. To the best of her ability, she told the story of Gram's experience: how she had come here after learning of Henry's death, and how she had encountered someone—or some*thing*—and how that spiritual experience had changed her life.

Glad she had read that diary entry more than once, Benita filled in the details now, right down to the Jersey Milk wrapper that stayed in the diary all those years. Throughout the telling of the story, Grace and Ramona did not interrupt even once, and the others didn't return. It seemed like a sacred moment to Benita, and she wanted to honor Gram in the telling of her story. Once she had told all she could remember, the other women sat in silent contemplation for a moment.

"That solves a mystery for me," Grace said finally.

Benita and Ramona both looked at her expectantly.

"Benita, I never told you this," Grace said. "Moments before your grandmother died, she said something that was puzzling to me, but that obviously meant something to her. She opened her eyes, but she wasn't seeing me, or the room, or anything I could see. She seemed to be looking beyond the ceiling, and she suddenly smiled the biggest smile. Then she said, 'Hi! I knew you'd come back for me.' And just like that, she was gone.

"At first, I thought maybe she'd seen my dad. Then, after you told me about Henry, I wondered if it was him she saw. But now I know. It was neither of them."

"It was the angel," Ramona said.

Grace nodded slowly.

Benita wiped a tear from her cheek. "His name was Aziel. It means 'God is my power.' And he was probably mighty powerful. Gram said he was the tallest person she'd ever seen."

"Her father was six foot four," Grace said. "So she knew what tall looked like."

"Wow," Ramona murmured. "Imagine seeing a real angel."

Suddenly, Grace chuckled.

"What's funny, Mom?"

"It solves another mystery, too. About ten years ago, Mom went over her will with me and when we got to the subject of funeral arrangements, she was adamant that we not put any angels on her headstone. 'Why not?' I asked her. 'Because they never get them right' was all she would say. I thought she was losing her mind."

All three women laughed until the tears came again. A sparrow flew down from a small evergreen, landed a few feet away, and hopped over to the edge of their blanket. Three pairs of eyes concentrated on the little bird, who seemed oblivious to them. He found some picnic crumbs and eventually flew back into the safety of the greenery.

"I have a thing about sparrows," Ramona said. "This will sound weird, I suppose, but . . . well, I might as well show you." She reached into her purse and pulled out a folded scrap of paper that was yellowed and obviously old. As Ramona smoothed it out, Benita could see it was a page torn from a hymnbook, page 272.

"This is the one thing I have from my birth mother." Ramona began to softly sing the words printed on the page before her:

More secure is no one ever, than the
loved ones of the Savior
Not yon star on high abiding, nor the
bird in home-nest hiding.

"As a little kid, my parents taught me that God sees each sparrow fall, and he cares infinitely more about me than he does about sparrows. Somehow, that stuck with me, and to this day . . . every time I see one, I remember: God is watching over me and he cares."

Benita looked at her mother, who was well aware of Gram's special relationship with birds in general and sparrows in particular. Benita could tell the significance of Ramona's words was not lost on Grace. Yet somehow she felt that an explanation in words would seem woefully inadequate. Then, Grace reached into her tote bag and pulled out the old green hymnbook of Henry's that Benita had given her. Wordlessly, she turned to where page 272 should have been and slipped Ramona's page inside. Once again, the old hymnal was complete.

Ramona clutched the book tightly to her chest while the other two women, one on either side, simply wrapped an arm around her and leaned their heads against hers. There they sat in silent communion, listening to the trickling of the shallow creek and watching the sparrows come and go. They were sitting there still when the others returned.

Uncle Jim looked tired. James's hands were filled with rocks and snails, Katie-Lynn's with goldenrods. The eight of them piled back into the van somewhat reluctantly. This truly was a special spot.

"One more stop," Grace said. As they returned to Roseburg, she directed Ken to turn north and continue to the edge of town. When they reached the cemetery, he pulled in and once more they all climbed out.

"My grandparents are buried right over in that corner." Grace led the way. "Mom brought me here a lot." The troupe made their way in silence to the corner of the cemetery, where they saw the name *Simpson* engraved in big letters across one stone. They gathered first around the grave of Cornelia's mother, and Katie-Lynn read the headstone aloud.

"Mary Sarah Simpson, February 16, 1895, to August 1, 1933."

"So young," Ramona murmured.

"She died on her daughter's twelfth birthday," Grace said. "Poor Mom. It must have been so hard. Uncle Jim would have been about your age, James, when he lost his mommy."

James reached over and took Jim's hand, but Jim seemed unaware of where he stood or the gravity of the moment.

Right beside Mary's grave lay another. "Charles Simpson," James read, not to be outdone by his sister. "November 3, 1885, to April 18, 1954."

Benita did some quick math. "Not quite seventy. And look at that, his wife was nearly ten years younger than he was."

"That wasn't uncommon back then." Grace continued walking. "Come this way, I'll show you my father's grave."

Lingering among the Simpson graves, Benita spotted Miriam's. "Guys, look! It's Miriam. This is the woman we think gave you Gram's phone number, Ramona. Gram couldn't stand her, though. She was bossy and always trying to tell Gram's dad how to raise his children."

"What?" Grace frowned. "Honey, nothing could be further from the truth. Gram had a wonderful relationship with her aunt Miriam. I remember."

"No, Mom, that can't be right," Benita insisted. "Are you sure you aren't thinking of her aunt Nonie?"

"She loved her aunt Nonie, too, but there was something really special between Mom and Miriam. I was pretty young when Miriam passed away, but I remember."

"Well, then, whatever caused it happened sometime after 1941, because as far as I read in the diaries, Gram felt no great amount of love for her nosy Aunt Miriam, that's for sure." Benita chuckled. "Nowadays we'd call her a royal buttinski."

She squatted to take a closer look at the gravestone and brushed away a pile of decaying leaves that had gathered in front of it. A gasp escaped her when she saw the stone's engraving.

"Mom! Ramona! Come and look at this."

CHAPTER 58

Skillfully etched into a corner of Miriam Theresa Simpson's gravestone was a finely detailed and beautiful sparrow. Below her name were these words: *Beloved Sister, Teacher, Mother, Friend.*

"Mother?" Benita asked. "Why does it say 'Mother'?"

"I have no idea." Grace studied the stone, shaking her head.

"Somebody probably got a good deal on a used headstone for the ol' girl," Ken joked.

"Ken, you're awful!" Grace slapped his elbow, then turned to Benita with furrowed eyebrows. "I honestly don't know, honey."

Each family member traveled his or her own private journey as they wandered the parklike setting for another quarter hour. Grace paused by her father's grave, remembering the day they'd buried him and the strength her mother had shown in the months that followed. Ken took the children to the corner of the cemetery where the war memorials stood. Together they found the name of their great-great uncle, William Simpson, Charles's brother who had died in World War I.

Ramona linked arms with Uncle Jim and wandered back to the graves of Charles and Mary. She stood patiently while his eyes scanned the surface of the stones and light began to dawn in them. He slowly raised a finger, pointing first to one and then the other. "Mother," he said. "Father." Ramona patted his arm.

David searched for stones reading *Roberts,* and when he found some, he called Benita over. "Would these be relatives of Henry's?"

Benita studied the names, trying to remember what she had read in Gram's diaries. Henry had worked that summer on his uncle's farm, she knew. They had a large family, but mostly girls who would have married and changed their names. These stones said *Benjamin Roberts* and *Emily Roberts.*

Benita thought hard. "Yes, I think Gram mentioned an Uncle Ben in her diary. And Henry had cousins about his own age—Elizabeth was one. I'm trying to remember the other."

David called his mother over then, and Benita let them share a quiet moment there together while she helped Uncle Jim back into the van. By the time the children were settled in their seats, Ramona and David had rejoined the group and they all headed back down the road toward the city.

James, Katie-Lynn, and Uncle Jim fell asleep in no time. Grace and Ramona chatted in the middle seat until eventually they, too, fell quiet and began to doze. Up front, Ken drove while keeping up a running conversation with David about the economy and business opportunities in the city. That left Benita to sit quietly with her own thoughts. She regretted not sharing the diaries, not finishing the diaries, not protecting the diaries. Yet today wouldn't have been possible had the diaries not been lost. This truth made her heart beat a little faster.

God, help me let it go, she prayed.

Benita looked at the two women resting peacefully, their heads touching. They had known each other for only twenty-four hours, but they were already sisters in every sense of the word. She knew the visit to the post-adoption registry tomorrow would reveal nothing they didn't already know. Grace was already making plans to repay Ramona's visit and had offered Benita and Ken plane tickets for later in the year. "Birthday presents," she said, "so you can enjoy a little getaway alone together and have a chance to meet the rest of Ramona's family." Benita was curious to meet the cousins whose voices, according to Ramona, sounded so much like hers.

She looked at the two men in front who had been introduced so recently but were already forming a fast friendship. She overheard David asking if the family could come to his home soon for a barbecue, to meet his wife, Gloria, and son, Evan, who was nearly the same age as James.

It would be wonderful to have an expanded family. Benita's family had always felt so small, and Gram had been the glue holding them together. Now, in a way, she would continue to be that glue.

Ramona's entry into their lives had also altered the atmosphere of her family's home. Since Benita's apology, it had felt as though a wall was finally coming down, and Ken had begun to express his pent-up grief.

She gazed at her two sleeping children—Katie-Lynn clutching a handful of rapidly wilting wildflowers and James wearing on his face evidence of everything he had touched, smelled, or tasted that day.

Benita rummaged in her purse until she found James's latest report card, which she'd tucked into a side pocket after parent interviews the previous week. "James seems a lot more confident and at peace," his teacher had written without further comment. Those words were more than enough to make Benita feel hopeful about James's future.

Another prayer rose to her mind: *Lord, help me leave a legacy for James and Katie-Lynn like the one Gram left for me.*

CHAPTER 59

After seeing Uncle Jim safely home, the family drove the last leg of their journey in silence. By the time they pulled into their driveway behind the store, darkness had fallen and the night was charged with crisp autumn air. Ken carried a sleepy Katie-Lynn up the stairs, followed by an equally worn-out James, while Benita checked on things in the store. Richard had left a note saying all was well.

Once the children were settled, the five adults sat around the kitchen table to share what remained of the unread diary. They gave Ramona the honor of reading the words aloud, and she spread the sheet out and took her time putting on her reading glasses before she began.

"Oh my. This is dated August 20, 1939. Cornelia would have been—what, eighteen?"

Benita knew that whatever Ramona was about to read, she had already read herself. She also knew it would be about Henry and marveled at the unlikely odds that Ramona should be given this particular entry to read aloud.

"Dear Diary,

"I've found him. I have absolutely found him. I don't believe in soul mates, but if I did, Henry would be mine. And if I didn't believe in heroes before, I do now.

"It was potluck Sunday, and I decided to take a saskatoon pie. The berries are finished now, of course, but I canned some last month and Aunt Nonie taught me how to thicken the juice with cornstarch, add a scoop of sugar, and make pie filling. So I made the pie yesterday and hid it from Jimmy to keep him out of it. He kept complaining that he wouldn't have a chance of getting any if that brute Stanley McKenzie got to it first.

"So as soon as the food was all set out and the blessing given, Jimmy made a bee-line for my saskatoon pie and helped himself to a slice. He took a big bite, his eyes grew big, he spit the mouthful out and came over to me. I tasted it, too. It was the saltiest thing I ever tasted. It was awful! I must have scooped a cup of salt instead of sugar into that pie.

"I told Jimmy we had to hurry and get that pie off the table before anybody else got any. But it was too late. Stanley McKenzie and his brother Burt had not only taken some, but each of them had a big bite of it in his mouth and they both ran to the edge of the churchyard to spit it out. Then they made the biggest theatrical performance out of it I've ever seen. You'd have thought I poisoned them.

"'Corrie made a pickle pie!' Stanley yelled, and he and Burt kept hollering 'pickle pie, pickle pie!' I felt mortified when everybody laughed.

"Everybody except Henry.

"Henry marched right over to the pie, picked up the whole plate, and started eating. He polished off all three remaining

pieces without so much as gagging or making a face. When he finished, he wiped his mouth on his sleeve and said, 'Delicious. You can make pie for me any time.'

"Now it was Henry's word against the McKenzies' and nobody could prove anything either way because the pie was gone. Henry made sure of it. He spent the rest of the day drinking a lot of water and taking endless digs from the guys, but he never complained once. When I thanked him for standing up for me, he shrugged. He told me the pie tasted good and those goons don't know nothing. Then he said anybody as beautiful as me could make a pie out of dirt and it would still taste great.

"I told him he'd never live it down. For as long as he stayed in Roseburg, he'd be known as the guy who ate Corrie Simpson's pickle pie.

"And you know what he said? He said, 'I hope so. I hope I'm known that way for the rest of my life.'"

Ramona looked up, a smile on her face. "Would it be too much to ask . . ." She paused to smooth the paper. "Could I keep this page?"

Benita smiled. She and her mother had already agreed that they would give the silver suitcase to Ramona to restore or to keep as is, whichever she chose, along with the few diary pages they'd managed to retrieve.

"There's one left." Ramona adjusted her bifocals and picked up the last of the scattered diary pages. "There's no date."

"One of the things I remember most distinctly about that day is how Aziel told me I would one day tell the world the truth about Jesus. What on earth did he mean? I've asked myself about it a thousand times. His eyes held such promise, like he knew. He knew! And yet, all these years later I have

never even mustered the courage to tell my sweet Stuart about the most significant encounter of my life. If I can't even bring myself to tell my own husband, how—when—will I ever begin to tell the world?

"I continue with this diary for my own eyes alone, hoping my life will somehow reflect the riches I know in my heart to be true. What makes it so hard to share the most important event of my life?

"Today as I pondered on this yet again, asking God 'when,' he pointed me to Habakkuk 2:2 & 3. 'And the Lord answered me, and said, Write the vision, and make it plain upon tables, that he may run that readeth it. For the vision is yet for an appointed time, but at the end it shall speak and not lie: though it tarry, wait for it; because it will surely come, it will not tarry.'

"I feel I'm failing you in this, Lord. But I trust you. In your time, God, this will happen somehow. Help me trust you. And your timing."

A peaceful quiet settled around the kitchen table as Cornelia's words sank in. Finally, Ken stood. "I have an announcement to make," he said. "This seems as good a time as any."

Three sets of female eyes turned to him expectantly, but he looked only at Benita. He grinned, pulled a brochure out of the drawer behind his chair, and pushed it toward her. It came from a local community college and lay open to a page where bright yellow highlighter ink circled the words *Interior Design Studies.*

Benita studied the page. "I don't understand."

"Let me finish." Ken cleared his throat. "As you know, the store has done steadily better. What you don't know is, I've been putting some money away. There's enough in the account to pay the tuition if you'd like to take this course."

Benita was speechless. It had become obvious that of the two of them, Ken was the more talented businessperson and belonged in the store. He was gradually starting to trust their other staff members more, too. Now Benita would have a chance to pursue a dream of her own.

"And by the time you graduate, I should have enough set aside to hire a decorator to spruce up the store a little. Provided I can find somebody who knows what they're doing," he teased.

"Benita, that's wonderful!" Grace smiled. "You can do my house, too."

"And mine," Ramona chimed in. "Way to go, Ken!" She beamed at him.

Benita threw her arms around Ken's neck, nearly knocking him off his feet. "So does this mean you'll do it?" Ken said. "Classes start right after Christmas."

"I'll register tomorrow." She kissed her husband squarely on the lips and held him close.

Cheers went up around the table, and Katie-Lynn padded out to the kitchen in her rumpled pajamas to see what was going on.

"Ewww. Why are Mommy and Daddy kissing?" She climbed onto Grace's lap, rubbing her eyes.

"Your mommy's going to school," Grace whispered, cuddling the sleepy girl. "And she *really* loves your daddy."

After everyone had gone home and Benita was preparing for bed, she noticed the dimples in the carpet where the silver suitcase used to sit. She knew that giving it to Ramona had been a good and right decision. After all, she and her mother treasured their own memories of the wonderful woman who had owned it. Giving up the suitcase seemed the least they could do for the daughter Gram had longed to know. Benita leaned down and ran her hand gently over the carpet, climbed into bed beside her husband, and turned off the light. She snuggled up to Ken, and he enveloped her in his arms and kissed her forehead.

A peaceful sigh rose from her lips, like a prayer meant for the ears of God.

EPILOGUE

Sixteen-year-old Jordan Martins grumbled as he pushed yet another shopping cart across the mall parking lot. He was still mad at his little sister, Meagan, for borrowing his iPod without asking. Now it wasn't working right. *That immature brat owes me big-time*, he thought. *Does she think iPods are free?* He had yelled at her and told her again how ugly she was, saying no boy was ever going to look twice at her. It was a low blow, but she deserved it. She was always getting into his stuff and never got in trouble. If his parents weren't going to do something, it was up to him to make her think twice about messing with him.

The wind was picking up, adding to his dark mood. He hated it when flyers and other debris got stuck in the carts and slowed him down, and he wanted to get inside before the rain came. Besides, it was time for his break. He yanked a piece of trash from a corner of a cart and looked around for a garbage bin. Before he could find one, however, something on the page caught his eye. The sheet was covered in handwriting that reminded him of the old-fashioned fountain-pen writing he had seen in his grandmother's penmanship book from her school days. He shoved the page inside his jacket on impulse and kept it there until break time.

Once he was settled into the basement staff room with a sandwich in one hand, Jordan retrieved the page and smoothed it out on the table. Some of the writing was smudged, but he could make out most of it.

April 23

Dear Diary,

Daddy passed away last week and I have just now found a chance to write. I don't know what has been more overwhelming . . . my grief over his loss or the revelation from Aunt Miriam. We got through the funeral and buried Daddy beside Mother. The next day Aunt Miriam came to help me sort through Daddy's things and clean out the old house. Before we began, though, she told me she held a long hidden secret she wanted to share with me . . . how when she was 25 years old, she became pregnant and knew she would lose her teaching position if it became known.

Instead, she went to the city for one entire school term. The folks back home believed she was teaching in a city school to expand her experience. None of them knew she'd actually had a baby girl, whom her brother and his wife took in and raised as their own.

Her brother.

Daddy.

Of course I didn't believe her. I thought she must be getting delusional in her old age, but then she pulled out a birth certificate with my name on it that clearly names her as my mother, and an adoption certificate with my parents' names.

Miriam, Mother, and Daddy had all agreed: Whichever one of them survived the others would tell me. I suppose if I had died first, I'd have gone to my grave without knowing this family secret. She said they even went so far as to pretend Mother was pregnant when Miriam's time came closer, all to protect Miriam's reputation in the community. Naturally, I asked about the identity of my father, but she insisted this was enough news for me for one day.

I've never been so angry in my life. I went to the creek, where I found a broken hockey stick and railed against the trees with it and shouted at the top of my lungs. How dare they? How could they keep such an enormous secret from me? Who was my father? How could they deceive me like this? This means Jimmy and I are actually cousins! I yelled and hit trees and kicked stones until my energy gave out. I swore, too, you better believe it. Then I flopped on the ground and sat there, staring at the water. I know Jesus heard it all, and I don't care.

I don't know how long I sat there. Long enough for sparrows to land, and I threw stones at them to scare them off. Stupid sparrows. I went home then, but I'm still mad.

Jordan flipped the page over.

April 24

I visited Miriam today, with every intention of giving her a piece of my mind. If my parents were there, I'd give them a piece too, but as the last survivor Miriam would have to take the whole load. On the drive over, though, something changed. It was almost as though a familiar voice spoke to me—not audible, but just as clear as if I'd heard the words with my ears. Gently, the voice said three things:

Corrie, who are you to be angry at others for keeping secrets?

I've given you someone who knows exactly how your loss feels.

I've given you a mother again.

In that moment, I realized Miriam had been through much the same thing as I had. Could this be why she was such a difficult person, why she so often wanted to be involved with my life beyond what seemed appropriate? How might I behave if my Mary Sarah was growing up in my brother's home?

By the time I reached Miriam's house, my anger had dissolved. Instead of lashing out, I ended up telling her about Mary Sarah, and that's when I got the biggest surprise of my life. She already knew. She had kept my secret too, even from Daddy, all this time. I now understand that, whether misguided or not, Daddy and his sister both kept secrets out of their deep love for each other. Do Jimmy and I love each other that much? I could fill pages with the memories we have together . . . fishing by the creek . . . sleeping on the front porch in the summer time . . . my teaching him how to drive, although I'm not sure who taught whom . . . my forcing him to dance with me for practice before my first big dance. What a good sport he was! There are a million precious moments like that recorded in my mind (if not in my diary!). I hope he knows how much I love him, even though I haven't always shown it.

Lord, help me be a good sister all the way to the end of my life, no matter who else comes and goes from our lives.

Jordan tossed the dirty diary page into the wastebasket with his lunch wrappings, but its words echoed in his mind through his entire shift. He had not missed the tears welling up in Meagan's eyes when he'd yelled those hurtful words at her.

I guess it wouldn't kill me to apologize when I get home, he thought.

Nicole Kwan sat at her husband's grave for the fifth day in a row. Had it really been only a week since they'd laid Kyle to rest here? It seemed like months. Three-year-old Mee flitted from gravestone to gravestone as though this was merely a playground obstacle course, and Nicole watched her with a tired sigh.

She still bore the numbness that had settled on her the day the flag-draped casket was carried to the cemetery by six uniformed men from Kyle's regiment. She remembered all the wonderful words that had been spoken about Lieutenant Kwan, about how committed he was to the cause and how firmly he believed that Canadian soldiers were making life better for disadvantaged people in Afghanistan. She remembered throngs of people standing in the rain to pay their respects, remembered the rifle salute, remembered the chaplain's words from the Psalms.

She also remembered the pain she had seen in Kyle's parents' eyes as they tried to grasp that their twenty-six-year-old son was lost to them. She had clung to her own parents with one hand, clutching Mee tightly with the other. If there was any good in this, she thought, it was that Mee would not miss what she had already lived without.

"But how will I go on?" she whispered. "God, if you can hear me, please help me. I can't do this. I need help."

"Look at me, Mommy!" Mee cried suddenly, running toward Nicole with her chubby little arms full of fall leaves. "Mee pick up leaves. Mee a good girl, Mommy?"

She dropped the armload into her mother's lap and Nicole swooped her up into a hug.

"Yes, baby. You are a very good girl." She smoothed Mee's curls and straightened her mittens. But the little girl would not be held down long. She scampered away to gather another bunch of leaves. Nicole was brushing away the first offering when she realized it wasn't all leaves in her lap. From the pile, she pulled two sheets of lined paper with old-fashioned handwriting on them. Curious, she began to read.

Dear Diary,

It is Valentine's Day and I can't believe it was only a year ago that I danced with Jimmy at the community dance in Roseburg. I never thought I'd say this, but I sure do miss my little brother. I feel as though I have lived an entire lifetime since then. Meeting Henry . . . our wonderful summer together . . . our big fight before he insisted on going off to that dreadful war . . . the nagging suspicion that I might be carrying his baby . . . then getting the most horrible news imaginable, that my Henry was dead. And then . . . the biggest event of all, my encounter with the angel down by the creek.

Nicole stopped reading. Had she read that right? She read the words again.

. . . the biggest event of all, my encounter with the angel down by the creek. In my darkest moment, the person I had so bitterly hated for five long years sent me an angel who offered nothing but love and comfort and hope. That visit seemed to go on for days, yet took only moments. I will never be able to explain it, and I'm afraid to speak of it lest people think I am a complete lunatic. All I know is this: that encounter remains as real to me today as it was that day, and it sustains me in my loneliest hours, of which there are many.

I can feel the baby moving a lot now, and it helps me to feel I am not so alone. Someone depends on me, needs me for life and sustenance and, eventually, deliverance. What a weighty responsibility! Already I feel such a deep love for this little one. I wonder whether he or she will look like me or like Henry . . . or perhaps a little like both of us. And then I remember I may never know, and my heart is broken in pieces.

I know I suffer the consequences of my own wrongdoing, but oh, life can be so hard sometimes.

The writing ended there, but Nicole felt as though she had been handed a priceless gem. Mee came running at her with another pile of leaves and dumped them in her lap, but this pile contained no surprise messages.

"Where did you find this, honey?"

But Mee was oblivious to anything but the leaves. Nicole spent the next half hour searching the cemetery for more papers, but found none. The days were growing shorter, and she knew it was time now to head for home. She skimmed the diary entry once again, then tucked it inside her coat next to her heart, where it seemed a fragile flame of hope had just been lit.

Besides fatigue, this hope was the first thing Nicole had felt in over a week.

Jenny Murphy clutched her cane a little tighter as she made her way down the sidewalk, her mop of a dog on a short leash to prevent the two items from tangling. These twice-daily walks around the block were becoming more challenging every day.

"Slow down, Molly," she scolded the dog. "You're not as young as you used to be."

Together the pair made their way through the creaking gate and up the walk to the front door of Jenny's tall, narrow brick house. Her neighbor Lou Warner waved at her from behind his rake in the next yard. A mere three feet separated their houses.

"Good morning, Jenny. Would you like me to come do yours when I'm through over here?" Lou had recently retired and, at 68, seemed like a spry youngster to Jenny.

"That would be lovely. And then come in for some tea." Jenny unlocked her door and let Molly scamper inside. She bent to retrieve a few pieces of trash that had collected in the corner by her steps.

"Oh, don't you go bothering with that," Lou called. "I can pick all that up when I do the leaves."

"Well, thank you, but I've got this batch." Jenny clutched the pieces to her so they wouldn't drop. "I 'spect there's a lot more where that came from, and we'll probably see it before this blustery day is done."

Once she was inside, Jenny dropped the trash into her kitchen wastebasket and washed her hands. She put the kettle on for tea, and when she turned to throw out the tea bag wrapper, she saw something in the collection of litter that she hadn't noticed before. It reminded her of the letters she used to write with her fountain pen back in the 1940s, and she carefully separated the page from the other trash and pulled it out of the basket.

It did, indeed, appear to be a letter of some sort, but it started in the middle of a sentence. With her free hand, Jenny poured boiling water into her apple-shaped teapot, a gift from a student years ago, and then she sat to read while she waited for the tea to steep.

> *. . . and Mr. Reynolds liked my presentation so well, he asked me to take it to the next Board meeting where they showcase one student's work each time they meet. "Cornelia," he told me, "this is the best presentation I've seen in all my years."*
>
> *I'm so nervous, I could throw up. But I figure it will be great practice. After all, if I'm going to teach, I'll be up front talking to groups of people every day. And not just students, but their parents too, at special events and such.*

Jenny read the paragraph again. She remembered a Mr. Reynolds from her Normal School days. Could this be the same person? Jenny couldn't recall any girls named Cornelia in her class, but her memory was fading more each day. The next entry gave her the clue she needed. Jenny had started Normal School in the fall of 1941. She probably missed Cornelia by a year.

> *We served our 1940 Thanksgiving Dinner in the cafeteria. With rationing and all, there was no turkey, but the cooks found enough chickens that everyone was able to eat their fill. We had plenty of mashed potatoes, gravy, stuffing, corn, and even apple pie. Apple trees grow on campus, and I was part of the crew that picked them last month and helped store them in the cellar.*
>
> *I miss Dad and Jimmy and wonder what they ate today.*

Jenny poured herself a cup of tea and pondered her unusual discovery while Molly lapped at her water dish. Through the window, Jenny could see that Lou Warner had finished his own yard and was now working on hers. She read the diary entry page one more time, then folded her hands on top of it and closed her eyes.

"Lord," she began, "I don't know why you brought this my way today, but you always have a reason for everything. Usually it means you want me to pray for somebody, but you'll have to guide me to the right words. So I pray for this Cornelia, whoever she is, wherever she is. Gracious, she's probably older than I am! Is she even still around, Lord? Perhaps not. Well, bless her if she is, God. And I pray for her family. You know who they are and what they need today. Bring peace and light to their home as only you can, Lord Jesus. May it be a place of unity and . . . and reunion, maybe. Yes, reunion. Bless them, Lord. Bless them richly with every good thing from your mighty hand this day. Guide them and draw them to yourself."

A knock on the door interrupted Jenny's prayer and she mumbled "Amen" as she shuffled over to show Lou Warner in for tea.

Two sixteen-year-olds sat on a bus-stop bench holding hands across the street from the community health-care center. The girl pulled her hand free and blew her nose into a tissue. The boy flipped through a fistful of brochures that he had already flipped through a hundred times. They had told the clinic they needed a half hour to think about it.

"How can I make a decision like this in half an hour?" she said. "I don't know what to do."

"You know I'll support you, whatever you decide." He wrapped one arm around her shoulder.

The girl gathered her brown hair into a ponytail and then let it drop. "I wish I could be that sure about everybody else. My mom and dad will die if they find out. They'll *die.*"

"Mine, too." He sighed. He wanted to kick himself for getting her into this mess. He also wanted to run far, far away and never have to face her again, whatever she decided. Deep down, he feared he'd do exactly that sooner or later—run. But for now, he would try to be there for her. He felt so helpless, watching the tears run down her face. "If we don't decide soon, they'll find out anyway."

"I know, I know. We're running out of time. Might as well get it over with, I guess." She stood and pushed the button that would make the pedestrian crosswalk light come on. As she waited, a transit bus slowed for her, but she waved the driver on. As it whizzed by, a swirl of debris floated up and landed at the boy's feet. He looked down briefly and then stopped and looked down again. He picked up a sheet of paper and studied it quietly, still standing in front of the bench.

"Come on," she said. "You're not going to chicken out on me, are you?"

"Wait. This is weird. I think there's something here we're supposed to see." He sat down again.

"We've looked at every one of those brochures a dozen times already. What more is there to know?" She kept her eyes on the clinic doors across the street.

"It's not a brochure. It's some kind of letter or diary or something. And it looks all old and stuff."

The girl crossed back to the boy and joined him on the bench again.

"I can't even read that," she said, looking at the page. "It's smudged and—I don't know, it's somebody's handwriting. It's probably private. Throw it away."

"No. We need to read this. We're supposed to read this. Listen." He began to read, his voice rising above the noise of the traffic as it thundered past just feet in front of them.

"Last night I dreamed it was all a horrible mistake, that I wasn't pregnant after all, and that a nasty big tumor grew inside me and the doctors were cutting it out. Everybody stood around me in the hospital room—Daddy, Jimmy, even Henry. Mrs. Marshall was there and Henry's parents and Aunt Miriam and some of the girls from school back home. I was afraid. They all said such wonderful things to me, telling me to be brave and promising it would all be over soon.

"Henry said we could get on with our lives after the operation and everything was going to be fine. And then one by one, they began to fade away until I was all alone again. I looked around the room but no one was there, not a soul. I started to cry and when I looked up, Jesus stood at the foot of my bed. I knew I was dreaming, because he looked the same as that silly Sunday School picture behind the attic mirror.

"'Corrie,' he said. 'It's going to turn out okay. I'm going to go through this with you, you're not alone.' Then he reached out his arms and suddenly, I had a baby in mine. I placed the baby carefully in his arms, and he smiled at the baby. I asked

if it was a boy or a girl, but he didn't answer. He turned and walked away, carrying the baby with him.

"Then I woke up. Strangely, I felt comforted. I believe God has a plan for my baby. He will make sure my little one is safe and loved. He won't let me down on this. I can trust him."

The boy and girl looked at each other with wide eyes.

"Where did you find this?" she asked, taking it from him with one hand while the other lay across her stomach.

"It just . . . sort of . . . landed at my feet." They read the page again. A bell from a nearby church began to peal.

"It's one o'clock," she said. "Our half hour is up." She looked up at him, her eyes glistening with unshed tears.

"I don't want to do this." The boy sighed. "I want to find a different way."

She nodded her head only slightly and let out an involuntary sob. The boy walked over to a nearby trash bin and tossed the brochures inside. The diary page, however, he folded carefully and put in his pocket. He walked back to the bench and held out his hand. The girl took it.

Together they followed the sound of the church bells and sat on the front step of the church until the priest, who was just returning from lunch, found them there and invited them inside to warm up.

Brent Beaulieu scraped a stick along the inside of his storm gutters until they were clear, and then he climbed down the ladder. His wife, Anita, had been after him about the gutters for weeks, and he wanted to make sure the job was done before she returned home from her weekend women's retreat.

"And those sparrows moved on weeks ago," she said. "Please clean that nest out of our eaves so they don't come back to use it again next year. They're cute little birds and all, but our patio isn't a poop deck."

Brent smiled, remembering her joke. He looked forward to her return and to how pleased she would be to see the work done. He raked up the gutter debris and added it to the grass clippings in his wheelbarrow, then he wheeled it over to the compost bin and dumped it in. Once he'd located the abandoned sparrows' nest under the overhang of their house, he moved his ladder to the right spot. As he climbed up, he wondered whether the nest would be worth salvaging as a science exhibit in his grade five classroom. But when he pulled it free from its space, one chunk stayed behind, leaving him holding a doughnut-shaped bird's nest. With his free hand, he cleared the remaining bits from the eaves.

He climbed back down the ladder, then studied the nest more carefully. *Birds will use the oddest things*, he thought as he examined it closely. Woven in with the crisscrossed twigs was an almost intact chocolate bar wrapper. The fine print was faded beyond recognition, but Brent could easily make out the words *Jersey Milk.* The most curious thing was the old-fashioned style of printing. It reminded him of the fonts used in the newspapers from World War II, now on display in his school's library.

I wonder how old that Jersey Milk wrapper is? He tossed the nest—chocolate wrapper and all—into the garbage can and brushed off his gloves. As he closed the can's lid, the shiny foil lettering on the candy wrapper glinted in the sun's rays and Brent had a second thought.

One of his students, little Katie-Lynn Watson, loved birds. She had just completed a report on sparrows, and he thought she would probably like to see this little nest up close, broken though it was. Brent reached back into the garbage can and retrieved both the nest and a clean piece of newspaper in which to wrap it. Then he laid it on the front passenger seat of his car so he would remember to give it to Katie-Lynn on Monday.

He could already imagine the smile that would brighten her face.

ACKNOWLEDGMENTS

It takes an army to publish a book. I'd like to offer my utmost thanks to my friend Julianne Dick, to whom God gave the picture of me seated atop a silver suitcase stuffed full of papers trying to get out. Thanks for your prayers, Jules! To Kimberley Peterson, my mentor at the Christian Writers Guild, for encouraging and teaching me. To my husband and first reader, Jon. When you cried real tears through that first clumsy draft, I knew we had a story. To our children, Nate and Dara, Mindy and Kevin, and Reuben and Jill, for their support and encouragement. To my wonderful agent, Jessica Kirkland, of the Blythe Daniel Agency, for not giving up. To everyone at Waterfall Press, especially my amazing editor, Shari MacDonald Strong. I know God hand-picked you for me. To my fellow Thesaurus Wrecks, for sharing this crazy journey: Michael Ehret, Kimberley Gardner Graham, Jim Hamlett, Clarice James, and Peter Leavell. I love you guys beyond words! To Mom, for sharing her one-room-school teaching stories. To my cheerleader, Dr. Lisa Graham, for raising the value of my autograph by a million percent. To every friend and family member who read earlier drafts, supported me, and kept me going. To everyone who has prayed for my health. Most of all, my thanks are due to my redeemer, Jesus Christ, master storyteller and main character in the greatest story ever told.

ABOUT THE AUTHOR

Photo © 2015 G. Loewen Photos

Terrie Todd is an award-winning author who has published eight stories with the Chicken Soup for the Soul series, created two full-length plays with Eldridge Plays and Musicals, and writes a weekly faith and humor column for the *Central Plains Herald-Leader*. Her debut novel, *The Silver Suitcase,* was a finalist in the 2011 and 2012 Christian Writers Guild's Operation First Novel contest. In 2010, she served on the editorial advisory board for the anthology *Chicken Soup for the Soul: O Canada*. She lives with her husband, Jon, on the Canadian prairies, where they raised their three children. By day, Terrie is an administrative assistant at city hall. She enjoys acting and directing with her local community theater group, the Prairie Players, and being grandma to four little boys.